the Goodnight Agency

the Goodnight Agency

BUCKLE UP.
THINGS ARE ABOUT TO GET **WEIRD**.

TYLER TORK

an imprint of
Roan & Weatherford Publishing Associates, LLC
Bentonville, Arkansas
www.roanweatherford.com

Copyright © 2023 by Tyler Tork

We are a strong supporter of copyright. Copyright represents creativity, diversity, and free speech, and provides the very foundation from which culture is built. We appreciate you buying the authorized edition of this book and for complying with applicable copyright laws by not reproducing, scanning, or distributing any part of it in any form without permission. Thank you for supporting our writers and allowing us to continue publishing their books.

Library of Congress Cataloging-in-Publication Data
Names: Tork, Tyler, author.
Title: The Goodnight Agency/Tyler Tork | The Goodnight Agency #1
Description: Second Edition. | Bentonville: Mad Cat, 2023.
Identifiers: LCCN: 2023942254 | ISBN: 978-1-63373-622-1 (trade paperback) |
ISBN: 978-1-63373-623-8 (eBook)
Subjects: | BISAC: YOUNG ADULT FICTION/Fantasy |
YOUNG ADULT FICTION/Paranormal, Occult & Supernatural |
YOUNG ADULT FICTION/Fantasy/Dark Fantasy
LC record available at: https://lccn.loc.gov/2023942254

Mad Cat trade paperback edition August, 2023

Cover & Interior Design by Casey W. Cowan
Illustrations by: cxojinu
Editing by Mari Mason, Laura Laud, Amy Cowan & Staci Troilo

This book is a work of fiction. Any references to historical events, real people, or real places are used fictitiously. Other names, characters, places, and events are products of the author's imagination, and any resemblance to actual events or places or person, living or dead, is entirely coincidental.

To all those who don't fit in,
and fight for justice.

One

Having used up her last aunt, Ruby Park stood on the doorstep of her weird uncle Simon in Chicago. A drift of boxes and bags accumulated around her as the driver unloaded her life from the van. She listened to the Blue Animals on her phone, singing along under her breath… *Break another one, break another one for me.*

She over-tipped the driver, just to use up the rest of the travel money—the last thing Aunt Meg had given her. Done. She faced the soot-stained brownstone. A tarnished brass plaque beside the door read, *Simon Goodnight—The Goodnight Agency.* She looked through the glass door, down a long, dark hallway. Light from a doorway midway down spilled out over polished floorboards and a threadbare strip of carpet.

Anger had propelled her this far, but now that she was on the spot, with no way back and nowhere else to go, apprehension gripped her. She'd met Simon three or four times at family gatherings, before all the trouble. They hadn't spoken much because she'd been at the kids' table. A stranger, really, and now she had to live with him. What if he was horrible?

Well, it would be embarrassing to be seen dithering on the steps. Might as well get it over with. She looked for a doorbell, found a frayed rope with a gold tassel, and pulled.

After a moment, the door jerked open, and her uncle goggled at her. "Oh, it's you." He looked a bit put out. Had he forgotten she was coming? "Come along and be quiet until I've done my business. Don't touch anything." He started down the hallway, then turned back to pick up the nearest piece of luggage—a large box of her specimens, individually bubble-wrapped.

"Careful with that!" Ruby got three suitcases through the door at once and dumped them at the foot of the stairs. Two boxes of books joined them. Then she followed Simon through a green felt door.

Walking into the study was like stepping into the past. The room was large and done in dark wood and red velvet, every wall covered with built-in shelves and every shelf packed with books, not a single paperback among them. Glass display cases and small, round lace-covered tables full of bric-a-brac stood on a floor covered with an overlapping arrangement of ornate, antique rugs. One corner held a huge, polished desk, overhung by a large stained-glass floor lamp. Evening light slanted in through tall, narrow windows.

Uncle Simon sat behind the desk, fitting in well with the decor in a dark green suit, black shirt, and red string tie with silver beads. Who dressed like that at home? Across from him, another man perched on a spindly-legged chair, leaning over the desk to sort through a collection of small items.

"Where the devil do you get these things, Simon?" The man pulled out a dog-eared catalog from a canvas bag on the floor.

"That would be telling." Simon glanced at Ruby, then his eyes flicked to a couch. Interpreting this as an instruction, she sat. She started to lean against the arm and put her feet up, but another look stopped her.

"This can't be real. There are only three of them, and I know where they are."

"You'd best call the people who have them to make sure theirs haven't gone missing."

"Oh, I trust you, I just don't think it's real."

"Take it with you while you check it out. If it turns out to be genuine, how much will it bring?"

"Hard to say. Nobody's sold one in decades. No papers on it, either, I suppose?"

Simon shook his head and ran a finger over his thin blond mustache. "A friend found it in his attic."

"Your friends have the most interesting attics. Thirty, at least." Reverently, he set it into a padded case on the desk and reached for the next item.

Ruby, bored, put her headset back on and listened to music, kicking her feet and looking around the room. Eventually the man stood, picking up his things. He was short and rotund, with thinning ginger-colored hair and a rumpled suit. He paused in front of Ruby.

Simon came up behind him. "This is my niece, Ruby. Ruby, this is Octavian McTeague."

Octavian glanced at Simon, then at her. He must be thinking what everybody thought when she was introduced by her aunts. How can this dark-skinned Asian-looking girl be related to blondie here? Mostly they assumed, incorrectly, that she was adopted. But he didn't ask, just held out his hand.

Ruby stood and managed a smile. His hand was cool and dry, with a slight tremble. "With a name like that, you must come from a large family."

Octavian looked again at Simon and raised an eyebrow. "Knows some Latin, does she? Yes, young lady. All boys, too. What are the odds, eh?"

"One in sixty-four. No," she corrected, blushing, and hating herself for doing so. "Two hundred and fifty-six if there are eight in all."

Octavian laughed, and his hand went to the breast pocket of his jacket. "My card. It's been a pleasure, but I must dash. I'm sure we'll meet again."

Returning from showing the visitor out, Simon sat in a padded chair and put his feet up on an ottoman, displaying red and gold brocade slippers with pointed toes. He rested his chin on steepled fingers and looked her over. She glared back, determined not to squirm under his scrutiny, despite feeling grubby and underdressed in a black t-shirt, travel-rumpled black skirt, and sneakers. While waiting for him to talk, she flicked the edge of Octavian's card with her thumbnail. Nobody had ever given her his card before, and she didn't know what to do with it.

"You look very much like your mother," Simon said at last.

"And you look nothing like her."

Simon's lips twitched. "Different mothers."

Ruby decided to test him. "According to Aunt Julia, different fathers, too."

Simon blinked. "Ha! Well, it's a theory. Whether we're related or not, Reno and I were the oddest of your grandpa Jim's brood. And the youngest, by a few years. We had a lot of adventures together. I hope you're like her in other ways besides appearance."

"Why, do you need something blown up?"

His smile vanished. She looked away.

"I refer to her ability to keep secrets and to deal calmly with the unexpected. I'm in an… unusual line of work, and my home is also my place of business. You must be both tactful and discreet. I'm also quite busy. That's why I was reluctant to have a child in the house."

"I'm not a child. I'm sixteen."

Simon shrugged and waggled his hand.

"I can take care of myself."

"Perhaps. But so far, you haven't demonstrated tact. I assume it's only for lack of trying." He took out a small black notebook from the inside pocket of his suit. "It must be understood how you deal with my clients who come here."

Another house of rules. Great. She sighed and waited.

Simon opened the notebook to a page marked with a ribbon. "If I'm available, I'll get the door. I see clients in this room. If I'm already with someone, or not at home, you let them in. Don't ask what they want, just show them into the drawing room across the hall. Never leave them alone in this room."

"Let in anyone who comes here?"

"If it looks like they might be a client. You'll get to know the look. They won't like to wait outside. You mustn't stare at them or show surprise or ask questions. In fact, it might be best not to look directly at them."

Not *look* at them? "What kind of clients do you have?"

"Unusual ones. Are we clear so far?"

"Okay." Ruby was mystified but managed to sound cool, she hoped.

Back to the notebook. "Other rules. Touch nothing without asking. Some things are delicate, others dangerous. Meals are at eight, noon, and seven. Be here at those times if you wish to eat. Home by ten unless by prior arrangement. Stay out of the basement. Stay out of the attic. Don't pry into my business." He looked at her expectantly.

"Got it."

He nodded and flipped a page. "I'll start you out with fifteen dollars a week allowance and a transit pass. If you think you need more, keep track of how you spend it, and we can talk. There's petty cash in the top right desk drawer. Use that for COD deliveries or if I'm away and you have to dine out or I send you out for groceries. Anything like that. If you take from the petty cash, write it in the notebook in the drawer. In case of emergency, if I'm not here, there's more cash taped to the underside of the third drawer on the right, which is locked. The key is in the spine of Collected Sermons of Wallace Blevin on that shelf. I figure nobody will try to read it. I certainly never have. Third drawer on the right. Don't open the other drawers." Simon tucked the notebook away. "Questions?"

"You trust me with your emergency cash?"

"Are you saying that's a mistake?"

"No." But she felt a flash of doubt. "It's—well—none of the aunts trusted me with anything. Because of my parents, I guess."

Simon frowned. "I sometimes can't believe we grew up in the same house. Maybe Julia really *is* onto something. All right, here's the deal. I don't assume you're the same as your parents, and in any case, I never knew them to steal anything."

"No," Ruby deadpanned. "Only destroy government property."

"You have nothing against the postal service yourself, I assume?"

"Not positively."

"Then you get the benefit of the doubt. Don't make me regret it."

"Okay."

Simon put the notebook away. "What happened between you and Meg? She was a little incoherent on the phone."

"She made it impossible for me from the start. I mean, it would've been hard enough because evidently nobody in that town ever met a non-white. But she made sure people knew my parents were in prison and why, so of course everybody at school was certain I was a terrorist."

"That must have been difficult. But what did *you* do? She said something about treeing the neighbor's son and threatening him with a pistol?"

"Yes, I chased him up a tree. He'd kept tormenting me and groping me, and nobody was doing anything about it. Anyway, it wasn't a real gun."

"I'm guessing he didn't know that. She also kept talking about owl pellets."

"That was probably the last straw," Ruby admitted. "I forgot they were in my pocket, and they went into the wash."

"What is an owl pellet, exactly?"

"You know cats and hair balls? It's like that. Anything an owl eats and can't digest, they cough up. Hair, mouse bones...."

"Yes, we wouldn't want that in the wash. And you were carrying it around in your pocket, why?"

"I dissect them, to see what the owl ate. Sometimes I can get a complete skeleton out. Then I glue it together."

Simon looked a little doubtful. He shrugged. "We'll be careful what goes into the laundry here, yes?"

"For sure."

"And there'll be no chasing people with guns, real or otherwise."

"Not unless it's absolutely necessary."

He gave her a long look. "If there's a problem, I *will* do something about it. Talk to me first. Any questions?"

Ruby paused, then took the plunge. "What exactly is it you do?"

"This is what I meant about prying into my business."

"Fine, don't tell. But when people ask?"

"If someone asks who has no business to know, I say I'm a financial adviser."

Ruby smiled. Aunt Edith's husband was in that line of work, and he had an often-repeated complaint. "Don't people try to get free stock tips?"

"Yes." A clock on the mantle chimed, and Simon turned to look. "Time to start dinner. Can you cook?"

"I can chop."

"It's a start. I'll show you your room—you get cleaned up, then meet me in the kitchen." He stood, rubbing his hands. "It's tarragon quail and carrot ginger soup tonight."

Fish sticks and mashed potatoes might be more her speed, but she grabbed two suitcases and followed him upstairs.

Ruby dreamed she was eleven again in her parents' apartment in New York. Through her closed bedroom door, she could hear the meeting in the living room, though she couldn't make out any words. She went into the hallway and stood in the living room doorway, watching, but though she could see the people talking, the voices remained muffled. Three other people besides her parents. She hadn't known their names or faces until the trial, but in the dream, she knew them.

She watched Jackson, a thin black man whose short, wiry hair was gray at the temples. He ate a pretzel, nodding as someone railed about something. Jackson saw her, gave a quick wink, and turned back to the others.

Ruby's mom came from the kitchen with a pitcher and glasses on a tray. Seeing Ruby, she stopped. "Back to your room, girly-o."

Ruby grabbed her mother's sleeve. "You have to listen," she whispered. "Jackson is a spy. He works for the FBI." Ruby knew she was dreaming, but somehow it seemed important to convince her mom, as if that could change what had already happened.

Ruby's mom laughed. "Don't be silly. Go on to bed." She walked away, shaking her head.

Ruby followed her into the living room. "Jackson is an FBI spy!" she shouted, and they all turned to look.

"I'm sorry," Ruby's dad said. "I don't know what's gotten into her." Jackson laughed, a deep chuckle. After a moment, they were all laughing at her. Ruby, mortified, turned to flee, but the carpet slipped from under her, and she fell....

She sat up, the first rays of dawn lighting the wall above her bed.

Tired from traveling, she'd gone right to sleep after dinner with her things still packed. Now she opened the curtains fully to see her room in good light.

It was small but pretty. The purple wallpaper had a raised fuzzy pattern of twining flowers. There was a large oak wardrobe, a roll-top desk, a dressing table with a yellowed, spotty mirror. A little sink in the corner, its plumbing hidden in a carved wooden cabinet. A small, dusty chandelier, and, of course, the bed—a heavy, dark four-poster with a deep purple satin canopy.

Her clothes fit into the wardrobe with much room to spare. There was no good place for her specimens and books. She'd have to ask for shelves.

With everything stowed, it was still almost two hours to breakfast. She drifted to the window, which overlooked the back yard. There was a little court, enclosed by a brick wall, with a gate to the alley. Winding paths led between flower and vegetable beds to a tiny patch of perfect lawn, on which stood a small white gazebo. Uncle Simon, she concluded, must surely be gay.

She dressed, slipped a paperback into her skirt pocket, and wandered into the hall. She nodded to the suit of armor as she passed. She looked up the narrow staircase which led to the forbidden attic, wondering what up there could be so secret. She trailed her fingers down the banister, passed through the old-fashioned dining room and the extremely modern kitchen, gleaming with copper and stainless steel, out the back door, down the steps. A rabbit looked up from nibbling a young lettuce plant and ran for the back gate, a leaf still held in its mouth. Following at a walk, she sat in the gazebo, put her feet up, and took out her book.

Sometime later, the doorbell rang. How could she hear it all the way in the back yard? A few seconds later it rang again, and she spotted the ringer over the back door. She looked at her watch. Early for visiting. Curious, she ran inside to look down the hall and through the front door glass. The visitor, short and a little hunchbacked, wore a gray hood and robe. Like a Star Wars Sand Person but without the glowing eyes. It looked away down the street, weaving back and forth. Simon came downstairs, tying the sash of his robe, and Ruby ducked out of sight. She heard the front door open and close, then the study door. She peeked out again, watching the empty hallway for a few minutes before getting bored and going to look for breakfast.

The pantry held a selection of reassuringly normal breakfast foods. She dawdled over her cereal bowl, reading, until Simon came in, resplendent in orange-brown silk pajamas and a terry robe. He picked up the cereal box, blinked at it, poured himself some, and got soy milk and orange juice from the fridge. "Don't you look energetic," he said.

She resisted the urge to ask about the mysterious visitor. "What's the plan for today?"

He set the things on the table. "First, school."

"But the term's over!"

"This school still has a week to run, but this is to arrange for next term. I've signed you up for a good one. Catholic."

"I'm not Catholic."

"Nor I, but it's the best school in the area. Not easy to get into. Are you going to eat that? I wouldn't ask except it's the last one. I had to call in a favor to get you admitted. We're to meet the principal today. Do you have any clothes that aren't black? A pretty hair ribbon, perhaps?"

"This is me. Deal with it."

"Well, it's up to you, but first impressions are lasting ones, so you might want to dress up a little."

"I don't see why. Ultimately, it won't fool anyone."

"Well… I'll tell you a secret, just between us. I got your records from your previous school and I… doctored them."

"You did what? What do you mean, you changed my grades?"

"No, the grades were fine. Well, I expect you to do better in English. No, I changed the teachers' comments about you. They now say you're eager and get along well with your classmates."

"Why would you *do* that?"

"To give you a chance to make a good first impression. Your teachers will read those notes, so that's what they'll expect, and they'll treat you accordingly. The other students will take their cue from them."

"But that's not me! They'll see that right away. I get along rotten with my classmates."

Simon shook his head sadly. "Then I'm in big trouble. They'll wonder what's up and talk to your old teachers. Couldn't you fake it for a while? Just long enough to prevent them from wondering whether they got the right person's records? You'll see they're much more diverse than the schools you've been going to."

Ruby put her head in her hands. "You're driving me crazy! How could you think this was a good idea?"

"I hear you've done some acting." Simon crunched his cereal, waving his spoon. "Play the part for a while."

Ruby lifted her head and gave him a brilliant smile. "Oh, hi!" she chirped. "Hey, are you going for cheerleading this year? Like, I'm for sure gonna try out. Dale's on the team, and he is so cute, and I heard he like broke up with Melody, you know?" Ruby's hand darted out and grabbed Simon's. He gave a little jump and pulled away, but she had a firm grip. "Oh my God, your nails, is that cute or what? Did you do the stars yourself?"

Simon pulled his hand away. "See? You can do it. People treat you the way you expect to be treated. You can fool them. It'll be fun."

"I don't want to be treated like a bimbo and have to talk nonsense. I'd rather be me."

Simon sipped his juice. "You can be you and still be agreeable. Unless, of course, you want people to dislike you."

"Of course not. I had lots of friends in New York."

"Before your parents were arrested. And since then, maybe it seems easier if you push people away before they get a chance to reject you. Lets you feel a little superior."

"You really don't get me."

Simon shrugged. "Maybe not. But these people don't know who you are, so you could give them a chance. Just try it for today, so your old uncle Simon doesn't get in trouble. Later, we'll do a little shopping, if there's anything you need, then stop for lunch. After that, I have an appointment near downtown. I could drop you off somewhere for a few hours—"

"The Field Museum."

"—then we'll come back here. Be ready in an hour and bring anything you need for the day."

In her room, Ruby looked at herself in the spotty mirror and sighed. "People will like you," she said without conviction. "You'll be very popular. School is fun. Whee." She took off her evil cat earrings and sifted through her jewelry box for a pair her mother had given her—little silver disks with holographic roses. She brushed out her wiry black hair, pushing it back over her shoulders instead of hanging in front of her face as she usually did. Totally unconvincing. Not perky enough. Too shaggy. She dug out a dark red scrunchie. Better. She gave the mirror a big smile. She didn't own any makeup. She'd have to get by on attitude.

Downstairs, Simon was nowhere in sight. She decided to explore the study. Not to touch, just to look. When he poked his head into the room, she was looking up at a skull on the mantle-piece. He took in her ensemble and nodded. "It'll do. C'mon, let's roll."

"That's a funny-looking skull." She followed him into the hallway. "Is it an ape?"

"Orangutan." Simon wrestled a large rolling suitcase out the door and bumped it down the stairs. "Make sure that locked. Sometimes it doesn't catch." Simon heaved the case into the trunk of a waiting Uber. The driver didn't get out to help.

He got in beside her. "I have a quick stop to make first."

"Not to worry. I always bring a book." But when the car stopped in front of a big concrete apartment building, she decided to practice her new chirpy persona on the driver.

By the time Simon returned, she'd managed to find out where the driver had grown up and why he'd left, seen photos of his family, and learned the name of the best Somali restaurant in town, which coincidentally was operated by his cousin. The trunk thumped shut, and Simon got back in, adjusting his tie and taking a comb from his jacket pocket.

St. Genesius Academy was a large brick building in the shadow of a raised expressway. Classes were in session, and once past the security checkpoint, Ruby could hear voices from the closed rooms as they walked down polished corridors. Bulletin boards were covered with the usual school detritus. "Look at this!" Simon exclaimed. "Lucky you, they really do have a cheerleading squad."

"I was definitely kidding about the cheerleading, and we will not mention it again."

"As you wish." Simon held a door open for her.

Ruby paused. "Look. I know what you're doing. The only reason I'm going along with it is because you're the last remaining relative who can stand me and who isn't in jail. But I'm not eager."

"Understood." Simon gave a little bow and motioned her into the principal's waiting room.

Two girls seated together looked up at Ruby as she entered. They were dressed identically in blue plaid skirts and light-blue blouses with a crest embroidered on the collar. Ruby gave them the high-wattage smile she'd been practicing and sat a few seats away. "Uniforms?" she whispered to Simon. "You didn't mention uniforms. Oh, hi!" she said as one of the girls came up on her other side.

The girl was tall and slender with honey-colored hair. "You're new, aren't you? I'm Ashley Tate."

"Of course you are. Ruby Park. I start junior year in the fall... *if* your principal likes me."

Ashley sat next to her. The other girl, who looked Mexican, with fluffy, curly black hair, took the next chair. "He'll like you," Ashley said. "Mister Erdrich is an old softie. Marissa and I run the spirit committee. Do you think you might join next term?"

When purple pigs fly out of my butt, Ruby thought. "Maybe. I just moved to town, and I don't know yet what kind of schedule my uncle's set up for me. He's full of surprises."

Ashley leaned to look past her at Simon, who was browsing

through a stack of magazines on a side table, then back at her, plainly wondering how they could be related.

Normally Ruby would've let her go on wondering, but that was inconsistent with her *Little Miss Friendly* persona. "I'm a mutt. Korean, white, and black. His dad was my grandpa, who remarried to my grandma."

"But you live with your uncle? What happened to your parents? Oh, sorry, I mean…."

"It's all right." Ruby dared to touch Ashley's hand. "It was two years ago. They were vacationing in Switzerland, climbing an Alp, and… there was an avalanche."

"Oh my God, that's awful!"

Beside her, Simon didn't make any sound, but Ruby could feel him paying close attention to the conversation. Her ears burned, and she decided to change the subject. "I don't talk about it much. What about you? What grade are you in?"

"I'm a junior, and Marissa is a sophomore. Well, for another few days, anyway."

Simon leaned forward. "Are you Sebastian Tate's daughter?"

"You know my dad?"

"I'm not sure we've ever spoken, but we're members of the same country club. I think I've seen you on the tennis courts."

"For sure. I'm in the tournament." Ashley's eyes flicked over him, plainly evaluating the cost of his clothes, watch, and haircut. She looked at Ruby again, weighing her in the same way.

"Ruby's just back from a long stay at my father's ranch in Montana," Simon lied. "They're a little rustic out there, and she's grown so much she'll need all new things. We're going shopping right after this meeting."

Ashley smiled. The discrepancy was resolved, and her brain no longer hurt. She and Marissa exchanged a significant look.

Marissa nodded.

Ashley turned back to Simon. "Let us take her instead! I know all the best places."

Simon's brows went up. "That would be very helpful. I have no idea how to shop for a young lady."

"Excellent! We can meet her right after school. Does she have her own card?"

"Eh no." Simon took out his phone. "You'll meet *us*. I must approve the purchases. You two exchange phone numbers while I go move an appointment."

As Simon went out to the hallway, the door to the inner office opened, and a man who resembled a pigeon in a brown suit beckoned to Ashley and Marissa. Marissa stood. "I'll get started. Hurry up."

"Here." Ashley handed over her phone, open to a new contact. "Put your number in, and I'll text you."

"Are you two in trouble? Called to the office?"

"Huh? Oh, no. Not this time, anyway. Final assembly planning."

"Sounds important." Ruby entered the number and handed back the phone. "I won't keep you."

Simon returned a minute later and sat beside her. "Well, that was decent of those girls. This will be fun, don't you think?"

Ruby was pleased and excited but saying so would give him too much satisfaction. She shrugged. "If you like that sort of thing."

Two

Over the next couple of weeks, Simon got her signed up for flute lessons, swimming lessons, and Ancient Egypt day camp at the Field, which he said, "could be useful someday." He encouraged her to socialize with Ashley and Marissa's crowd, which mainly involved hanging out in mall food courts or going to someone's fancy house. It was clear he meant to keep her busy and away from his reclusive clients.

Despite the lecture he'd given her on how to deal with callers—which he repeated a couple more times over meals—he never let her answer the door. Whenever the bell rang, even once when he was with someone in the study, he rushed out and hustled them in, shutting the door to whatever room he put them into. She knew he always shut the door because she always happened to wander past, to check whether the mail had come, for instance.

Anyway, there weren't many callers. More often, Simon went to them. There were a few late-night or early-morning visitors and a few phone calls. Ruby wondered how they set up appointments. Maybe by email. There was a computer in a small, modern office adjoining the study, but Simon had set up a separate password for her.

Try as she might, she was unable to accidentally read any of his email.

She did explore the basement, of course. She was always up early and didn't like to wait for breakfast until Simon awoke, so she generally had a little pre-breakfast. She was alone in the kitchen every morning, with the basement door right there. One day, she gathered up all her courage, and a large metal flashlight in case of opposition, turned on every light, and crept down the wooden stairs.

It was a large open space, concrete-floored, wooden-pillared, with exposed rafters and the usual machinery and pipes, though unusually clean and free of spider webs. Boxes were stacked against one wall, and a workbench on the other side had tools hung over it in neat rows. The only odd thing was the three arched alcoves at the back, each about eight feet square, with stone walls and ceilings.

Ruby stood in the middle alcove and ran her fingers over the wall. In several places, something had scraped parallel grooves into the stone and the mortar, rough-edged and a quarter-inch deep in places. She turned to look out into the main room. This was just like a little cell if there had been bars. She shivered. What could've been in here trying to claw its way out through stone walls? She hurried back upstairs into the sunlight, leaving everything as she'd found it.

One night, she heard low voices in the hallway and footsteps on the attic stairs. Two ascending but only one descending. Opening the door a tiny crack, she saw Simon pass. Was someone spending the night in the attic?

Simon said nothing about it over breakfast the next day. Ruby's eyes bored holes into his newspaper until he noticed the quiet and lowered it. "Eat up. You'll be late for soccer practice."

"Living in this house, I'm bound to run into some of your clients eventually, you know. When they come downstairs to use the bathroom or to murder me in my sleep."

"Nobody has ever been murdered here. And the attic has its own bathroom."

"Even so, if I'm not ready to meet them now, why should I be ready to come across them later by surprise?"

Simon folded his paper and set it down. Ruby waited. "All right," he said at last. "You can't bother whoever might, or might not, be in the attic. But day after tomorrow, I'll take you to meet someone."

Ruby whooped, came around the table to give him a big hug, and promised, "I'll be cool, you'll see." Then she ran upstairs to dress for soccer.

As it happened, though, she had a chance encounter the next day while riding back from the mall with Marissa and Marissa's mom. Marissa said, "Wow! Who's that big guy on your doorstep?"

Ruby, who'd been playing a game on her phone, looked up. Standing at the door was an enormous man, maybe seven feet tall and powerfully built, in a wide white straw hat and a long white coat, despite the sweltering heat of a Chicago summer. "I don't know. One of Uncle Simon's clients, I guess." She kept her voice casual, but her heart beat faster. She got out of the car, waved goodbye, and hurried around a tall white Hummer limo and halfway up the stairs.

The man turned, and she stopped, shocked, despite having expected something out of the ordinary. He was perhaps the ugliest person she'd ever seen, with a wide, dark-lipped mouth, practically no chin, squashed nose, and tiny ears high up on his head. His skin was brown and seamed, and a long, jagged scar crossed his cheek, lending a sinister aspect to a face that would've been disturbing even without it. His face was covered with heavy reddish stubble, highlighted by the spots of sunlight filtering through his hat.

"I'll, uh, let you in," she stammered, gesturing with her key. The man nodded and stepped aside. Her hand shook, so it took her three tries to get the door open. He followed her in, taking off suede gloves so large that Ruby could've worn one like a hat. As he hung his coat and hat, the light caught the back of his hand, and Ruby could see it was covered with hair. Not tiny, fine hairs, but thick fur that seemed to have been shaved recently. His nails were long and somewhat pointed. Ruby swallowed and held open the door to the drawing room. "I guess Simon's out. If you could wait here?"

As he lumbered past her, Ruby got a whiff of soap and cologne and an undertone of something animal. He looked at and dismissed the chairs, which were too small and delicate, and lowered himself onto the window seat. It creaked under his weight. He tugged the edges of his tailored suit coat and smoothed his trousers.

"Would you like anything while you wait?"

He looked at her with his big brown eyes—definitely his best feature, not that it was much of a contest. "Wather. If you pleathe." His rumbling voice seemed to come all the way up from the bottom of his size-forty shoes.

"Water, right." Ruby closed the door and walked quickly to the kitchen, where she leaned against the wall and took a few deep breaths. As she came out with a large glass of water, she saw Uncle Simon through the front door, juggling two bags of groceries and his keys. She ran to open the door and held out her arms to trade him the water for the groceries. "There's someone to see you. I'll put these away."

The stranger was in the study with Simon for half an hour. A phone call was made—Ruby could tell by the lights on the hall telephone, visible from her vantage point on the stairs. When the man left, he was laughing. He clapped Simon on the back, making him stagger. "Nex' week." He collected his things and let himself out.

"You have another visitor." Ruby ran down the stairs to be there when he opened the door of the drawing room. A small, mangy dog got up from the middle of the floor, wagging his tail. "He was nosing around the front door and seemed to want to come in. Thought he might be a client."

Simon nodded and closed the door. He went into the kitchen for a moment, then the study, bringing out a large, flat board. He set the board—a Ouija board—on the floor in the drawing room. From his other hand, he set down a bit of leftover apricot chicken from last night's dinner—on a small china plate, naturally.

The dog sniffed at the Ouija board, then the chicken, devouring the latter. He trotted over to see whether Simon had more.

"Nope. He's just a regular dog." He led it out onto the street. "Next time you can test for yourself." He vanished into the study, leaving Ruby to wonder whether he'd called her bluff or whether some of his clients really might be dogs. Clearly, they weren't all entirely human. "We're still on for tomorrow, right?" she shouted through the door.

Fresh from swimming practice, hair frizzy and smelling of chlorine, Ruby clattered down the stairs from the elevated train, dodging around slower travelers, and consulted her phone for further directions. The place Simon had told her to meet him was around the corner and two blocks down. He was already waiting on the sidewalk, looking too warm in a three-piece suit of brown tweed, an off-white shirt with little pleats in the front, and a floppy bow tie. He wore gold cuff-links, and a thin gold watch chain hung across his chest to a small vest pocket.

Ruby looked him up and down. Two-tone shoes, too. "What century does your client live in?"

"Very amusing. This is just what I felt like wearing."

"What's on the chain?"

Simon pulled it out. His cell phone dangled from the end.

"Do you know the sign language alphabet?"

"Yes."

Ruby spelled out *L-A-M-E*.

"Don't say lame. It's offensive."

"Pathetic? Ridiculous?"

"Those should be all right." Simon glanced at the phone as he put it away. "We're a bit early, but it shouldn't matter. Now, remember. This guy, he's harmless. He can't leave his tank."

"His *tank?*" Ruby looked at the building. Whoever the client was, he couldn't live in the shoe repair shop to the left or the Chinese restaurant supply place to the right. The plain metal door before them must lead to a stairway. She looked up at the second floor, grimy red brick with just two small windows. "What is it you do for these, uh, people, anyway?"

"The details are confidential, but mostly, whatever they can't do for themselves. Some don't want to appear in public, some can't work with technology, some can't make themselves understood. But they're people, of one sort or another, so you must treat them with respect. Are you ready?"

Her heart beat a little faster. "Sure."

Simon took from an inside pocket the black leather notebook he carried with him everywhere. He flipped through it and punched a code into a keypad beside the door. There was a click, and he pushed the door open.

A narrow set of stairs led upwards to a small alcove. They paused at the top. Simon rang a doorbell and waved to a camera in the corner. The door clicked open on an ordinary-looking apartment living room, with overstuffed furniture, a beige carpet, a TV, and stereo.

The woman who crossed the room to meet them was middle-aged and cheerful looking, in a colorful print dress, with her graying copper hair in a loose bun. She paused, confused, when she saw Ruby. "Mister Goodnight?" She had a pleasant Irish accent.

"Flora, this is my niece. She's here to meet Seymour. Ruby, this is Seymour's nurse. How's he doing?"

Flora fluttered her hands. "A little better, I think. You know it's hard to tell, but he seems to have more energy. He tells jokes. That's a good sign. The doc was here yesterday, and she says maybe next month he can go home."

"Good, because I have another job for you as soon as you're free."

"Oh, it's not them patchwork things again, is it? They give me the heebie-jeebies."

"Flora, a little professionalism."

"I can't help it, sir. Those ones just take me wrong. I know they're all God's creatures—theoretically. But they're not nice like Mister Seymour."

"Hm. Well, the patchwork things are set up to take care of their own now, so they won't need you anymore. But there's plenty of demand for a good nurse. In fact, if you know anyone else who might be suitable...."

"Since you asked before, I've been thinking of my sister Maureen, in fact. She's got her green card now and heaven knows could use the work. She hasn't got her certificate here yet. Would that be a problem? She's certified back home. As you know, we both grew up knowing bogles, so she already has some idea."

"I'll interview her, but you know the rules. Mum's the word until then. Ruby!"

Ruby had drifted over to the shelves near the TV, flipping through a collection of DVDs, most of which seemed to be of the underwater monster genre. Simon gestured her over. "Come on. Let's step into the lab and see what's on... the slab."

She followed him through yet another heavy steel security door into a large windowless room, too warm, with fluorescent lights. It was filled with a variety of machines making humming, beeping, and chugging noises. The place smelled of the ocean, warm mud, and sulfur. There wasn't actually a slab. Instead, in the center of the room, connected to the machines with tubes and wires, sat a large square glass tank, chest-high for her, filled with opaque brown sludge. There was a stirring, and something pale and pink swiped along the edge. Then a warty brown bump rose above the surface, and a single red eye the size of a baseball blinked open and stared at them.

Ruby stood transfixed, crushing Simon's hand. He nudged her and pointed at a computer monitor hanging above the tank.

It showed a scene from an online virtual world. A chubby, brown-skinned avatar waved and smiled, then its fingers danced as it typed a message in midair. *"Hello, Goodnight,"* it wrote. *"It's been a while."*

"Morning, Seymour. Sorry I don't stop in more often. You know how it is, press of business. This is Ruby."

"Charmed," the avatar typed and bowed.

How was it doing that? Did it have a waterproof keyboard in the tank? "Pleased to meet'cha."

"Seymour makes his living online. Making buildings and custom objects in MMOs. He gets royalties from a couple of games, I believe?"

"Blobbypus is the one you might have heard of," Seymour typed. *"The other sank without a trace."*

"I've played Blobbypus," Ruby said, surprised. "It's pretty good. But I didn't know it was autobiographical."

The sludge churned. The avatar laughed silently, then clapped. *"Very good. And what is it you do with your days?"*

"I'm going to be a naturalist."

"She haunts the Field Museum and the aquarium, keeping people from getting their work done."

"You should get in touch once you finish your education," Seymour typed. *"I could sell you some unusual specimens."*

They chatted for a few minutes more. Then Simon shooed her into the other room, saying they had private business.

Ruby snooped into the contents of the shelves, then settled on the couch to watch the beginning of *Creature from the Black Lagoon.* Flora came in from the kitchen after a while, wiping her hands on her apron, and sat to watch with her.

"The nice thing about the Internet," Ruby said after a while, "is nobody can tell you're a tentacled sea creature."

"That's so."

"He should have a DVD jukebox, so he could watch these without having someone put the disk in for him."

"He copies them to his computer. He's got a—you will pardon the expression—*monster* hard disk. Hush, now, I like this part."

Three

Ruby had decided she should be ready for anything when answering the door, but this guy looked pretty normal—the usual number of heads and limbs, non-transparent, no tiny face where one of his eyes should've been, nothing like that—just a regular, weedy man with protruding eyes and a weak chin poorly disguised by a scruffy beard. Judging by his wardrobe, he believed he was in Hawaii. "Is Simon in? I have an appointment."

"Come. He'll be down in a minute." Ruby showed the man into the study and waited with him.

He wandered restlessly around the room looking at the books and knick-knacks, up to the front to look out the window of the little office—not as if looking for someone, just too much nervous energy. He looked at his watch. "Will he be long?"

"I think he's on the can if you must know. I'm sure he heard the bell. Can I get you something?"

He shook his head. "You're new. What do you do here?"

He was really starting to piss her off. "I live here."

"Where you from? Your English is real good."

Ruby gave him a long, squinty look. "Manhattan."

The man flopped into a chair, looking down at a Persian carpet. "Does all right for himself, doesn't he?"

"He has an… exclusive clientele."

"Oh, you don't have to be careful with me." The man waved his hand. "I'm Polacek." As if that would explain it. "We're in the same line of work," he clarified. "Simon and I. He gets all the Sasquatch business, you know. They're rich as mud."

Sasquatch? "I guess they like his fashion sense."

"Ha! You might be right. For sure they're snappy dressers. Snooty bastards. Well, no matter. I'll be in the money soon, too." Polacek laid a thin briefcase across his lap and drummed his fingers on it. "Pretty soon."

"Here he comes." Ruby was disappointed to lose the chance to quiz Polacek further but also relieved to escape his twitchiness. "See you later." She had to hurry anyway or be late for her flute lesson.

When she returned from the lesson, she found Simon in the garden, sourly examining a chewed-up lettuce plant. "Ever eaten rabbit? I know in my profession I shouldn't be prejudiced, but I have to admit I can't stand rodents."

"Rabbits aren't rodents. Here, wait, I'll show you." She ran up to her room and returned with a skull in one hand, a squirrel skeleton in the other. The squirrel was posed, looking alertly over its shoulder. Simon waited, arms crossed. She held out the skull. "This is a cottontail—the kind of rabbit I've seen eating your lettuce."

"You've seen it. Did you chase it away?"

"Um. They'll run, but they come right back when you leave. Anyway, compare the teeth with this squirrel. See, the rabbit has two extra incisors. They're not rodents, they're lagomorphs."

"It's not a rodent because it has two extra big teeth, the better to eat my vegetables with. Lovely."

"There are also differences in the digestive system."

"The better to digest my vegetables with. I see. Well, thank you for the zoology lesson. Strangely, though, knowing rabbits better hasn't made me love them more."

"The only place they can get in is that gate in back. Just put some chicken wire across the bottom so they can't get through the bars."

"Put chicken wire on my nice wrought-iron gate."

Ruby shrugged. "Or fence the vegetables. If you decide to eat them, I'd rather have a hamburger. But you could save me one for the skeleton."

Simon gave her a squinty-eyed look and turned back to his weeding. Ruby sat on the steps to watch. "What'd Mister Polacek want?"

"Are you prying into my business?"

"Only if you feel like sharing. He already told me you're in the same line of work."

"Hm. It affects you, so I guess you should know. He's going away for a while and wants me to cover his clients while he's gone. We trade off, or we'd never get a vacation."

"Just like country doctors."

Simon wiped his brow on the back of his gardening glove. "Pretty much. So, I'll be extra busy. There's always something that can't wait." He looked around the yard. "There's too much to do around here, too. How'd the lesson go?"

"I'm afraid I'll have to give it up, or I might damage the flute."

"How could that happen?"

"I might dent it on my teacher's head."

"I see. Maybe you need a different teacher."

"And a different instrument. We can return the flute, can't we?"

"What instrument?"

Simon had insisted music lessons were non-optional, and all his suggestions for instruments were among those found in an orchestra. Still, nothing ventured, nothing gained. "Electric guitar?"

Simon stood, thoughtfully took off his gloves, and tucked them into a pocket of his gardening apron. He looked at her. "You're a leftie, aren't you?"

"Right. I mean, correct."

He took off the apron and held it out to her. "Hold that." He went inside, and a few minutes later returned with a dusty guitar case. He brushed it off, sat on the steps beside her with the case on his lap, and opened it.

"Oh, my God," Ruby breathed. It was an electric guitar—beautiful, bright, metal-flake blue with red and gold flames.

"It was left to me by a friend." His hand drew bright whispers from the strings. "Someone ought to be using it."

"It's too nice a one for me to learn on." She was guilt-stricken and a little panicked because Simon seemed to be getting choked up.

"It's all right." He closed the case, latched it, and set it on her lap. "Just remember it's a loaner and don't bash anyone on the head with it. And no amps in the house. I'll buy you headphones." He stood abruptly and went back inside.

Ruby sighted across the net and gave her paddle a preparatory waggle. Marissa's dog, McSchmidt, watched from the couch. In the next room, Marissa's little brother had the TV on too loud.

Marissa returned the serve with spin. It ticked off the table edge and rattled away under the couch. McSchmidt ran after it. "Ha! Fourteen— nine, me. Ready to concede? We could play *Star Raiders.*"

"No, I know you can whip me at *Star Raiders*. With ping-pong, I have a chance." Ruby shifted the couch to retrieve the ball.

"You've gotten better. Hey, did you see Joey Ergot is going with Dana now?"

Ruby did a couple of practice bounces. "Is Joey the tall boy with the ears from Penny's party?"

Marissa laughed, making her miss Ruby's serve. "No, silly, that's Jonah. And I wasn't ready."

"You were ready when I hit it. I can't help it if you burst out laughing when I haven't made a joke. Fourteen—ten."

"Come on, you really don't know who Joey Ergot is? From *Over the Line?*"

"Oh, on TV? He's got long brown hair that hangs in his eyes? And who's Dana?"

"Hello, the model? How can you live in this country and not know this?"

"Secretly, I live in a different country. We read books there instead of *People* magazine. C'mon, my serve still."

"You're a little odd." Marissa bopped the ball back. "It's a good thing you're funny."

Ruby sighed theatrically. "You've found out my secret. I'm odd. I thought I was hiding it so well. Ready?"

A long volley ended with the ball rolling into the next room. "Fifteen—ten," Marissa announced. "You know what else though? I think Conrad likes you."

"Your serve. Conrad… Conrad. Ashley's brother? I didn't think he could tell Ashley's friends apart."

"He noticed you all right." Marissa bounced the ball on the table and caught it again. "He said you were smart."

"Marissa, a boy saying you're smart does not mean he likes you. I know this from personal experience."

"It was more the way he said it. 'That Asian girl is pretty smart. What's she doing hanging around with Ashley?'"

"That's not a compliment of me. It's a dig at his sister. Anyway, Ashley's got a brain, too, when she chooses to use it."

"I don't think that's what he meant. You haven't seen…. Well, anyway, *I* think he's cute."

"Yeah, he cleans up pretty good." Ruby picked up the paddle. "Are you serving or what?"

When Ruby was collecting her things to go, Marissa told her to wait, ran into her room, and returned with a handful of magazines. The top one was called *HeartBeat,* had a cover crowded with photos of people she'd never seen before, and promised 212 proven fashion secrets. "What are these for?"

"To improve your camouflage," Marissa said. "If you like them, I'll save you more. I'll send you links, too."

"Oh… thanks."

"People magazine, as if!"

Four

Ruby sat on her bed, headphones on, trying to teach herself some chords before her first guitar lesson. There was a scrape and a thump from above. Ruby paused and looked at the clock. Simon had said he might be late, but it was almost eleven and still no sign. It was majorly creepy to be alone in the house with whatever was in the attic.

She closed her lesson book, then opened it again, then closed it and got up. She was tired of imagining. She'd rather know. Leaving the guitar, she went into the hallway and up the narrow attic stairs, not hurrying and not too quietly. She stopped at the top, collecting her courage.

She knocked softly.

Something moved in there—she imagined it shuffling and breathing right on the other side of the door.

"It's silly we're living in the same house and haven't met." Silence. "I'm going to the kitchen to make myself a snack. I'll be there for a while. If you want to talk."

Still no reply.

On her way down, she stopped in her room for the guitar. Sitting on a stool at the kitchen counter, she attempted a scale. She'd turned partly away from the door but could still see it in the corner of her eye.

Half an hour went by, and she'd almost forgotten she was waiting, when she saw something move. She stiffened but kept playing. After a minute, she turned to look, braced for the worst.

He was short, shorter than her, bald, and pale, with a low forehead, large yellow eyes, huge pointed ears, a small upturned nose, and wide mouth. His white, sleeveless t-shirt was slit on the sides, to allow for the hanging folds of skin between his arms and his body. He looked at her expressionlessly and blinked slowly.

"H-hello. Have we met before? You look familiar." It was the line she'd decided on while waiting, hoping to break the tension with a joke.

But the strange little man didn't laugh. "Perhaps," he said in a high, squeaky voice, "you've seen my picture in the paper."

When he spoke, she could see his teeth, wide and white and shark-like, and she realized she had, in fact, seen that face before, or something like it. "You're Bat Boy!" she said, excited. "My parents used to get that paper."

"Yes," he chirped. "Thank heaven it's gone out of business. Told the most awful lies about me. Of course, I'm not a boy anymore, but the name Batman is taken. So please, call me Wally." He moved a little closer, and Ruby forced herself not to shrink back. The teeth were his most alarming feature. They looked like they could rend flesh. But he moved slowly, with a rolling walk, nonthreatening. He sat on a stool. "What are you drinking?"

"Hot strawberry milk. Well, it used to be hot. Want some?"

"Perhaps tea instead? Earl Grey?"

While Ruby fussed about with cups and spoons, Wally leaned over to look at the guitar. "Nice axe. Custom Strat. May I?"

"If you're careful. It belongs to Simon, and it's sort of a treasure."

Wally set the headset on the counter and turned the volume to max. He picked up the guitar, his arm membrane cradling the body, a vein visible where it stretched over the end. He strummed, adjusted the tuning. He fiddled with a knob, then launched into a driving frenzy of chords, finger-picking, and drumming on the strings. He threw his head back and gave a maniacal laugh, displaying every pointed tooth. "Wipe out!" he squealed and continued to the end, laughing again when he was done.

"All right, that's disturbing. Don't do that again." The microwave dinged, and she dropped a teabag in.

"Only song I can sing anything like the original."

"Are you left-handed too?"

"Both-handed. I get them mixed, in fact. Dr. Fortunato says I have a weird brain. Go figure." Wally played quickly, plucking the strings with his long fingernails, in a series of runs reminding her of the flight of a crazed hummingbird.

"You're really good."

"Yeah, well. Don't get out much. Lots of time to practice."

"I haven't heard you playing upstairs."

"Didn't bring mine. Just here a few weeks. I travel light." He looked at her lesson book. "You're just starting. Show you some stuff? Here, take it. Play me a C."

In about an hour, she learned a series of chords well enough to get through the changes fairly smoothly. "Now you can play twelve bar blues," he said. "Amaze your teacher. Go ahead and do it again, and I'll sing the blues, cause baby, when you're feeling low, it makes you feel just a tiny bit better. Just repeat, I'll pick it up on the second go-round."

Ruby started playing, and Wally said, "This here is the Bat Boy Blues. Written tonight, special for you." And, swaying, he sang into a spatula.

I woke up this evening, and things were not okay.
Woke up this evening, things are lookin' gray,
'Cause I'm still the Bat Boy, just like yesterday.

I've got the Bat Boy teeth and got the Bat Boy ears,
Got the Bat Boy nose, for sure the Bat Boy ears.
When plastic surgeons see me, they run away in tears.

Got me these here wings, and yet I cannot fly.
Got me these old wings but not much use to fly.
Prolly gonna break my neck if I ever even try.

There was slow applause from the doorway, and they spun, startled, to see Simon there. "Wow, what happened to you?" Ruby said. He stood in his sock feet, clothes a mess, the first time she'd seen them less than perfect after nine a.m. His shirt had a torn sleeve, a missing button, and a large green stain. His trousers were coated with mud, the tie was missing, and on the suit jacket he'd draped over his arm... "Is that *blood?*"

"Don't worry, it's not mine. I'm okay. But you"—he gave Ruby a hard look—"do you know what time it is? And I thought we had an understanding about going into the attic."

Wally shook his head. "She didn't go in the attic, Simon. I chose to come down."

"And," Ruby said, "I don't recall agreeing to a particular bedtime. Besides, I was worried about you."

"Well, no harm done, I suppose." Simon grumbled. "But go to bed now, please. And Wally, wait for an all clear before you come out again. If someone were out front, they could've seen you in the hallway."

Simon led the way, opening the drawing-room door to block the view from the front door. "You can knock on my ceiling when you want to come out," Ruby whispered to Wally. "What's the all clear?"

"The button behind the painting at bottom of stairs. Three long, one short."

Ruby got into her pajamas and brushed her teeth, practicing chord positions with one hand. "C, C, C, C," she sang to herself. "F is a hard one, F, C, C, G, F, C, C." She rinsed her mouth. "Oh, Papa's in the big house, Mama's in the big house too. Papa's in the big house, Ma-a-a-ma's in there too. Baby, I've got troubles, what's a girl to do?"

She slid between cool sheets and was soon dreaming of looping crazily through the night sky, looking for bugs to eat, while bats in sombreros flew alongside, strumming ukuleles.

Ruby had the newspaper set out on the table, sausage cooked, and an omelet in the pan when Simon showed up downstairs the next morning, late and bleary-eyed.

"What's the plan for today?" she said.

"What are you doing? You don't cook." He tugged the knot tighter on his robe and leaned over the pan. "You're overcooking those eggs. Take mine out now, please. No, I'll do it. You run outside and get some basil. Damn, you already got some. Do I smell coffee?"

"Sit, I'll take care of it. I know you had a hard night."

Simon sat, looking at her with suspicion as she set food in front of him. He picked up a fork. "What is it you want?"

"Nothing much." Ruby plunked herself and her plate down across from him and reached for the salt. "Just thought you might like some company on your rounds today."

"Ho ho, no. Don't you have guitar, swimming, and something else?"

"You and I both know swimming is just to get me out of the way. I'm a marvelous swimmer already. Second fastest in my class. And about the guitar...."

"Yes?"

"Well, Bat B—*Wally's* a great teacher, I think. He taught me a lot, and I wasn't even a little tempted to bash him."

"He's only here a little longer."

"What for? Never mind. I know, you can't say. But I could work with him while he's here and start regular lessons after."

"Did you even ask him? Anyway, he only knows rock and blues and bluegrass."

"What, if you please, is wrong with that? I hope you don't expect me to play Beethoven. He's bored out of his mind. I'm sure he'd love to do it. And I can meet more of your clients today."

Simon took a sip of coffee. "You can't come with me. They're not all sweethearts like Seymour. They don't like anyone knowing their business or where they live. And you have to give this teacher a chance. She's very good."

"Is that a no, then?"

"A definite no." He picked up the paper. "If Wally wants to teach you too, though, I don't mind."

"Well, that's something." She stood. "Do you want more coffee or anything?" She got juice, and on her way back rubbed her knuckles on his head. "Getting a little thin on top there, Unc."

"What?" He smoothed his hair. "No, it's not."

She shrugged. "Suit yourself."

He turned a page. Was he reading the continuation of the headline article, *Killer Strikes Again—Still No Bodies Found?*

"If there are no bodies," Ruby asked, "how do they know there's a killer?"

"What?" Simon looked where she was pointing. "Oh, I don't know. I never read that lurid stuff. Lots of blood on the ground, maybe." He looked at the clock. "I have to hurry." He took his last two bites and stood, coffee cup in hand. "I might be late again," he called over his shoulder. "If there's nothing in the fridge, get take-out. The eggplant parmesan at Marcelo's is nice."

She tidied up, then went to prepare for her day. As she passed the bathroom door, she saw Simon leaning over the sink, toothbrush sticking out of his mouth, trying to see the top of his head with a hand mirror. She smiled as she walked to her room and murmured, "That's for the uniform."

Five

Ruby stopped by the zoo on her way home. She made faces at the orangutans to see whether they would make faces back. One did. Then she went to the Field Museum and walked through the "History of Man" exhibit, looking at the tree of human ancestry painted on one wall. She found an anthropologist she'd pestered on a previous visit, Dr. Rora, in the diorama of Australopithecus, squatting to insert a stone tool into the hand of a hominid figure seated on a log, scraping a skin.

"What was wrong with the old tool?" Ruby asked.

"Ruby, hi. This *is* the old tool." Dr. Rora pushed her hair back from her face and reached for a glue gun. "He dropped it. What's up with you?"

"What do you think about Sasquatches?"

"Bigfoot? I think they're imaginary."

"Some people think they're leftover Gigantopithecus."

"If they really existed, they might be descended of them, though they probably evolved a lot in all that time. But if there were huge animals living up in the woods of the Pacific Northwest like people claim, we'd have found some by now. At least dead ones." Dr. Rora stood and looked over her handiwork from different angles.

But what if they weren't in the woods anymore? Maybe they'd all moved to Chicago and had their own gated community. "Change of subject. Is there an orangutan skull in the museum?"

"Not on display, but we can look in back if you like."

She didn't get home until after six, carrying two chili dogs and large fries. She went into the study and stood, guitar still strapped to her back, greasy fast food bag in one hand, sipping at her cola from the other, while she stared at the skull on the mantle. Definitely not an orangutan. Too small and narrow for a Sasquatch. Too bad she couldn't show it to Dr. Rora.

Leaning the guitar case against the wall, she went out to the gazebo to eat and read. It had become her favorite spot—sitting on the rail and leaning against the brick fence, which was cool from being in the shade all day. From there, she had a good view of the gate. She'd declined Simon's offer of a pellet gun to pot any rabbits entering that way.

The woman at the door was in a brown burka, only her eyes visible in the concealing garment. The eyes, and the skin around them, were dark reddish brown, like mahogany. Ruby opened the door. "Simon's away until late, probably."

The woman nodded. "You help me." She had a heavy accent Ruby couldn't place.

"Come in, and I'll call his cell." Ruby stepped back to let the woman pass.

She moved gracefully, the robe swishing around her ankles. It was made of a heavy, slick fabric that clung where it touched. "It is well. You help me. I do not understand if."

"What?" Ruby opened the study door, but the woman didn't enter. "If I don't call him, he'll be upset. Who are you?"

"Who?" The woman stood looking at the guitar, which she'd

leaned against the staircase when she came in to answer the door. "You play well."

"Not really."

The woman drifted into the study and over to the desk. "You help me. Why don't I?"

"Why don't you what? I have to call him, but why don't you tell me what you want so I can tell him?"

The woman unpinned her head shawl, and with one movement, swept it off and opened the front of her garment. Beneath, she wore a low-cut brown unitard. Aside from the dark patch around her eyes, and a pale strip starting at her chin and running down the middle of her chest, her skin was tiger-striped, dark reddish-brown and cream. Her hair had the same colors, braided into a helmet of corn-rows. "I must see this in the all-around." She held out a thick, yellowed card a little smaller than an envelope. "I know it, but I have forgotten."

Ruby took the card, handling it by its edges as the woman had. Printed on it were two identical photos of a sturdy man in an old-fashioned athletic suit, barefoot, legs apart, holding a rod in each hand. But no, the photos weren't exactly identical. They'd been taken from slightly different angles. Someone had drawn on it with red and blue ink, swooping, curving lines that each ended on the end of a rod and on the ground at his feet, passing in front of the man and behind. These lines too were slightly different on the two sides. In one case a little bit of line was visible between his legs, for instance, and in the other it was hidden. "This is a 3-D picture, isn't it? Like a View-Master slide."

The woman smiled a little desperately, and Ruby could tell she didn't understand.

"I'll call Simon. He'll know what to do."

Simon didn't answer.

"I left a message. He'll call back soon."

"The interval is short."

"Are you saying you're in a hurry?"

"Teela." She held out her hand.

"Hi. I'm Ruby." The woman's hand was fever-hot, though she looked healthy.

"You help me now. Simon does not call."

"You could wait longer than fifteen seconds to decide that."

"Figure it out, begin. The interval is short."

"How short?"

Teela held her hands apart about ten inches.

Ruby rolled her eyes. "Fine, I'll try to figure it out." She turned the card over. The back was blank except for some unrecognizable symbols in one corner.

"It is old." Teela nodded.

"It looks like an antique. Hey, I know someone who knows antiques. Wait here."

Ruby pulled out her phone and scrolled back through the photos to the one she'd taken of Octavian McTeague's business card. Teela had taken a book of impressionist art from a shelf and sat cross-legged on the floor, robe spread out around her, looking at the pictures. Ruby stepped around her and into the office, pulling a chair over to the doorway where she could both reach the phone and keep an eye on the visitor.

Someone picked up after three rings. "Mister McTeague? It's Ruby Park. Remember me?"

There was a pause. *"Oh, yes. Probability Girl."*

"That's me. I'm sorry if it's late to call. I have a weird question." Ruby described the card. "What do people use to view those?"

"Oh, you see them in antique stores all the time with boxes of the cards. They're like goggles on a stick with a frame to hold the card out in front. I'm sure if you google you can find pictures of them. Try 'antique 3-D viewers.'"

Ruby started typing the search on the computer. "Is there any way I can get one right away?"

"You have to view it right now?" McTeague sounded amused. *"I*

don't think anyone's still open, and anyway they come in different sizes. You could make your own, I suppose."

She paged through the pictures in the search results. "How? It looks like they have lenses."

"A pair of reading glasses might work."

After a little more research, Ruby took some petty cash, left another message for Simon, and moved Teela into the drawing room. Teela brought along a small stack of illustrated books. "I'll be right back," Ruby said. "I'm going down the street to the all-night drugstore. If the phone or the door rings, please don't answer because you'll just confuse them."

"If, if. Everyone says this, and I do not know what it means. You say if with something that's not true. Nothing rings."

"Never mind. Just stay here and don't answer."

"Plus two!" Teela called after her.

What? Sea monsters were easier to talk with. "Plus two, okay! Same to you."

Under the harsh fluorescent lights in the drugstore, Ruby stood at the rack of reading glasses. They came in different strengths, starting with +0.5 and going up to +4.0. "Plus two," Ruby murmured. She picked out one pair of each strength anyway. She could return the extras later. After all, the interval was short. She didn't want to risk having to make another trip.

She ran back to the house, but Teela was gone. The books she'd been looking through were piled in front of the study door, which was still locked. But she'd left her picture card on the hall table, so maybe she'd be back. Ruby sat on the steps and dumped the reading glasses out onto the floor. She picked up the +2.0 pair and put them on, holding the card up in front of her face and trying to see it in 3D. This only made her cross-eyed, so she cut a piece from the back of a legal pad from the office and held it up to make a barrier in the middle. The picture sprang into three dimensions, and Ruby could see how the lines swooped and wove. She experimented to find the best viewing distance, then went scavenging for materials.

As she was finishing up, the back door opened. She ran to the kitchen, pliers and coat-hanger wire in hand. "Oh, it's you. I asked you to stay put."

"I have found a place of no electric. You are ready."

"Almost. Wait here." Ruby poked the ends of the clothes-hanger wire through the sides of a battered felt hat she'd found in the hall closet and taped the cardboard divider to hang from it. "Put that on. Okay." The card fit nicely into the wire framework Ruby had bent with pliers. "These are the *plus two* glasses." She watched Teela closely for a reaction. "I got other ones if it's not right."

"Again with *if!* This is well. You find them, and so it is."

"How did you know plus two was right?"

Teela ignored the question. She was too busy digging into an inside pocket of her robe. "This is payment." She put something into Ruby's hand.

"What are they?" Three small, shiny brown objects, like beans. Ruby thought of *Jack and the Beanstalk.* What might these grow into?

"They are shouts. Useful for you. Come now, collect my things." Teela turned toward the door, then stopped. "Bring light. No electric. On your arm."

Collect *what* things? Teela still had everything she'd come with. And what was on her arm? Teela wanted light but without electricity? Ruby had seen some candles and matches in a kitchen drawer. She set her "shouts" on the counter and got them out.

She found Teela near the gazebo, arms held up like the man in the picture, a short, thick stick in each hand. "Light," Teela said. Ruby lit a candle and held it out. Teela tucked one stick under her arm and took it. "A thing you must know." She held the candle up to her face, flame licking at her chin.

"Hey! You'll burn yourself."

"I do not burn, though I walk in fire." Indeed, the flame seemed not to affect her. "You also do not burn, for you do not follow."

"If I follow you, I will burn?"

"Again if!" Teela shrugged. She held the candle to illuminate the card. "I am ready, but you have electric. Please take it away."

She had electric? Where? Ruby patted her pockets. She was sure she'd left her phone inside.

"On your arm, as I say."

Oh. Digital watch. Ruby ran to the house and left the watch on the steps, then returned in time to see Teela toss the hat aside and start swinging the sticks through the air. After several looping movements, she plunged the sticks toward the ground. Suddenly, she erupted in a halo of fierce red and blue light, shouted something, then there was darkness.

Ruby blinked, the lights still swimming in her eyes. After a few seconds, she could make out a dark area on the lawn. Teela had fallen. Perhaps she was hurt, fireproof or no. She ran over to help, but Teela wasn't there—just her clothes. The two sticks also lay there, their ends resting on a small, burned patch of lawn. Simon would love that. She cautiously touched a stick. It was a little warm.

She folded the clothes, piled everything else on top, and took it all inside, picking up the beans as she passed. But when she set everything down on Simon's big desk, the beans were gone. She retraced her steps, turning on every light, but they were nowhere to be found. Well, they would turn up... maybe.

Six

Ruby held up her swimsuit and sighed. She'd tried to wheedle Uncle Simon into getting her a bikini, the better to fit in at Marissa's birthday party. But he proved wheedle-proof, so she had a one-piece. She crumpled the suit and threw it into her backpack.

As she came down the stairs, she found the study door open. Damn! She'd hoped to sneak out before Simon woke. She paused in the hallway, then walked quickly and quietly past the doorway.

"Hold on a moment!"

So much for luck. Ruby backed up. "Yes?"

"A word with you. Sit." Simon had Teela's belongings piled to one side and the card on the desk right in front of him, face down. He'd been looking at the odd characters on the back with a magnifying glass.

"Woof!" Ruby sat across from him.

He raised an eyebrow.

"I did call you several times, but she was anxious and in a hurry."

Simon leaned back, making his chair creak. "Tell me all, omitting no detail, however slight."

Ruby did, then asked, "Who is she? Where is she from?"

Simon shrugged. "Doesn't sound familiar. Just passing through is my guess."

"She's not a regular client? How'd she know to come here?"

"They have a system, like hobo signs. Do you know what those are?" Simon opened a desk drawer and pulled out a small card. "When migrants roamed the countryside, they had a secret language of marks they would make on trees and fence-posts. One sign meant a mean dog, one meant they might get a handout at that house, and so forth."

Simon tossed the card across the desk. "After I set up in business, I found this symbol scratched into the nameplate by the front door." He pointed at the card, his business card. The logo looked like a crescent moon with two curved lines across the bottom.

"So you had a new nameplate made with that as your logo. I've noticed it."

He nodded. "When I get new clients who don't seem to be from around here, I assume they followed the signs. Now, about these shout things...."

"I looked all over for them. I can't understand how they even got out of my hand." She made a fist to show how she'd held them tightly.

"I was about to say, I consider it your problem. You helped the client, the payment is yours if you can find it."

"Oh. Well, okay. Thanks! But what's a shout good for, anyway?"

"I haven't a clue. Don't look so surprised," he said, irritated. "Compared to all there is to know, nobody knows much. Next time, I suggest you negotiate a payment you can understand before providing service. And, speaking of payment, I expect you to reimburse the petty cash. I notice you forgot to write down the amount."

"Oops. Yeah, sorry, I was in a hurry. No problem, I'll return all the reading glasses and get the money back."

Simon passed her the glasses. "It only takes a moment to record it, and it's less work than having to remember later."

"Next time I'll do it that way, for sure."

"There's also the matter of a small, burned patch in the lawn."

Fifteen minutes later, Ruby stood on the front steps and took a deep breath of relief. That hadn't been as bad as she'd feared. She'd been sure Simon would be furious. Instead, he'd been just annoyed, and after a point-by-point critique of her actions—leaving Teela alone in the house near the top of the list—he'd let her go without even telling her never to do any such crazy thing again. From Simon, that felt almost like approval.

She dropped by the drugstore to return the glasses, then ran for her train. Once she settled, breathless, in her seat, she opened her pack to take out a book. But Marissa's magazines were in there too, and the party was in a few hours. She dropped a magazine into her lap and stared at it with distaste. It was pink. "Yeah, all right," she muttered and opened the cover.

Though the party was in Marissa's honor, it was being held at Ashley's because she had room. This, Ashley apparently felt, put her in charge of the event. The day was a scorcher, and everyone was wet from the pool by the time she announced it was time for cake and presents. Marissa settled in at the head of the table, grinning as she vigorously dried her curly black hair.

As Ashley made preliminary cut marks, Ruby counted candles on the cake. "You're only fifteen? What'd you do, skip a grade?"

"Um, yeah." Marissa blushed. "Don't make a big deal about it, okay?"

"Start on the presents," Ashley directed. "We're on a schedule here."

"Mine first!" Penny reached into the pile for a small box.

Marissa was pleased with the little gold earrings Penny gave her and loved the scrapbook from Ashley and scrapbook supplies from Sophie—she and Ashley had collaborated. When she got to Ruby's present, she felt it before opening. "A picture! Not of you, I hope."

"No, I wouldn't want to scare people when they saw it."

She tore into the wrapping paper and withdrew a framed picture. "OMG it's McSchmidt! Cute, he's got a ping-pong ball in his mouth. Ruby, this is really good! Did you paint this yourself?"

"It's just a little watercolor. I'm used to painting animals."

"But how did you do it? From memory?"

"I took his picture."

"Let me see," Sophie said. "Cool. What kind of name is McSchmidt, anyway?"

"Part Scottie, part German Shepherd. Ruby, thanks, I love it!"

Ashley's schedule called next for games, to wait out the time—exactly one hour, not a minute less—which Ashley's mom required between cake consumption and a return to the pool. The rubber-ball bolo game was fun, but Ruby didn't care for the cut-throat style of croquet the other girls seemed to enjoy, so she settled on a deck chair to read and halfway watch.

Right after a smash of Ashley's sent another player running across the yard to retrieve her ball, Ashley looked back at the house and said, "Is that boy staring at me?" She had a dangerous tone of voice.

The other players turned to look. The boy standing next to the sliding door into the house was tall, red-haired, wore a button shirt and cutoffs, and held a notebook. He did seem to be looking at Ashley, though he looked away, embarrassed, when everyone looked at him.

"It's that dork friend of my brother's," Ashley said. "The math genius. Who does he think he is to stand there looking at me?"

"Ashley," Marissa said, "let it go. Come on, so he's a jerk, big deal."

"No, I don't think so." Ashley started walking toward the boy, sandals flapping. Marissa and Penny followed. Ruby set her magazine aside, sensing whatever was about to happen might be more interesting than an article about acne.

The boy looked at Ashley again as she walked up to stand about two feet away from him. He seemed nervous but stood his ground. "Hey, carrot top," Ashley said. "What's the big idea staring at me?"

"I'm just waiting for Conrad." There was a defiant tone in his voice. "I guess I can stand here and look around if I want."

"But you weren't looking around. You were looking right at me. As if you wanted something." Ashley moved a little closer. "Did you want something?" The boy backed up, his calves bumped into a potted palm and his arms went up to keep his balance. His notebook flew away to land on the concrete.

Marissa tugged at her elbows. "Ashley, come on, don't spoil the party."

Ruby had, by this time, stood and moved closer herself. She looked down at the papers spilling from the notebook. A drawing of a robot, very detailed, with gears and pulleys and cables to work the limbs, and a basket of eggs on top of its head. A sheet titled "Flocking Behavior," showing several birds in flight, arrows between and around them, labeled with equations. A page of tiny, dense handwriting with a Venn diagram, two circles labeled "green leafy vegetables" and "edible items." The circles did not intersect.

Ruby had the sudden conviction that she would rather be friends with this one boy than with all of these girls.

Particularly Ashley, at the moment. She'd moved even closer, and the boy looked panicked but didn't back away again. She stepped right up to press against him with an evil grin.

The boy's eyes got wide, and they flashed down to where her chest touched him, then immediately away. "He looked at my breasts!" Ashley said. "Is that why you were staring, you wanted to see my breasts?"

"Ashley, cut it out," Ruby said.

"No, no, if he wants to look at them, I think he should. In fact…" Ashley stepped back, reaching for the strap of her bikini top. "…he should have a good look."

Ruby snapped. Without even thinking about it, she reached down for a large nylon bag that had held pool toys, took it by the edge, swooped it around once so it filled with air, then up and over Ashley's head and down past her waist, where she pulled the drawstring tight.

"Hey!" Ashley yelled, starting to struggle.

Ruby grabbed her, pinning her arms, still holding the drawstring rope in one hand. "You need to cool off." She dragged Ashley toward the pool.

"Let me out!"

"And you, a Catholic school girl. You should be ashamed." Ruby spun Ashley, making her stagger, then released the drawstring cord. Ashley, off balance, fell into the water. Shrieking and choking, she fought her way out of the bag.

The other girls had followed, some laughing, some just appalled, and they were all beside the pool when Ashley surfaced, spluttering. "You bitch!" she screamed at Ruby, face red. "That was suicide! You can just forget about getting onto Spirit Committee now! Or cheerleading!"

"Oh no," Ruby said dryly, arms crossed. "Not that. *Anything* but that."

"You brought it on yourself." Ashley seemed oblivious to the irony. She swam for the ladder. "I think it's time for you to leave."

"In fact," Ruby said, "I was just thinking I had something better to do." She looked back at the house, but the boy had gone. "Damn. See ya! Marissa, happy birthday, bye!"

Marissa, standing on the sidelines looking amused, wiggled her fingers. Ruby ran inside and through the house. She found the boy at the front door, ready to leave. He had scooped up his notebook and papers in a hurry, and they were in disarray. His face was white, freckles standing out. He turned to glare at Ruby as she ran up. "Who the hell asked you to butt in?"

"I… what?"

"I can manage without your help." He left, slamming the door.

"Well. You're welcome." She thought about going after him but decided not to in her bathing suit. Anyway, why give him another chance to yell at her? She went to collect her things and change, disappointed.

By the time she got home, Ruby had worked up a fine wallow of self-pity. She didn't indulge often, but the situation seemed to justify it. She'd made a powerful enemy—while she didn't care about Spirit Committee and cheerleading, she knew Ashley could find lots of other ways to make things difficult for her. The other girls wouldn't defy Ashley to be her friends. All this for the sake of a boy who'd practically spat in her face.

Smooth move, girl.

So wrapped up was she in her own misery and anger, walking quickly home from the station with her head down, that she pulled up just short of bumping into someone on the sidewalk. She stopped, looking up at a tall, sneering young man in a dirty denim shirt with the sleeves torn off, displaying crude tattoos. Behind him were two other boys in their late teens, equally disreputable-looking. "You're in a big hurry," he said.

Ruby looked around. There was nobody else on the street, just houses where probably nobody was home at the moment. Uncle Simon lived in a nice neighborhood, but the commuter rail tracks were on the border of a not-so-nice area. These boys must come from the other side.

"Let's see what's in the bag." The tall boy held his hand out.

She knew better than to try to fight three older boys who might possibly be armed. But what was in the bag was almost a hundred dollars from returning the reading glasses, which Uncle Simon expected her to return to petty cash. Plus, this had been a bad day so far already, and her level of affection for the human species, and for boys in particular, was way down in the red zone. Doing the smart thing wasn't really her style, anyway. She narrowed her eyes, jutted out her chin. "You really don't want to mess with me today."

The boy laughed, turning his head to catch the eye of the other two, who also laughed. Then he lunged toward her, too fast for her to back away, and grabbed the loop on the top of her backpack, some bracelet he wore scratching her neck.

"Let go!" Ruby tried to jerk the bag out of his hands. She put a hand on his dirty old shirt, pushing him away. "Back off!"

The results were far more dramatic than she'd expected. The world went blue for a second, and she could barely hear her own voice, though she'd shouted plenty loud. The tall boy let go of her, and all three staggered back, falling hard, without trying to break their falls. The blue faded, and Ruby staggered a little herself, off balance from being released. A car alarm went off, and every dog in the neighborhood started barking like mad. From the brick building beside her, a fine powder of red dust sifted down. "Holy shit." Ruby walked to the tall boy, who'd looked like he'd cracked his head pretty good on the sidewalk. He was out but still breathing. A small trickle of blood ran from one ear.

A second-floor window opened across the street, and a skinny black woman leaned out. "What was that?"

"Um, I don't know. What'd it sound like?"

"Sound like a bomb went off."

Ruby thought fast. "That's what I thought. I ran around the corner to see and found these guys. Maybe they set it off. But I think they're hurt. Will you call an ambulance?"

"Yeah, I'm gonna do that and the police too. They can't set off no bomb in my street. You wait there." The woman ducked back inside.

What the hell had happened? Ruby looked at the hand she'd put against the tall boy's chest. It looked normal. Then it occurred to her she should be far away when the police and ambulance showed up. Given her parents' history, the last thing she wanted was to be associated with any sort of explosion. She did the rest of her thinking while running toward home.

She lived in a weird household, and that had to have something to do with it. But there was nothing weird about her, she was just a witness to strange events. Nobody had zapped her with a superpower ray or fed her a potion or even given her anything unusual.

But wait. Someone had given her something. Teela had paid her with three beans which then mysteriously vanished. She'd even called them "shouts," and shouting was what Ruby had just done, in a big way.

There had to be a connection. It was super ridiculous, but it wasn't her imagination. There were three boys, unconscious on the sidewalk, showing something odd had happened, and she couldn't think of a better explanation.

She reached home, ran up the stairs and into her room, and threw herself onto the bed. Now that the danger was past, irrationally, she was feeling all the fear she hadn't felt at the time, and she needed a few minutes to breathe and calm down.

So, she'd used one shout. Presumably she had two more, and she'd have to be careful not to set them off accidentally. It was unsettling, like walking around with a bomb in your pocket, and she was even unsure what set it off. Did she have to touch someone and yell? Did it matter with which hand? Or would it happen anytime she yelled? Let's hope not because that would be super inconvenient. But there was no way to be sure without maybe wasting one.

She'd just have to remember to keep her voice down. She scowled. Super inconvenient! As if she needed one more reason to feel miserable. She'd burned her bridges with Ashley, boys were stupid, and now she couldn't even yell at people. She got up and drew the curtains to make the room as dark as possible, then lay down again to dwell on her suffering for a while.

After a while, there was a light knock on the door. "May I come in?"

"If you must," Ruby replied, her voice muffled by the pillow over her face. She heard the door open and a chair being moved into place beside the bed. Peeking out, she saw Simon standing beside the chair, looking at her shelf of skeletons.

"Nice work. I didn't know you had so many. How do you clean off the bones?"

"Those that are too big for owls to eat, I use beetles."

"Beetles?" Simon looked around the room, a little anxiously.

"Don't worry. I don't have any at the moment, and anyway I won't bring them inside."

Simon sat. "You're home early. Is something wrong?"

"Nothing murdering Ashley wouldn't solve."

"If you have eight hundred dollars, I could arrange that for you," Simon joked. At least, Ruby hoped it was a joke.

"Also, some boys tried to rob me, but I beat them up. I'm through with boys forever, by the way, so I won't need that bikini after all."

"That's good." Often, Ruby couldn't tell whether Simon was playing it cool or hadn't heard a word she'd said. This time, though, he seemed distracted.

"What about you? Is something wrong?"

"I heard today that Polacek is dead. His wife called."

For a few seconds, Ruby drew a blank. "Oh. The twitchy guy." She almost objected that she'd just talked to him the other day but realized that was stupid. People could die a minute after you talked with them. "He didn't look sick. What'd he die of?"

"Carelessness." Simon rubbed his hand over his chin. "I don't understand what he was even doing here in town. From what he said, he should be vacationing in Bermuda. What did he tell you?"

There was no response. Simon looked up to find Ruby staring at him. "What?" he said.

"You honestly think you can get away with a one-word answer on this one? Look, Mister Mystery Man, I get the whole confidentiality thing, but really? Carelessness? Carelessness is getting run over by a bus. He was doing something for work, wasn't he? Something someone will want you to do, now, since evidently, he screwed it up. How do you think it is for me, you out all hours of the day and night, you come back covered in blood, and wave your hands and say 'No problem, it's not mine.' Like that's supposed to stop me worrying? Sure, of course!" Realizing her voice was rising, Ruby paused, took a breath, and resumed more quietly. "Fine. Don't tell me a goddamn thing! Get yourself killed. It's your life. But what about me?"

It wasn't just this. It was everything, the whole rotten day. She shoved her face into the covers, overwhelmed with fear and anger and injustice. "It's not fair, it's not fair!"

Simon stroked her hair and thumped her gently on the back. "I'm sorry. Of course, it's a legitimate concern, and I should've talked with you about it before. Come on downstairs, and I'll show you how I've provided for you if anything happens to me."

"Argh!" Ruby screamed softly. She flipped over and curled up under the covers. "Go away, go away!"

He got up, and after a moment the door closed. She stayed under the covers and cried herself to sleep.

Seven

In the dream, Ruby was left to wait outside at a cafe table while her mother made calls from a phone booth. This was weird because her mom's cell phone was in her purse, sitting on the table beside Ruby, and as far as she knew, it was working.

In fact, as she sat there slurping the last of her milkshake, the cell phone rang. Mom was too far away to hear it. Ruby dug the phone out of the purse, checked the caller ID, and answered.

"Hi, Dad."

"Hey, Frijoles. *Where's your mom?"*

"Hold on, I'll get her." Ruby picked up the purse. Her mom was just dialing another number and started talking as Ruby came closer. "Hey. Yeah, listen, we need a really ripe limburger. Have you got a couple of pounds? The party's on Sunday." She looked down at her daughter, who stood waggling the cell phone at her. "Just a sec, dear. No, the others don't know yet. Uh-huh. Right, I'll pick it up tomorrow." She hung up.

"I know you weren't really talking about cheese." Ruby hadn't said that at the time because she hadn't known, then. She handed over the cell phone. "Don't do this, you'll get caught."

Ruby's mother knelt. "Sweetie, we have to make a statement."

"Can't you just start a blog, like a normal person? Why do you have to blow something up? Did you ever think maybe this isn't fair to me?" But her mother was talking into her cell phone, no longer listening. Ruby started to shout. "You can't do it—you have a kid. It's not fair!" But her mom just scowled and shushed her.

Ruby woke and threw the covers to the floor, setting the wind chimes on the bed canopy jangling. The sun hadn't set yet. She got up to wash her face, staring at her red eyes in the mirror over the lavatory. "All right. It's all business. Get professional, girl." She fixed her hair, then went downstairs.

Simon was on the phone. He motioned her to sit, finished the call, scribbled some notes, and looked up. "Are you all right?"

"Yes. I'm sorry for the scene. I've had a hard day. What can I do to help?"

He looked at her narrowly, then leaned back in his chair, clicking his pen. "I'd like to figure out what Polacek was up to. He was always full of crazy schemes, and I figure one of them got him killed. Did he tell you anything?"

"He didn't mention a vacation," Ruby said, trying to remember their conversation. "He expected to get a lot of money soon. Perhaps if you tell me what happened to him?"

Simon sighed. "This is second-hand from his wife, based on what the police told her, and she was sort of hysterical, so I don't know how reliable it is."

"Okay." The thought that Polacek had a wife who would miss him gave Ruby a funny, twisty feeling inside.

"It sounds like he was attacked and, um, partially eaten by a large animal. He was found in Higsbee."

"Partially eaten?" Ruby felt a little nauseated, remembering the man she'd met and wondering which parts were missing. "What kind of animal?"

"They didn't say."

"Where's Higsbee?"

"A neighborhood a ways to the south."

"Wait, wait. The Higsbee Killer."

"Sorry?"

"Remember that gory article you didn't read in the paper? Most of the bodies were found there. Actually, that's where they weren't found, just blood and a few little bits. Maybe there's not a killer. Maybe there's just a hungry animal. It kills them and drags them off. Or eats them bones and all. Some animals do. But it would have to be huge to eat a whole person."

Simon leaned forward, brow furrowed. "There are abandoned warehouses and tunnels around there to hide in. But wouldn't someone have seen it? What about tracks?"

"I don't know. But, invisible giant animals that leave no tracks sound like your department. You think maybe someone paid Polacek to deal with it?"

"Maybe, but that doesn't make a lot of sense. If it's a normal sort of animal or a person, they could let the authorities deal with it. Or, if it's something that's not from around here, the Guardians would deal with it. We already pay them to do that sort of thing. Why pay someone else for the same?"

"Sorry, who are these Guardians?"

"A secret police force. A lot of them are also in the regular police. When there's a problem, they take care of it so it doesn't end up on the news. And, you know, there are rules about what you can tell people who aren't already in on the Scene. They enforce those."

"The scene?"

"The *Scene,*" Simon clarified. "The whole underground network of creatures the general public doesn't know exist. I've relied on your common sense to know you shouldn't tell your friends about the things you've seen, but as you're learning more, I suppose you should learn the rules as well. They're over there, third shelf up, yellow book titled *Principles of Badminton*. Study it when you have a chance."

"I will." She meant it. She was intensely curious about what secrets it would warn her not to tell. "But since I'm basically back to zero in the friends department, I have nobody to spill the beans to anyway."

"Oh? I'm sorry to hear that. And a little later, I'd like to hear more about it, but right now I have exactly"—he glanced at his phone—"three minutes. Things are a bit crazy. I'm still covering for Polacek, and his death has thrown everyone into an uproar. In fact, there's a matter you could assist with if you have time."

"My calendar is suddenly pretty wide open, so you're in luck. What do you need?"

"Netta—Polacek's wife—has gone all to pieces. Someone has to arrange the wake and funeral service, and I just don't have time, until someone else moves in to take his place."

"You want me to set up the funeral?"

"Some parts. Mainly food and transportation for guests. I know it's a lot to ask." Simon frowned. "In fact, it's a big responsibility. Maybe I should ask—"

"I can do it! You'll have it catered?"

Simon hesitated a moment longer, then nodded. He pushed a file folder across the desk. "These are the companies we can work with. These are all outfits that don't ask questions, but if there's a name listed, make sure you talk only with them. If I've left out anything important, text me. Have them reserve the date, and we'll leave the number of guests open for now." Simon stood. "Look it over while I get ready, see if you have any questions. I'll let you know any special accommodations we'll need and how many to expect. Probably two to three hundred."

Ruby took the folder while Simon stood and took his suit coat from the back of his chair.

Ruby made calls most of the afternoon, lining things up for the ceremony. She'd hoped to learn more about the Scene at the same time, but that didn't work out. Everything on the list was either ordinary stuff she could just order, like folding chairs, or things whose names she didn't recognize. She didn't want to just ask what they were because some of these folks seemed a little paranoid. If they realized she didn't know what she was asking for, they might just hang up. She tried to get some hints, for instance, by asking, "So what type of Model B Binding Rig are you sending?"

"The standard, same as always. Why, ya need something special?"

Well, the ceremony should be instructive, anyway.

Simon was out late—he hadn't called, of course—so Ruby got Chinese for herself and Wally. The mangy little dog she'd let in that one time followed her home, wagging his tail hopefully and looking at her, then at the bag.

"Scram. Uncle Simon doesn't like dogs who can't spell, so quit coming around." She hurried up the steps but glanced back at the dog, who looked at her forlornly.

"Oh, all right." She opened the carton of mandarin beef, dug out a piece, and tossed it. The dog caught it in midair, gobbled it down, and stood ready for more.

"No more. And if you learn to talk somehow, please don't tell him I fed you."

As she turned back to the door, a flash of light caught her eye from the window of a parked car across the way. She pretended to be looking for her keys, which were actually in her hand, to give herself an excuse to not turn away just yet. A little orange glow confirmed it. Someone in the car, facing her, had lit a cigarette.

They could just be waiting for someone from one of the other houses. Or they could be watching the house. Simon would want to know. Flustered, she let herself in and texted him. Then she opened the drawing room door to block the view down the hallway—really, they should put a shade on the front door. She closed all the window curtains, then buzzed Wally down for dinner.

When he came, he brought along the guitar and a gray plastic case, which he set on the kitchen floor.

"What've you got there?" Ruby asked.

"Amps. Can't do electric proper without 'em."

"Uncle Simon said no amps. Anyway, where'd you get them?"

"Just little ones. I'll explain it to him." Wally rubbed his hands together. "What'd you get us? What's this say? Moth fried rice? What?"

"I thought you'd like that. And here." She handed over a carton labeled "mandarin dragonfly"—actually the mandarin beef. Ruby had borrowed a Sharpie at the restaurant to label the containers herself.

"Hilarious. Mocking my infirmity." He pulled the bag over and looked inside. "You get moo shu like I asked?"

After they'd eaten and put away the leftovers, Wally showed her how to set up the amp and one new chord. "Yeah!" she said, as the first one blasted out of the speakers.

"Yeah! But turn it down a little." Wally reached for the knob. "We don't want the neighbors to call the cops. Anyway, I have sensitive ears." After she'd played for a while, Wally pulled a harmonica out of his pocket. "Now you know enough chords for 'Like A Rolling Stone.' You like Dylan?"

He had to teach her the words, but soon she was belting them out and strumming along recognizably, if unevenly, while Wally played harmonica.

When they reached the end, Ruby laughed. "That was great!" She was about to go on, but then a voice from the dining room called out, "Hello?"

"Crap!" Wally whispered and dove behind the counter. Ruby headed for the kitchen door to head off the visitor, but Marissa sailed through before she got there.

"Sorry, I couldn't find the doorbell, and the door was open, so I came on in. Was that you playing? Wow, nice axe! But who were you talking to?"

"Nobody. It's just me." Ruby, distracted by the watcher across the street, must have forgotten to push the door hard enough to latch.

"You were singing *and* playing harmonica?" Marissa dodged around Ruby, who'd tried to block her way with the guitar neck. Marissa leaned to look behind the counter.

For a frozen moment, Marissa's and Wally's eyes met. Then Marissa backed away. "Oh! Oh! Oh!" She turned for the door.

"Wait!" Ruby grabbed her arm. "It's okay! He's a friend."

"That... that...."

"His name is Wally."

"But he's got... oh God!" she squeaked.

"Calm down," said Ruby. "You'll hurt his feelings. He's not that bad."

"Yes, I am!" said Wally from behind the counter.

"Stop helping." Ruby took Marissa by both shoulders. "Deep breath. Okay? Give him a chance. You'll like him."

Marissa closed her eyes for a second and relaxed a little in Ruby's hands. "Okay. It was just, you know, no warning."

Wally rose slowly from behind the counter, giving Ruby a look, then turned to Marissa. "Pleased to meet you, miss." He extended his hand across the counter.

"Um, hi," Marissa visibly braced herself before stepping forward to shake his hand—briefly.

"Maybe someone," Wally said, "should check the door? We don't want anyone else coming in."

"Right." Ruby headed for the front.

"I'll come with you!" Marissa said. "Oh my God!" she whispered after they'd left the room. "What happened to him?"

Ruby shrugged. "He was born that way."

"I'm sorry. I should've checked before coming over, but your phone was busy, and you didn't answer your email, and I had to see you."

"Did you come by yourself?" Ruby looked out through the window of the door, thinking Marissa's mom might be waiting outside. There was no sign of her, but the watcher across the street was still there. Or at least, the car was there, its windows dark.

"Yeah, I took the train."

"You want to be careful near the station. I almost got mugged today." Ruby pushed the door, making sure it latched. "Why'd you come?"

"I had to see you! You'll never guess. God, I'm so embarrassed!"

"What, about that thing at the party? Look, I'm so sorry I spoiled things...."

"No, no! Dunking Ashley was awesome! Best party ever. She totally deserved it. No, this was after you left. That guy, Ashley's brother...."

"Conrad. Deep breath."

"Right. Conrad caught me after the party, and he asked me out."

"Like on a date?"

"Ye-e-ah! And I thought, OMG!"

"You didn't say OMG, I hope."

"You think I shouldn't say that?"

"Not if you want to be taken seriously. But why are you embarrassed?"

"I thought you'd be upset because before, I told you he liked you."

"No way. I didn't believe it, and anyway, he's not my type. I'm not sure I have a type, in fact. What'd you tell him? Do you want to go out with him?"

"Sure I do, but I had to talk with you first. I said I'd let him know. Should I, do you think?"

"Myself, I don't see why not, but your parents might think he's too old for you. In fact, is it even, you know, legal?"

"I think so. He's Ashley's twin, so two years older than me. It's certainly legal for us to date. But you're right, I better ask my folks first. I haven't been on a date before."

"Me, either." Ruby tried to imagine how her own father might react to the news that she'd been asked out for the first time. "Maybe it would be better to talk to them in person."

"I suppose." Marissa looked a little deflated. "I wanted to call him back now, though, before I chicken out."

"My mama always told me it never hurts to make them wait a little while. Come on and visit for a spell." She strolled on back to the kitchen, singing "Anticipation."

Marissa's impatience to get home, perhaps combined with some remaining discomfort at being near Wally, made the visit short. When she left, Ruby insisted on walking with her to the station. "It's dark. I'd worry about you."

"What, you can protect me?"

"You might be surprised."

Ruby was careful to pull the door shut this time. It felt almost absurdly good to be walking through the warm night with her friend, talking about unimportant things—Ruby was mostly up to speed on beauty tips from the magazines but still woefully behind on celebrity romances.

"Look, though. There's no point in my learning that stuff now, is there? Since Ashley's going to blackball me from everything anyway. Which, by the way, what got into her? I mean, yeah, she's always been bossy, but when did she turn into the Queen Bitch?"

"She's not normally like that. Only when she's provoked."

"Aren't you afraid to be seen with me?"

Marissa shrugged. "Ashley's not the whole world. It's a big school, and there are lots of folks who don't give a fig what she thinks. You still want to be popular, don't you?"

"I haven't totally decided yet."

"Listen, at my last school, they called me Miss Brainiac, okay? Here, I got to start all over because nobody knew me from before. This is way better."

"You've certainly reworked your image. But what about after you finish school?"

"Hey, I'm still making A's, I just don't brag about it. And I'm in a bunch of activities, which helps get you into better colleges. I'll tell you what I'm gonna do—confidentially, okay?"

"Sure."

Marissa pointed. "See that there?"

"The bright star?"

"The planet Mars. I'm going there."

"That sounds like fun. If you find any Martian critters, bring me back specimens, okay?"

"You're laughing at me now."

"No, no! I'm sure you'll get to Mars. That's a terrific ambition."

"You know there are no critters."

"The last few weeks, I've been finding out a lot of things everybody thinks they know are wrong. I seriously can't rule out critters."

"Okay, whatever. Listen." As they approached the station, Marissa stopped. "Two things. First, I love the painting. You really paid attention to what I like. That is so sweet."

From anyone else, Ruby would've winced to hear herself described as "sweet." She managed a weak smile. "I'm glad."

"And the other thing. How often do you jam with Wally?"

"Every night. He's just here for another couple weeks, and he's teaching me a lot while we have the chance."

"Do you think it'd be okay if I join you tomorrow night?"

It would be embarrassing to have Marissa hear her pathetic playing. "With your drums? They're not portable, are they?"

"I got a little electronic set." Marissa held her hands apart to show how big. "For my birthday."

"That reminds me. I thought Hispanic girls were supposed to have a special big party for their fifteenth. *Quince* something."

"*Quinceañera*. Yeah, my folks don't do that kind of thing. They're very assimilated. But I noticed that change of subject. Can I come over tomorrow?"

"I'll ask Wally. And Simon. But I can hardly play at all—I suck big-time. It might be boring for you."

"You were doing okay. You need someone to help you keep time, though." Marissa gave a little, wicked smile.

"Subtle. Give me a call after you talk with your parents about that date."

"I'll call. Answer your phone!"

Arriving home, Ruby let herself in and started upstairs, but a loud harrumph from the study made her back up to look between the railings. "You're home."

Simon, seated behind his desk, beckoned her over. When she walked into the room, she found Wally in the other chair beside the desk.

Simon looked at her without expression. "I hear we had company while I was out."

Well, shit. "Um. Yes, Marissa did stop by."

"And you let her in while Wally was downstairs?"

"She let herself in. The front door didn't latch."

"It didn't latch? Or you failed to latch it?"

Ruby closed her eyes. "Look, I know—"

"I thought you understood this is serious business. Is your friend going to talk about this? Do you think Wally wants to be in the papers again? Do you think I want to be?"

"I know. And I'm really sorry, but we need to get that door fixed."

"No excuses. I've explained the stakes to you. This could be serious trouble. I have to call someone about this, see what we can do."

Wally raised a hand. "Now, Simon. I'm sure the girl won't talk. She was a little startled at first, but she's cool. And you can't blame Ruby for everything. She was about to get rid of Marissa, but I was curious to meet her, so I stood up for a look. My choice."

Simon put his face in his hands. "Wally, you can't keep doing that sort of thing."

"How's a fellow supposed to make any friends if he's always hiding behind the furniture? I figured any friend of Ruby's would be okay. You mustn't call the Guardians for this. It's my call, and I say it's fine. I only told you because I thought you needed to know."

Simon regarded them both with suspicion. "I can't look at either of you right now. We'll discuss this further tomorrow, miss." He shooed them away, and they went, Ruby following Wally's narrow butt up the stairs.

"Thanks," Ruby mumbled when she was sure they were safely out of earshot. "You didn't need to lie for me."

Wally shrugged. "Figure I can take the heat easier than you."

"I really am sorry I endangered you. I'll be much more careful from now on."

"Good." He paused at the base of the attic stairs. "And do get that door fixed, yeah?"

"Yeah. Oh, hey! Marissa wants to get together again and jam. She plays drums. Maybe tomorrow. If that's okay?"

"Sure, why not? I'd love some company. But maybe I should be the one to break the news to Simon, hm? She'll be my guest."

"That'd be great! You're the best."

Wally brushed his long, curved fingernails against his chest. "So all the ladies tell me." He gave a little bow. "Until tomorrow."

Eight

Ruby leaned against the door to shut it and stood for a moment appreciating the air-conditioning after the noonday heat. "I'm home!"

"Back here!"

Ruby set her backpack beside the stairs, paused to examine a large black medical bag that partially blocked the hallway, and headed to the kitchen. Simon was at the stove, scraping from a cutting board into a pot. A man she didn't recognize sat at the counter, cutting hotdogs into pieces. He was tall and gaunt, dressed in faded denim, with tanned skin and long, sun-bleached hair in a ponytail. He waved the knife at her.

Simon looked up. "This is Ruby. Ruby, this is Spider Terboositer. He's an old friend."

"What kind of name is *Terboositer*?"

Spider gave a slow grin. "Mine."

"Here, let me do that, you're too slow." Ruby washed her hands, then took over the chopping. "What are you making? I can't believe you're cooking hotdogs. I thought you didn't allow them in the house."

Simon picked up the cutting board and dumped the pieces into a bowl. "These are organic beef franks, not 'hotdogs.' I'll also need that onion diced fine."

As she chopped, Ruby glanced up at Spider, who'd turned his stool to lean against the counter. He held a beat-up pack of playing cards, which he proceeded to cut one-handed, flipping one half of the deck over the other with his long, yellow-stained fingers. He wore a tarnished silver ring with multiple strands woven into a sort of knot.

"You're not from around here."

"Nope."

"In town for long?"

"Nope." He cut the cards again and fanned them out in a circle.

The door to the basement opened, and Ruby looked up, startled. A woman came out, holding a bottle of wine, which she brushed off and held out for Simon's inspection. Simon nodded. "Ruby, this is…."

"Dr. Fortunato. I saw your bag in the hall."

"Call me Alice." The woman smiled warmly and held out her hand. She was short, plump, with dark brown skin and short, frizzy black hair, and wore a tent-like dress with a bold print pattern of black and red zig-zags. She had a slight accent, maybe Canadian. "Good to meet you at last. I've heard a lot about you from Simon."

Ruby was never sure what to say when people said they'd heard a lot about her. "Um, really?" She looked curiously at Simon. "How do you get him to give out information? Do you have truth serum in that bag?"

Alice laughed. "I have many tricks, not all of them in my bag."

"Onion!" Simon said.

"Gotta work." Ruby moved back to the counter. "Come talk to me. Spider here is a man of few words. Hey, Seymour's your patient, isn't he? How's he doing?"

"You know him?"

"We met once, and I chat with him online. He says he's feeling great, but you know, I have no way to tell really."

"He should be going home soon."

That wasn't exactly an answer, but Ruby decided not to press for details. Spider might not know about Seymour, and in that case, Alice could hardly say he had a bad case of barnacles or something. She was starting to pick up Simon's habit of secrecy, she realized. "Coming through with onions." She maneuvered around Alice and scraped them into the bowl Simon pointed to.

Lunch was served in the courtyard at a card table. Franks and beans, potato salad, and "oven-fried" chicken, which as far as Ruby was concerned, meant baked chicken, but it was all pretty tasty. Spider proved he could, in fact, string multiple words together. He told an amusing story, in his cracked and dusty voice, about an old Indian who had beat him in a series of increasingly improbable bets. "He offered to go me double or nothing for my bike, so I could win back the fifty dollars, the case of corned beef, the set of antique false teeth allegedly once belonging to Sam Houston, and the white Ford pickup truck worth perhaps two hundred dollars, but I decided I should cut my losses while I still had wheels. But I really think I would've won that time." He leaned back, putting his hands behind his head. "You put on a good feed, Simon. What's for dessert?"

After lunch, they went back inside, and the adults started talking about people Ruby didn't know. Bored, she wandered off to check her email. Marissa's status report on the date situation was that she'd talked her parents into letting her go provided it was a double date. She logged in to Seymour's favorite virtual world and found him working on an aviary that someone was paying him to add on to their virtual house. "I'm having trouble getting the birds to take off and land realistically," Seymour typed. "You do it. I'll pay you."

"I don't know how to program them," she typed back.

"I'll program. Just show me how the wings are supposed to move and tell me when it looks right."

She was busy researching online for videos and charts of birds taking off when Spider poked his head into the study to ask where the bathroom was.

"Upstairs, first on the left." Then when she didn't hear the door close, she leaned her chair back to look out from the office.

Spider had paused to look at the skull on the mantel. He gently picked it up, then noticed her watching.

"This is Micah, isn't it?"

Ruby's heart beat a little faster. "Did you know him?" She tried for nonchalance.

"Alas, poor Micah. I knew him, Ruby. He and your uncle used to be tight. He managed their band, you know, before. Fleeting Expletive. Where be your hot licks now?" he asked the skull, then set it back on the shelf, brushing his hands on his jeans. "The others broke up after he died. Too bad, I thought they were going places."

"I never met him. He must've been an odd-looking man."

"Well. No weirder than Mick Jagger. Their audience probably dug it. Besides, who could tell much under all that hair?"

"What instrument did he play?"

"Electric guitar, vocals."

Ruby thought she could guess where that guitar was now. "How did he die?"

"Dunno. He was old, you know, though he didn't look it. Three hundred and something. Think he was the last of his kind." He wiped his hands on his jeans, went out, then popped his head back in. "You got someone at the door." And he was gone again.

Ruby got up to see. Standing on the stoop was a slender figure in a brown burka, dark face peering in from behind a veil. "Uncle Simon! Teela's back!"

She opened the door, and Teela sailed in. "Why didn't you ring the bell?" Ruby asked.

"It is not necessary. You are here to let me in."

Simon came out from the dining room, but Teela, who was

removing her veil, said, "Ruby helps me." She paused. "Or do I say, is helping?"

Ruby took the veil and hung it up. "Will help."

"I can help you this time," Simon said. "But come away from the door, the house is being watched."

"Ruby helps, it is good." Teela put her hand on Ruby's shoulder.

"As you like. Your client, apparently." Simon gestured them toward the study.

"I don't know what to do!"

"You did okay last time. Call me if you need a hand." He went back into the dining room.

Teela sank cross-legged onto the study carpets, uncovering her head and opening the front of the robe. Underneath, as before, she wore a unitard, this one black.

"Your hair!"

Teela grinned and ran a hand over her bare, striped scalp. "Teela does not burn, but hair burns. Is well, it returns." From her robe she withdrew a metal plaque a little larger than her hand, pewter-colored, with black symbols on it. "Problem is to know value of this mark."

The plaque was irregularly shaped and heavier than it looked, rough on the back. There were nine or ten groupings of symbols on the polished surface, and the symbol Teela had pointed out appeared in four of them. It looked as if it'd been written by hand, but the lines were deeply inscribed in the metal, the grooves filled in with a shiny black substance, chipped loose in a couple of places. None of the symbols were familiar, except one that looked like a plus sign. "Are these equations?"

Teela shrugged. "I must get wet to find the answer."

"Okay. Anything else you can tell me?"

Teela shrugged off her robe and folded it, acting as if she hadn't heard the question. Ruby sighed. "All right. I don't know whether I can do this, but if I can, what are you offering in payment?"

"If! Ruby, you can. I have no more shouts, but what would you?"

Ruby had given the matter some thought during the last minute or so. "Simon keeps going away and not telling me where he's going. Do you have any way I could keep track of him?"

"It makes you worry."

"Yes, I worry about him."

"He always comes back."

"So far. But I think he does dangerous things, so I still worry."

"So, you will spy in secret." Teela considered, clicking her tongue. "I can do this thing. It requires something he always carries with him. But you do not like this plan."

"Why not? Though I can't think of anything he always has with him. Even his cell phone, I think he ditches sometimes. He never answers it when I call him, anyway."

"We do not do this because… I do not know the words. Simon visits persons with secrets. He writes in his black notebook. The person tastes the link of you with the notebook. The person is angry with Simon."

"What's the black notebook got to do with it? Oh, of course! That's something he always carries. But how did you know?"

"You tell me this."

"I never did! Can you read minds? But I didn't even think of the notebook."

"I do not understand *read minds*. A mind is not a book."

"Huh." Ruby looked at her suspiciously. "Anyway, I think you mean someone might notice the link. All right."

"Other plan, of a way to always find him, is better."

"Yeah, if I could always find him, that would be good enough."

"It needs an animal that knows him. The little dog works."

"The little dog who keeps hanging around hoping to be fed? How do you know about that?"

"You tell me this. You find dog today, and I arrange this. It is a good price."

"What will you do to the dog?"

"No harm."

"Okay, deal." Ruby slapped the metal plaque thoughtfully against her palm. "Now let me see whether I can do my part."

"I am absent for an interval. I take my things I leave before."

"You want your sticks and stuff? Sure, hang on." Ruby hurried out of the room and back to the kitchen, then screeched to a halt. Simon and Alice were seated together at the counter, leaning toward each other, foreheads touching, gazing into each other's eyes. Alice's hand lay on top of Simon's, and his other hand rested on her knee.

"S-sorry," Ruby stammered and backed into the dining room.

Simon came out after a few seconds. "Did you want something?"

"Are you and—is she—hell. I thought you were...."

Simon raised an eyebrow.

Saying, "I thought you were gay," was perhaps not the best move at that point. "Never mind." She was recovering her equilibrium. "Alice, really?"

"We're just friends."

"I don't do that with any of my friends. Anyway, I just wanted to know where you put Teela's stuff from last time."

"In the cabinet under the stereo, bottom shelf, on the right."

"Thanks. Next time I'll call out before I come in."

"Appreciated."

Ruby gave Teela her things in a leftover grocery bag and saw her off. She messaged Seymour that she'd get back to him about the birds, then tried for about an hour to decipher the plaque, without much progress. Most of the groupings she guessed were equations, but some, concentric circles with dots inside and lines of various lengths sticking out, might be pictures of something. She figured out the symbol for "equals," and others that were probably used like parentheses, but she could only guess at others. Maybe a walk would clear her head, and anyway, she needed to find the dog.

Ruby scanned the plaque into the computer and emailed a copy to Marissa with minimal explanation. Then she stopped by the kitchen, asked Simon to keep Teela entertained if she returned first, and left the house with two pieces of leftover chicken in a zipper bag.

The dog was where he often was, hanging around a deli two blocks away. He looked skinnier and mangier than ever and still no collar. He trotted happily over to her, and she fed him out of her hand. "You want to come on home with me, boy?" Evidently he did because he walked alongside, nails clicking on the sidewalk.

Ruby went down the alley and let herself in through the back gate because she suspected Simon wouldn't be happy to see the dog inside.

Spider was in the gazebo, smoking a cigarette that looked home-made. "That's one sorry-lookin' dog."

"You want him? Maybe sitting next to you, he'd look better by comparison."

Spider mimed receiving a knockout punch. Ruby shook her head and led the dog to the back door. She thought he was too big to get out through the bars into the alley, but just in case, she gave him the other piece of chicken to encourage him to stay, while she went in to see where things stood.

She found Simon preparing to go out. Alice stood holding her bag, waiting for him. "Teela's not back yet?" Ruby said.

"Nope. I've got clients to see. I should be back in time for dinner. Spider's going out too, I think."

Good. Ruby wouldn't have to explain the dog. She bid them goodbye and went to check her email. Marissa had answered, "Where did you get this?" and added some guesses about which symbols meant what. "You should get Kirk to look at it."

Ruby called Marissa's cell. "Who's Kirk?"

"The redhead you rescued from Ashley."

"Oh, him. Someone said he was a math genius. But I don't think he'll talk to me. He seemed pretty steamed."

"He can't resist a puzzle. Call Conrad, he's got Kirk's email address. If you write a subject like 'Bet you can't solve this,' he'll read it. Speaking of Conrad, I don't suppose you can dig up some boy and come with us on that double date?"

"You'd better ask someone else. I don't know anyone." This wasn't strictly true—there was a boy named Tim in her swim class who talked to her occasionally, and she had an idea he'd like to get to know her better. But he also annoyed her by consistently swimming faster than her, and besides, his voice was too loud, and he laughed like a sheep. Asking him out would definitely fall into the category of giving him the wrong idea.

"Okay. I'll ask around, but I want your opinion of Conrad, so you're my first choice."

"If something turns up, I'll let you know."

"We're still on for tonight, right?"

"Yeah. Uncle Simon didn't like it much, but Wally gets to decide who he jams with. Are your parents really okay with this?"

Marissa paused. "Um… there are some things parents don't need to know?"

"Marissa!" But yeah, Marissa's parents would want to meet Wally before they agreed to any such thing, and that would never work. "Yeah, I guess that's the only way to do it. But they know you'll be here, right?"

"Oh, sure."

Ruby next dialed Ashley's house—a man answered.

"Is Conrad there?"

"Conrad! A girl on the phone for you!"

"Hello?" Conrad said after a minute. *"Who is it?"*

"I'm Ruby Park." When this didn't get a response, she added, "I threw your sister in the pool last week."

"Oh, yeah, the Asian girl. What's up?"

"Is that what you call me, 'the Asian girl'?"

"I'll use your name now I know it."

Ruby was dying to ask why he was interested in going out with Marissa, but she couldn't think of a way to do it that didn't diss Marissa. Why shouldn't he want to, after all? On to business. "Your friend, Kirk, I want his help with something. Can I have his email address?"

"I don't know. After the party, he said he was sick of girls. He might not like it if I let you pester him."

"It's something I think will interest him. Can I email you it to forward to him?"

There was a pause. *"I guess that would be okay."* He gave his address.

"I'm in a hurry."

"If I agree he'll be interested, I'll send it on right away and text him to tell him to read it."

"That's great. Thanks!"

Ruby waited for a "You're welcome" or "Goodbye," but there was silence on the line. She was about to say goodbye herself when Conrad spoke.

"There's something else I wanted to ask. You're Marissa's friend, aren't you?"

"Yeah…." Where was this going?

"I don't suppose you could find yourself a date for Saturday?"

"Jeez, not you, too. No, probably not. I don't know anyone." No one who could appear in public, anyway. "I'm going to send that email now, okay?"

When Teela returned, she still had the same grocery bag she'd left with. Ruby brought her into the study. "I couldn't figure the plaque out, but I'm trying to get help with it. I hope that's okay."

"It is well, but do not say who wants it." Teela set the bag down and pulled things out to set on the desk. "In the interval, we work on the dog." A rusty metal ring almost two feet wide, an orange crystal, and a pottery crock stopped up with a large cork came out of the bag. A dark blue substance encrusted the rim of the crock.

"Are you sure? I don't know whether I'll be able…."

"I am sure. Bring the dog. No hurt. It makes him better."

Ruby had been about to ask for more reassurance on that score. "So long as it doesn't harm him, okay?" She went to the back door and whistled, and the dog gladly followed her. Meanwhile, Teela had uncorked the crock and gotten a paintbrush from somewhere. She carefully painted a line of blue glop on the inside of the ring.

"Let me set out some newspaper. Simon won't like drips on the floor."

"Teela does not make drips." She looked at the dog, who looked back at her, wagging his tail tentatively and whining. "It is well." She dipped the brush and painted more, closing the line, and held the ring out. "Make it be dry."

Ruby held the ring by the outside edge, careful to not smear it. "I'll use a hair dryer. Do you want to wash your paintbrush? There's a sink…." But Teela reached out and tapped the brush on the edge of the crock, and all the paint fell off into the crock with a little plop, leaving the brush clean. "Hey, where can I get brushes like that?"

Teela smiled and tucked the brush away in her robe. "Another time." She drifted over to the bookshelves.

Ruby brought the hair dryer downstairs, mindful of Simon's rule about leaving people alone in the study, and worked on the ring there. Teela had settled on the floor with a stack of picture books, the dog beside her. One book was open to a photo of a bleak but majestic landscape, brown mountains impossibly steep against an orange sky. Ruby looked at the caption. "Mars. I have a friend who wants to go there. But wait, I guess you already knew that."

"It is not pleasant. Too cold."

"I expect she'll bundle up." Her cell phone rang, and Ruby shut off the hair dryer and carefully leaned the hoop against the desk before picking up. "Goodnight residence."

"What is this you sent me?" The caller sounded irritated. *"Is this some dumb game?"*

"I recognize that attitude. It must be Kirk."

"Ha ha. You're the one who dunked the bitch Ashley, right?"

"I didn't do it for you, so don't feel like you need to thank me." Ruby looked at her nails, one of which had gotten chipped somehow. "It was for the good of all mankind. Horrors must be quenched."

There was a pause. *"I guess I was a little horrible myself."*

"Well, it is rude to stare."

"To you, I meant. I was just really upset about the whole thing and you all standing around watching."

Ruby supposed this was the closest she would ever get to an apology. "Well, we live and sometimes we learn. Anyway, what'd you think about my email?"

"They're definitely equations." Kirk started to sound enthusiastic. *"I even recognize some of them."*

"Wait, wait. How can you do that?"

"They're famous equations from physics and fluid dynamics. The form is familiar, and so you can guess what the terms mean...."

"All right, too much information. Do you have the answer?"

"It's like someone picked easy-to-recognize equations on purpose," Kirk continued as if he hadn't heard. *"So anyone would be able to figure them out even without knowing the symbols. And then there are pictures of atoms, with measurements, so you can tell what the units are. You know what it reminds me of? Those things they put on space probes as a message to aliens. Except this doesn't use our units, so it's more like it's from the aliens. Where did it come from?"*

"I don't know. But do you have the answer?"

"If you don't know, how did you know which term you wanted to solve for?"

"I can't tell you. But do you have the answer?"

"Well... sort of. I would have to take a measurement."

"What measurement?"

"Density."

Ruby closed her eyes and counted to five. "Density of what?"

"Whatever object you're trying to move through the extremely odd liquid in the big equation."

Ruby looked over at Teela. "Hang on." She put the phone on mute. "Teela."

"Teela is the object." She nodded.

"I have to measure your density."

Teela turned a page, not looking up. "Teela is ready."

"Fine." Ruby went back to the phone, about to ask Kirk how she was supposed to do the measurement but remembered Teela saying she would have to get wet, and the answer came to her. Nice not to have to ask Kirk every little thing. "Okay, I'll do the measurement and call you back. At this same number?"

"You're not gonna tell me what this is about?"

"I really can't explain. I'm sorry."

"This happens later," Teela volunteered.

"Thanks. I can tell you someday, not now."

"Who's that talking in the background?"

"Bye!"

She took Teela upstairs to the bathroom and looked at the big claw-foot tub, then at her. "You'll fit." Ruby put in the plug and turned on the hot water. "Hot here, cold here, see? Make it a comfortable temperature, and I'll get the other things we need."

When Ruby returned, Teela had draped her robe over the toilet and was sitting in her unitard on the edge of the tub, stirring it with her hand. "I need to weigh you. It is just you traveling again, or will you take anything with you, like your clothes for instance?"

"Only I may go."

"Then you should...." Ruby began, but Teela had already grabbed the collar of the unitard and pulled it down. She stepped out of it—the stripes did, indeed, cover her whole body except for the belly—and stepped onto the scale.

"Three hundred ten, honest?" Ruby looked with amazement at the trim figure. "Do you eat rocks?"

"Only a few."

"Huh. All right, into the tub. Get all the way under, and lie still until the water settles down, so I can mark the depth. Do you understand?"

Teela slipped in with barely a ripple, leaving just her nose above water. She waited for the surface to calm, then breathed out and lowered herself gently. Ruby made a pencil mark on the porcelain, then rapped on the side. "Okay, come out now."

Teela didn't stay wet when she got out—the water rolled off as if she were oiled. She dressed and sat on the toilet to watch Ruby repeatedly fill a pitcher at the lavatory and dump it into the tub.

"By the way, those bean things you gave me?"

"The shouts."

"Yes. What exactly do I have to do to make them go off?"

"One raises either hand thus and speaks loudly."

"Perfect, thanks." Ruby poured in a final half-pitcher to reach the pencil mark, wrote down a total, then followed Teela downstairs to finish her calculations.

"Eighteen point seven eight pounds per gallon."

Kirk snorted. *"Pounds? Gallons? I thought you were a scientist."*

"That's what I had handy. I can convert it to metric for you if you can't manage it."

"Pshaw. The measurement was made on this planet?"

"Sure, Astro Boy. In my own bathroom. Besides, who told you I was a scientist?"

"Marissa."

When had he talked to Marissa? A couple hours before she hadn't had his contact info. Ruby could hear keys clicking in the background. *"The answer is seven point oh three."*

Ruby wrote it down. "Is that all? Weren't you just fussing at me about units?"

"No units. You asked for the value of backward-z-squiggle. That's the value."

Teela, meanwhile, had picked up the metal hoop and touched it to make sure it was dry. She took a Sharpie from a pen holder on the desk and drew an arrow on the edge of the hoop. Then she took up the orange crystal and ran it around the edge of the hoop in the direction of the arrow, making the metal ring. She stepped over to the dog, who had fallen asleep curled up on the rug, shook him awake, then lowered the hoop around him.

"Yikes! Call you back. Thanks!" Ruby hung up the phone and hurried over to where the dog had been, but there was now empty floor. Or not quite empty. There seemed to be a pale flickering form, vaguely dog-shaped, standing in the hoop.

"You must call him," Teela said, "so he steps out."

"H-here, doggy." The flickering shape moved toward her, its legs flashing out in odd directions. As it left the circle, Teela quickly picked up the hoop and brought it down again over the white shape, and it was gone. Or, no, there was a small, vague flickering.

"Call him again. No harm."

"What have you done to him?"

"Call him."

"Come on, doggy." Ruby felt a little silly addressing empty air. The flicker drifted in her direction.

Teela watched intently, then picked up the hoop. "It is done."

"I thought you were just going to give him super tracking ability."

"This he has. Who he knows, he can follow. You must teach him to track." Teela held out the hoop, and Ruby took it gingerly. "Look through this to see him better."

Ruby held the hoop up in front of her face. It was a little shimmery, like a giant soap bubble, and when she looked through, the vague white dog shape was again visible. She clucked her tongue, and it scampered toward her, dancing around her feet.

"Use the crystal as I do. Throw food in. He likes to eat, though he has no need. Thus, you train him to do your wish." She demonstrated again with the crystal, pointing out the direction of the arrow. "This way to close." She scraped the crystal along the rim, and the soap-bubble look went away. She pointed at the arrow. "This way to open." She set the hoop down. "Now Teela goes. It does not matter."

"All right. Outside, like before?"

Teela didn't answer, just reached into her robe and pulled out a small brass cube of spheres connected by notched rods. Each rod had a bead on it, each a different color.

"Seven point oh three," Ruby said, but Teela was already adjusting the cube, sliding the beads to different positions on their rods, where they clicked into place on the notches. "As you knew," Ruby muttered. "Wait! What if it's wrong?"

"If!" Teela sounded amused. She held out her hand, smiling. "We meet again."

"Until then."

Teela paused, holding on lightly to Ruby's hand, and looked at her consideringly. "I recall, you walk a narrow path, with chaos to both sides."

"What do you mean, you recall? What chaos?"

"The details escape me. Be strong. You must carry the burden yourself." Teela dropped Ruby's hand, popped the cube into her mouth, and silently vanished, her empty clothes settling to the floor.

"Radical." Ruby bent to pick them up. "Hope that really was the right number."

As she was shoving the bag of Teela's belongings into the cabinet, her phone rang, showing Kirk's number. Before she could speak, he said, *"What's going on? Why did you say 'yikes?' I thought you were going to call back."*

"You got the right answer. Anyway, it seems to have worked."

"What worked?" Kirk sounded frustrated.

This was fun. "Tell you what. Are you free Saturday night?"

Nine

Marissa showed up with a flat, black nylon case over her arm. "This feels so weird."

"You're not afraid, are you?" Ruby herded her up the stairs.

"Well… maybe a little."

"Listen, under that bug-eyed, shark-toothed exterior, Wally really is a nice guy. He'll give you shit, but you just have to give it right back."

"I can do that," Marissa murmured. "Oh, cool, is this a real suit of armor?"

"Probably. Whenever I ask Uncle Simon whether something of his is real, he just gives a little half-smile and says, 'You tell me.' So it's on my list to figure out." As Marissa reached for the visor, Ruby debated with herself whether to warn her and decided it'd be more fun not to.

"*Eep!*" Marissa stepped back quickly, letting the visor drop with a clang. She gave Ruby a reproachful look. "*That* wasn't real."

"It's a Halloween mask. Simon has a strange sense of humor. Up these stairs." Ruby bowed and held her hand out toward the narrow, dark stair. "After you."

"Ah, no, thanks, after you."

When Ruby knocked, the answer was a maniacal laugh followed by a creaky, "Come in, my pretties!" She rolled her eyes and went in. Marissa followed after, sticking her head in first.

It was Ruby's first time in the attic too. It was a tidy little apartment, narrow and with corners cut off by the slope of the roof. The main room had a window overlooking the back courtyard, with two doors to other rooms. Wally stood behind a counter in a compact kitchen, putting ice into a glass. "You girls want a snack? Afraid all I have is moths, but they're real fresh."

"Moths?" Marissa said. "Um, no, thanks. I just had dinner. Anyway, in my family, we only eat moths at Easter."

Wally laughed. "A soda, then?"

"I'll have one," Ruby said.

"Help yourself." Wally came around the end of the counter and moved the mini amp from the floor to the coffee table. "Use a coaster, Simon says."

Marissa pulled one of the chairs closer, unzipped her bag, and handed a cable across to Wally with a reasonably steady hand. Ruby smiled and started opening the catches on her guitar case.

"Ruby, how are the fingers?" Wally asked.

"I soaked them in tea like you said, but the tips still feel like they've been mushed into hamburger."

"Try super glue. But you'll get calluses soon enough, I promise. You practiced the finger-picking pattern I showed you?" He passed her a scribbled paper.

"'House of the Rising Sun?'"

He handed a sheet to Marissa, too. "You read drum tabs? That's from memory, so if it don't sound right, change it. Choke the cymbal on the intro, okay?" He took out his harmonica. "Ruby, take your headset over there and practice till you can play it. Marissa, let's go through it a couple times."

Ruby listened to them start to play. Marissa was discouragingly good, though Ruby also wondered how difficult drums could really be. Wally looked over at her in a way that clearly said, "Get going," and she put on the headset and leaned over the guitar.

The next morning, at breakfast, Ruby sat across from Simon and listened to Jimi Hendrix on her phone—Wally's homework assignment. When the doorbell rang, she got up to get it, then froze in the dining room doorway when she saw the two men in rumpled suits on the other side of the glass. She ripped the headphones off. "Cops."

"Don't say 'cops.'" Simon put down his newspaper. "It's low-class. They're police. Or more exactly," he said, getting a look at them himself, "detectives."

He adjusted his robe, unobtrusively pressing a bit of carving on the edge of the staircase as he passed. There was a distant "thud," and the floor vibrated slightly for a few seconds. "Don't be concerned. We have nothing to hide."

"Sez you."

Simon opened the door. "Good morning, gentlemen. What can I do for you?"

"Can we come in? We need to talk." The shorter, heavier man flashed a badge, while the other peered over his shoulder, looking around the hallway.

"Certainly. I'm always glad to assist." Simon led the men into the study. The taller detective scrutinized Ruby as she followed them in. She fidgeted with her phone, which she'd pulled off the headset cord and held concealed in her hand. She glanced down at it, pressing buttons to start recording audio. Trying to look casual, she leaned against a table, then moved away to sit on the couch, leaving the phone behind.

"Who is this?"

"My niece lives with me."

The short detective looked doubtful, as most people did. "We won't want her in here. NMI, why don't you take her out and interview her in another room?"

"She's a minor. I assume you meant to ask my permission first?" Simon said frostily.

"Are you her legal guardian, sir? No? Who should we call?"

"Please don't bother Aunt Meg. I don't mind talking to him." Keeping her voice steady was a major effort. In fact, she minded a lot. But if they called Aunt Meg, they'd get an earful of information about her parents that Ruby would much rather they didn't know. She gazed earnestly at Simon, willing him to understand.

Simon paused, then nodded. As Ruby followed the detective from the room, her eye registered a blank space on the mantle, and she paused, surprised. Micah's skull was missing. She looked around the room. Lots of things were missing. She looked a question at Simon, and he frowned and shooed her out.

As she and the detective sat facing each other in the drawing room, her heart raced. She tried to look calm and slightly curious.

The detective pulled a small, tattered notebook from his pocket and flipped it open, thumbing through the pages. He wore a scratched-up wedding band, and his large hands had something dark in the creases, maybe engine grease. He looked up. "That man really your uncle?"

"Yes."

"So you're adopted."

Not that he probably cared, but this cop wasn't making a good first impression. "No," she said. "He is."

He raised an eyebrow and made a note. "Name?" After this and a few other preliminaries, he said, "I'd like you to think back to the twenty-fourth, this past Friday. Where were you from, oh, six p.m. onward?"

Ruby thought. Friday was the new day for music lessons, so she'd been at Mrs. Esterhazy's house until five, then…. "I was at the Field Museum until about seven, then came home on the train. I stopped for take-out. Someplace near here, I think the Bluebell. Then I was home the rest of the night."

"You got home about what time?"

"About eight."

"Who else was here during that time?"

Ruby could tell from the way the detective leaned forward slightly that this was the real point of the questioning. He wanted to know where Uncle Simon was then, and she hadn't seen him all evening. She could still say he'd been here, but what if Simon admitted being out or if they had evidence otherwise? What could she say that would least likely contradict whatever other information they had? "Nobody. But I was tired, so I went to bed early, like eight thirty. I don't know when Uncle Simon came home, but it was before one, because I heard him in the bathroom then." That, at least, was true.

He just sat and looked at her for what seemed like a really long time. Ruby started to kick her feet. "Was there something else?"

"What does Goodnight do for a living?"

"Financial advisor."

"It's funny he doesn't have an ad in the phone book or a website or nothing."

It wasn't a question. Ruby said nothing.

The detective stood and walked to the window. "Yesterday a woman came into this house. A woman in a brown veil."

Ruby suddenly knew what he was going to say, and her heart fluttered. Stupid, she'd been so stupid! She'd even *known* someone was watching!

"She left," he continued, "then came back, but she never left the second time. Is she still here?"

"No. She left again around five thirty. I let her out myself." Ruby's brain was racing. "Hey, how do you know about her? Are you watching our house?" Of course she knew the answer. She just wanted time to think.

The detective didn't let himself get distracted. "By which door did she leave?"

"Which door?"

"Front or back?"

Did they have someone watching the alley? It would be hard to miss someone exiting that way. "Front. But she'd taken off the burka then. She said it was too hot. She had a white dress on underneath."

He looked skeptical. Damn! She should've waited for him to ask. He sank down onto the window seat. "What's this woman's name?"

"I don't know, just one of Simon's clients. A walk-in, I think."

"A what?"

"No appointment. Just walked in off the street."

"Your uncle wasn't here when she came back."

"Yeah. That's why she left." Ruby tried to look eager. "Hey, did she break the law? Are you following her?"

"I'll ask the questions."

Ruby waited, wide-eyed, for him to do so. He made more notes. "Your uncle threw a suit coat away recently. It was cut up and stained."

Blood-stained, Ruby thought. "You dug through our trash?" She was honestly, this time, incredulous. "Don't you need a warrant?"

"So you *do* know about it."

Damn. "I know he ruined a suit coat last Tuesday night." Good thing it hadn't happened on the Friday the police found so interesting.

"That would be the twenty-first?"

"If that's a Tuesday."

The detective made a note, then tapped his pencil on the page. "Did you know Alasdair Polacek?"

"I knew a *Mister* Polacek who died recently, but I never heard his first name. If it's Alasdair, no wonder he didn't use it, poor guy. I only met him once."

"How does your uncle know him?"

"Through business, though they might've been sort of friends, too."

"They were competitors?"

Where was this going? "I'm not sure. Uncle Simon doesn't talk about business much."

"He knows the widow, though."

"Slightly, I think. Enough that we're helping with the funeral." That was surely no secret, since she'd overheard Simon on the phone with the Medical Examiner's office. "I've never met her. Are you investigating his death? Do you think you'll release the body by Friday afternoon? The funeral director wants to know."

The detective looked at her, stone-faced. "It won't be an open casket in any case."

"I know, but they expect to cremate something on Saturday."

"Jesus, you're a cold kid." He flipped back through his notes and started asking about Simon's movements on other nights, for all the good that did, then repeated all his earlier questions a few times, as if to catch her in a lie. Finally, he sent her away and went into the study, shutting the door.

Ruby sat on the stairs. It was another half-hour before the police left, without any prisoner, to her great relief. Every minute they'd been in there without her knowing what was going on, she'd been more certain they'd arrest Simon. As soon as the front door closed, she ran into the study. Simon was at his desk, still in his robe, looking unperturbed. Micah's skull, and the other missing knick-knacks, were back in place as if they'd never moved.

"Don't you have a lesson of some sort in thirty minutes?"

She walked forward to stand next to the little table and put her hand unobtrusively on her phone. "What did they want?"

"Apart from being curious about people who come into my house and don't come out again?" he said dryly.

"Yeah, sorry. Do they think you murdered Polacek?"

"They don't tell me what they think, but I wouldn't be surprised. They must be under a lot of pressure to come up with something.

I suppose they're questioning people who knew any of the Higsbee victims, and as you can imagine, my alibis tend to be weak."

Of course—because his clients wouldn't want to talk to the police to confirm them. "But they've been watching us for a couple of days. You didn't know any victims besides Polacek, right? They don't have any other special reason to suspect you."

"Don't they? You tell me."

"I hate when you do that! All right…." Ruby paused to think. "Well, I guess they always talk to everybody who knew the victim. There's no point in that if it was really a giant animal looking for dinner, but they don't believe that, do they?" Ruby wasn't sure she believed it herself. It would be hard to miss, wouldn't it, a large animal roaming around eating people?

"And?"

"And… you're mysterious, and they might think you do something illegal for a living. Which for all I know some of it might be."

"Yes, yes. And?"

"And there's that suit coat. Careless of you to just throw that in the trash, Unc. When they get their lab results back, what kind of blood will it be?"

"Not human, which is all they care about." Simon looked at his watch. "You'll be late if you take the train. I'll call a ride."

"I'll wait out front." Ruby went into the hallway and looked at the phone, stopping the recording. The new file was forty-three minutes long. Excellent!

She slipped the device into her pocket.

Returning from the train station that afternoon, Ruby rounded a corner and happened upon one of the boys who'd stopped her the other day hanging out in the doorway of a tobacco shop. Not the tall one—one of the minions. He saw her, too, looked nervous, and started to walk away.

"Hang on a second. I want to tell you something."

He stopped walking and turned to look at her, wary.

"What's your name?"

"Jimmy."

"I'm Ruby. Look, Jimmy. I have a friend who comes here at night. A Mexican girl, curly black hair, this tall. I want you to know if she gets any trouble from you or anyone else, I'll come after you and your friends. And I can find you, just like I found you now."

"What'd you do to us?"

"I used my magic. You want to see it again?" Ruby raised her hand.

"That's all right!" Jimmy backed up a couple of steps.

Ruby let her hand drop. "Are the others okay?"

"They said we all got a little concussion, and Spike's kinda deaf on one side, but he'll be all right." He licked his lips. "Look, we ain't gonna mess with you no more. But could you show me how to do that shit?"

Ruby tossed her head. "You either got it or you don't."

When she got home, Ruby went straight to the office to upload the recording from her phone onto the computer. She'd tried to listen on her ear buds, but the sound picked up by the crummy mic was too faint to make anything out. She donned headphones, loaded it into a sound editing program, and fiddled with it until it was as good as it was going to get. That was still none too good, but she was able to understand most of it by listening closely. The detective started out asking Simon what he did for a living.

"Chiefly, I'm a freelance financial advisor."

"But you also...." There was a pause, and Ruby imagined the detective consulting his notes. *"You also are a notary and a paralegal, and you have a private detective license."*

"I offer a portfolio of services."

"Who to?"

"I'm afraid I can't disclose that."

"I could come back with a warrant." The detective sounded annoyed.

"I would of course comply with a warrant to the extent required by law, but first, please talk with Captain Susan Urbana in this precinct. She'll tell you I run a legitimate business." Simon paused. *"I may also be able to arrange for her to interview some of my clients if it's really necessary."*

"Urbana's in Vice. This is a homicide investigation."

"However, they might talk with her. I doubt they'll talk with you."

"Oh, they'll talk to me, once I get my hands on them."

"Good luck finding them."

There was a long, low-voiced conversation Ruby couldn't make out much of, though the words "obstruction of justice" came through once. Footsteps. The detective said, *"You own a firearm."*

"Yes."

"You're licensed to carry."

"I seldom do, however. I keep it locked in my desk."

"May I see it?"

"Is that relevant to your investigation?" Simon's voice was calm.

"Is there a reason you don't want me to see it?" A pause, followed by metallic clicking sounds, before the detective spoke again. *"Silver bullets. You kidding me?"*

"Silver plated, actually. Just as effective, much less expensive."

"Effective for what? What would you need these for?"

Frustratingly, Simon's reply was inaudible, though she listened three times. She continued the playback.

"You are full of shit," the detective said. *"Here, put it away."*

There followed essentially the same series of questions Ruby had been asked. The detective seemed skeptical of Simon's story of how his jacket had been ruined. *"Let me get this straight. You were attacked by a masked, machete-wielding animal rights activist because you were wearing leather shoes?"*

"I guess it was the shoes. He kept screaming, 'Leather is murder.' He

tried to hit me with the machete, but I blocked it with my jacket, got the blade tangled up. Then he threw the blood on me, pulled the blade loose, and ran away."

"You were attacked with a big-ass knife and didn't call the police?"

"There was no point, since I didn't get a good look at him. It was dark. I'm sure I couldn't identify him."

"Did anyone else witness this supposed attack?"

"I don't think so. The street was empty."

The detective made a sound of disgust.

There was only a little more before the end and nothing new. Ruby sighed, shut down the computer, stood and stretched, looking speculatively at Simon's desk. She shook her head and went to the kitchen, brushing Micah's bony chin in greeting as she passed. She made tea to soak her fingers in, then while waiting for it to cool, found a note on the counter. *Out late. Leftovers in fridge. Spider might stop by. I said he could sleep on the couch if he didn't get a better offer. Can you explain two dead rabbits in the back yard with broken necks?*

Ruby suspected she knew what was going on there. She scribbled on the bottom of the note, *SPECK (Strategic Plant-Eater Control Kontraption) installed and working. Happy birthday (early). Did you save me a rabbit for the skeleton?* Then, taking her bowl of tea, a few cut-up slices of bacon, and her hoop and crystal, she went out back. "Here, Speck!" she called and whistled. Soon, through the hoop, she could see a white shadow dancing around her feet. It was time to start training.

Ruby opened the door and looked past Marissa to the boy standing at the bottom of the steps. Marissa seemed nervous, looking over her shoulder at him.

"Jimmy," Ruby said, a little dangerously, as Marissa edged past her, "what's going on here?"

Jimmy seemed at a loss to explain, but Marissa answered. "He said he was supposed to protect me. He knew your name, so I thought it was probably okay."

Ruby looked sideways at him. "I didn't ask you to do that."

Jimmy looked down. "Well, you sorta did, though. You said if anyone else gives her trouble, you're coming after us."

Oh, okay—she had said something along those lines. She hadn't expected this reaction, though. "Marissa, why don't you go on up? I want to talk with him for a sec." She looked at Jimmy. "I thought you would just pass the word to leave her alone."

"She's actually pretty safe on this side. But I want you to know we looking out for her."

"Who's *we?*"

"You know. Me and Iggie. Maybe Spike. He won't make any trouble, anyway."

"Look. You don't need to do this again." She felt guilty for having terrorized Jimmy. She should do something to make it up to him. "Wait here, I've got something for you." She ran into the study and got ten dollars from petty cash, recording it in the notebook as "tip."

When she handed over the money, Jimmy looked surprised and a little amused, but it vanished into his pocket. "All right. You want anything else, ask after me at Green Way Market." He nodded, turned, and walked away.

Marissa hadn't gone up. She was still waiting at the bottom of the stairs. "What's going on? Are you bullying the local hoodlums? It's like they're in awe of you. How do you know that boy?"

"I didn't bully him, just warned him off."

"And then gave him money."

"Well, he went to all that trouble to escort you."

"I didn't want an escort. It was creepy."

"It won't happen again."

Marissa paused on the landing, putting her hand on Ruby's arm to stop her. "There's something I'm not understanding here. Why would boys like that be afraid of you?"

Ruby chewed on her lower lip for a moment. "All right. But this is absolutely secret, okay? Cross your heart and all that."

"Okay, I promise. Spill it."

"They think I'm some sort of wizard. They think I can blast them with a spell."

"How did you convince them of that?"

Deep breath. "I actually did blast them."

Marissa gave her a look. "Yeah, right."

"No, really." Ruby paused, uncertain. "Look, I can't show you that spell, because it's too noisy. But come now, and I'll show you my other trick."

"Come where?"

"Just out back. This way."

Ruby collected a few things from inside, then turned the lights on in the courtyard and went out onto the path. "Here, Speck!" she called. In the growing dark, Speck was dimly visible even without the hoop, jittering in front of her face.

Marissa stopped on the steps. "What is that?"

"My nearly invisible dog. Flying dog." Ruby looked around for a stick—not easy to find in that tidy yard—and settled for a wooden plant stake. "Fetch!" She threw the stake toward the back. Speck darted off in a straight line, right through a patch of tall grasses, then the stake rocketed back around the grasses. Ruby held up her hand, and it slapped into her palm. She looked at Marissa, standing open-mouthed on the stairs. "I think being invisible has made him smarter. He's easy to train."

"What? How...?" Marissa sputtered to a stop, then started over. "This is too much! There's no such thing as what you're doing there!"

Ruby shrugged. "Okay." She threw the stake again, and Speck zipped off and caught it before it hit the ground. When she didn't hold up her hand, the stake just dangled in front of her.

Marissa stalked over and took it, running her hands over it. "What's the trick?"

"You try."

Marissa looked at her, looked at Speck, then tossed the stake into the neighbor's yard. Speck went straight through the brick wall, then sailed back over, returning the stake to Marissa. She dropped it, picked up a different stake, and threw it straight up as hard as she could. Speck darted upward and caught it as it started its descent.

"Look at him through this," Ruby nudged Marissa, who stood captivated watching the stake drift down. Ruby handed over a tuna fish can with the top and bottom cut out, which she'd treated with the blue paint. She'd needed something to drop treats through for training, and the big ring had been too unwieldy.

Marissa held the can in front of her face and watched Speck finish his descent. She moved it around, looking at other things through it, then reached for it with her other hand.

"No, no." Ruby grabbed her wrist. "Don't put your hand in, or it'll be all pins and needles. You won't be able to play drums for half an hour." She took the can and pulled a fish-shaped cracker from her pocket. "Good boy." She dropped the cracker through the can, where Speck swooped to intercept it.

"Where did you get this stuff?"

"I promised not to tell." Ruby ran the crystal around the rim of the can and put both objects back into her pockets. "Now, come on. Wally will be wondering what happened to us."

"But wait a minute…!"

In the dream, Ruby was playing on the computer in her parents' apartment when a banging on the door made her jump. "Police! Open up!"

Ruby's dad ran through the room and grabbed the Rolodex from the kitchen counter, opening a window and throwing the Rolodex out. He ran to the bathroom. There was a crash from the apartment door, but it held. A cabinet slammed open in the bathroom. The toilet flushed.

Ruby looked outside to see where the Rolodex had gone. The building across the street was one story higher than their top-floor apartment. There were police cars in the street—he wouldn't have thrown it down there if he didn't want it found, so it must be on the roof of the other building. She shut the window.

There was another crash from the door and pounding feet in the hallway. Ruby threw herself behind the couch. "Here's one! Lie down! Down!"

"Bedroom's clear! Where's the woman?"

"Hey, there's one behind the couch!"

Ruby tried to shrink further into the corner, but her ankles were grabbed, and she was dragged out, shrieking and kicking. She tried to hit with her fists but, dream-like, couldn't connect with anything.

"It's a kid." The officer grabbed her arms and pulled them behind her back.

"Cuff her," someone else said. "Bring everyone, we'll sort it out down at the station."

Ruby woke, sobbing in fear, her legs tangled in the covers. She kicked loose and rolled off the bed, stumbling to the little sink, where she threw cold water on her face, then leaned over the basin, hair dripping.

There was a gentle knock at the door, and Ruby whirled, heart pounding. "What?"

"Are you okay? You shouted."

It was Simon. She started breathing again. "Just a bad dream."

There was a pause. "I was on my way downstairs to make cocoa. Would you like some?"

"Yeah." Ruby wiped her face on her sleeve. "Yeah, that'd be great. I'll be down in a minute."

Ruby found Simon bent over the stove, stirring a saucepan. "I always just nuke it," she said.

"I know." Simon continued stirring. "Grab some mugs?"

"I don't like police." Ruby set the mugs on the counter.

"Did their visit upset you? They have their uses, but most of them do have a narrow and inflexible view of things."

Ruby watched him pour from the saucepan without spilling a drop, two quick pours ending with the same amount in each mug. He sprinkled mini marshmallows on hers from a bag on the counter, and they ticked their mugs together. Ruby took a tiny sip of the too-hot cocoa. He'd made it with a lot of cinnamon and a bit of cayenne powder. "What if they arrest you?"

Simon blew on the surface of his cocoa. "They'd have to let me go eventually. They don't have a case. It's not actually a crime to be mysterious—yet. You can manage for a while if it comes to that, right?"

"Well, sure, I suppose. I can go to Flora or Dr. Fortunato if I need an adult for something. Or call an aunt if I'm really desperate. That's not the point, though."

"The point then is what?"

Ruby sipped—still too hot. "The point is, the point is, there's no guarantee. Innocent people go to jail sometimes. It's not just the police. What if you get eaten by a Sasquatch or something? I would—I'd miss you."

"I see." Simon set his cup on the counter and pushed on the handle to rotate it. "I'd miss you, too. Not if I were eaten, of course. But that's unlikely, especially by a Sasquatch. They're non-violent."

"Oh, be serious."

Simon looked her in the eye, seriously. "Ruby, do you ever visit your parents?"

Ruby looked away, angry.

"They must miss you. They're not that far, and money's not a problem if you want to go. Don't you want to see them?"

"They made their own choice about that, didn't they? You can use explosives to express your political views, or you can be with your kid. Not both."

"Yeah. That's hard. But I know they still love you. And Ruby?" He waited until she looked at him. "I won't leave you by choice."

"Okay." Her voice was a little husky. She looked down at her mug, and they sat a while in silence, drinking their cocoa.

"Where are you going on your date?" Simon asked at last.

Change of subject—good. "Conrad's driving us to a new games place, Port Ganymede."

"This is your first date, isn't it?"

"It's not a real date for me. Kirk and I are just doing chaperone duty. It's not like he's interested in me or anything."

"Are you interested in him?"

"I don't think that's really any of your business."

Simon nodded. "I would have an awkward talk with you about biology at this point, but since you're a naturalist, you must know the basics."

She rolled her eyes. "It's a little unnecessary, even for non-naturalists. There is such a thing as the Internet. You don't need to worry about me."

Simon shrugged. "I'm not really worried. You're a sensible girl, and I know you can defend yourself if need be."

"What? How do you know that?"

"Word's been going around the neighborhood about a mysterious explosion that knocked out three boys. When the guy at the deli told me about it, I realized I'd heard someone else say 'three boys' recently."

"Um, yeah, that was me. I didn't realize you were listening."

"Halfway. I'm guessing you found those 'shouts' Teela gave you?"

"Turns out I had them all along." Ruby held out her hand. "Here."

"You'll save them as a last resort, of course."

"Of course."

"Seriously, be extremely careful with that kind of thing. Don't do things that are hard to explain. Actually, you should have something else, something more subtle." Simon finished his cocoa and set the mug aside. He thought for a moment. "Here, take this." His tugged a ring off his little finger and held it out to her.

Ruby took it. It was still warm from his hand, a narrow silver band with a pointy black stone mounted in it. "What does it do?"

"It's a hungry stone. If you scratch someone with it, it'll weaken them for a few seconds, slow them down. Long enough to get away if they're holding you."

"Okay, nice! Thanks." It fit her middle finger. She held up her hand to look.

"One other matter I wanted to discuss… this 'Speck' thing…?"

Ruby held up her hand to stop him. "The details are confidential, I'm afraid. Teela insisted."

"Really." Simon drummed his fingers on the counter. "Okay, for now. But since it kills small animals, I'd like your assurance it can tell the difference between rabbits and the neighbor's cat. She's been known to wander into our yard."

"Ah. I'll see to that first thing tomorrow." How exactly, she'd have to think about. "Which neighbor is it?" Could she borrow the cat for a training session, maybe?

When she put her mug in the dishwasher and turned to leave, Simon said, "Sweet dreams!"

Ruby looked at him over her shoulder. "We'll see."

Ten

The building where the memorial service was to be held was low and gray with a ramp sloping down into underground parking. The caterer's van turned onto this ramp, and their cab followed into the echoing, fluorescent-lit space. A panel truck marked "Thorvaldsen Moving" was there ahead of them. Two men in orange coveralls wrestled a huge wooden crate from the back of this vehicle down a ramp. It seemed to have been constructed to fit the truck and had "Piano, fragile, this side up" stenciled on it. While Ruby and Simon waited for the elevator, she watched the movers trundle the crate to the freight elevator, open the doors, and squeeze in beside it.

Ruby knew she hadn't ordered a piano. "Was that one of the guests?"

Simon nodded. "Several, actually."

"We still don't have a body, right?"

"Unless the police have slipped it into the casket without telling me, which seems unlikely." Simon looked at his phone.

The meeting room upstairs was nicer than the exterior of the building had led her to expect. The florists had already been there and left tasteful silver vases of lilies on small tables along the dark-paneled walls. Guests were already milling around the back of the room—about half were regular folks, mixed with a fascinating variety of other creatures. A woman with uncontrolled blonde ringlets, a pale, blotchy face and puffy red eyes, Ruby guessed must be the widow, Netta. She held the hand of a boy who looked about ten, who scowled at his polished shoes, looking ill at ease in a suit and tie.

A short, bald, older man wore a dark suit, its buttons straining. He must've grown since he bought it. A tall old woman in a dark red jacket stood beside him, her veined and spotted hand resting heavily on the gold knob of a carved wooden cane. Her eyes scanned the room alertly, and when they caught Ruby's, her other hand raised to beckon.

"Someone's summoning me," Ruby said. "Imperiously."

Simon looked and sighed. "Might as well go. I have to ask the security people why there's no guard on the garage ramp yet. I want to make sure those detectives aren't admitted."

"What will the detectives think about that?"

"Nothing worse than what they'll think if they do get in. Go on, talk with Ms. Wheelwright, but try not to let her touch you."

"What? Why not?" But he was already gone. Reluctantly, Ruby wound her way around the chairs. The old woman watched her approach with glittering gray eyes and took a couple of steps toward her. The man she'd been with seemed a little relieved at her departure.

Ruby came to a stop before Ms. Wheelwright, who looked her up and down. Ruby wore a new dress, since Simon had declared her best wasn't up to the occasion. It was more girly than anything else she owned—sleeveless with a square-cut neck that highlighted her almost total lack of cleavage. At least it was black.

Ms. Wheelwright stood a little straighter, the dim overhead lighting glimmering on a gold-set cameo pin on her lapel. "You're the new girl, then." Her voice was rough, almost a whisper.

"I'm Simon's niece."

"One more to keep the chaos in check," Ms. Wheelwright

whispered. Her eyes flicked to the casket at the front of the room. "We lose one, we gain another. Perhaps you will be more effective."

Though Ruby hadn't been terribly impressed with Polacek herself, it was a little tacky to criticize him in front of his grieving family. However, they weren't nearby—the sullen boy was getting a low-voiced lecture from his mother, and the man, who might or might not be a relation, seemed to have focused his attention on a tray of cheese and cold cuts.

"No danger from the outside at the moment," the old woman murmured. "But the inner forces are in discord." She reached out a hand and took a step closer. Ruby, a little alarmed, stepped back. "Oh yes," Ms. Wheelwright said sardonically. "Fear the old woman, for she is mad."

Ruby flushed. In fact, Ms. Wheelwright did seem a bit unhinged, but her mockery was still embarrassing. And Simon had just said try not to let her touch her, not under no circumstances let her. Defiantly, Ruby stepped up within Ms. Wheelwright's reach.

The wrinkled hand came up to rest on her head, a cool thumb touching her forehead. Ruby suddenly felt dizzy. Things rushed away from her, those intense gray eyes sparked at her as if from the end of a tunnel, and the world went crinkly with light. A roaring and a babbling filled her ears, and she staggered back against a folding chair. "You are not the one." Ms. Wheelwright's voice seemed to come from a great distance, sounding disappointed but resigned.

Ruby sank into the chair and put her head in her hands. After a few seconds, the world swam back to normal. When she looked up, the boy was standing nearby, looking at her. Ms. Wheelwright had turned away and was instructing the bald man what food to put on her plate.

"Are you all right?" the boy asked.

"I think so. What'd she do?"

He shrugged. "She does it to everyone. They let her because she's rich and does charity for… these people." His gesture encompassed the hall. "I'm not the one either." He stuck out his hand. "I'm Ray. Raymond Polacek."

"Ruby Park," she replied, taking the offered hand which, as she'd feared, was sticky. "I'm sorry about your dad."

"Yeah." He kicked at the carpet. "Mom's real upset."

"How are you doing?"

"I'm strong. I'm gonna get 'em when I'm big."

"What do you mean? Get who?"

"The ones who killed him. I'll kill 'em back."

But if it was really a big animal, there was no "them" to get. Did he know something she didn't? "The police will catch them before then."

A sneer expressed Raymond's opinion of the police.

Ruby felt a stab of pity for him. She took his hand again. "Nobody expects you to be strong right now. It's okay to be sad. You can still get them later."

Raymond jerked his hand away. "What do you know?" His lip quivered. "You're just a dumb girl!" He darted to the far end of the row of chairs, where he sat by himself, facing the wall.

Ruby looked around and found Simon standing nearby, looking at her. He raised his eyebrows, and she raised hers back. "What?"

"Never mind. Did you enjoy your chat with Ms. Wheelwright?"

"It was…." Ruby paused for the right word. "Mind altering."

"Hmph. I did warn you. So, are you The One?"

"No. What happens when she finds them?"

"She hasn't said. Myself, I think the elevator doesn't run all the way to the top floor. Whatever her delusion is, if it included actually finding someone, she's had over fifty years to do it. I think she just likes looking."

"Has she tested you?"

"No. I don't believe in humoring her." Simon turned to watch the door. He seemed to be looking for someone.

A few more people had entered, including Dr. Fortunato and a couple of Sasquatches—judging by its dress, one was female, though Ruby wouldn't have guessed otherwise. The two were of similar size, both craggy-featured and muscular. The female's deep blue dress was long-sleeved and high-collared. She also wore white gloves, which probably all saved on razor blades, and both their outfits were well-fitting, with nice detailing. It had to be all custom made.

The movers with the giant crate had also finally shown up, after what must have been a circuitous route. They had the crate on a wheeled platform, which they rolled into the back of the room through a sliding partition. They locked the wheels and unlatched the end that faced the front of the room.

Ruby watched, interested to see what might come out, but was distracted when Mrs. Polacek returned and made a beeline for Simon.

"Simon, there you are, thank God. I've been... I don't know what. It's just horrible what they're saying now. How can he be missing?"

Ruby looked over at Raymond, but he was still sitting where he'd been. Who was missing?

"I don't know," Simon said. "I only just heard about it myself. Captain Urbana will be here soon. She might know more."

"Well, my God. Who would even do such a thing? And how? Isn't the place guarded?"

"Netta, it doesn't make sense to me, either. Look, some wibbles just came in. Why don't you go get them settled? When I find out more, I'll tell you right away."

Once Mrs. Polacek was out of earshot, Ruby asked, "Polacek's body is missing? This is why the police haven't returned him—because they've lost him?"

"Apparently." Simon watched Mrs. Polacek wade in amongst a crowd of wibbles, who held their long, fuzzy green arms in the air, reminiscent of baby birds wanting to be fed.

Simon turned to face her. "She kept bugging them about when

they would be done with the autopsy, and they kept putting her off, and she finally got them to admit it today. I was wondering what was taking them so long, on such a hot case."

"So, he's been missing all along?"

"Since early on, anyway." Simon looked at his phone.

"Someone broke in and took him. Is the place guarded?"

"Like I told Netta, that's all I know. About all we can say for sure is he didn't walk off on his own. At least...." Simon paused a moment. "No, definitely not in this case."

"You think someone took him because the autopsy would prove he wasn't really killed by a giant animal?"

"Or because it would prove he was." Simon glanced toward the door again. "Ah. Here's Captain Urbana." He hurried off to greet the new arrival—a short, muscular woman with graying hair pinned back in a bun. She scanned the room with a dispassionate glance.

Ruby suddenly remembered the piano crate and turned to look. Nothing had come out. Instead, the open side, which faced the front of the room, was blocked off with a curtain of white gauze. Apparently, whoever was in there meant to watch the show from inside. A caterer stopped at the crate with a tray of what looked like very overripe pears and pushed it under the edge of the gauze.

A variety of guests, of all types, were milling around, talking, finding seats. Ruby remembered she had her own job to do and went to the podium to make sure the microphone was working.

"Excuse me?" someone squeaked behind her. She turned to find a slender, light-blue creature of about her height, dressed in a yellow jumpsuit with many zippers, pockets, and brass buttons. It stared at her out of one large blue eye in the middle of its face. Below was a soft mouth fringed with stubby cilia. "Are you assisting with the arrangements?"

"Yes. Can I help you?"

"The box." The blue thing rested one long-fingered hand on the casket, a pale box of plain wood which, for reasons nobody had explained to Ruby, had three daggers protruding from the lid. "It's empty, yes?"

"Yes."

"Is that all right? The ritual is otherwise the same?"

"It would be better to have him here, but yes, nothing else changes."

The blue creature paused, looking down. "May I speak first? I am, that is, a little nervous." His gesture encompassed the room, now more than half full. "I don't wish to wait."

Ruby hadn't been told anything about who was to start things off. "Sure. When people are settled, you can begin."

As she descended from the little stage, the male Sasquatch caught Ruby's eye. Ruby had missed breakfast and was eager to check out the food but waited for him to pick his way through the pack of wibbles.

Ruby had thought she'd gotten over being afraid of odd creatures, but when the Sasquatch squatted to talk to her, she found herself talking an involuntary step back. He gave a thin-lipped smile, briefly showing large yellow teeth, which was less than reassuring.

This wasn't the same one who'd come to the house a couple of times. He was a little smaller with striking, alert pale blue eyes and bald patches above the ears. A scar tracked from his forehead into the thick hair on his scalp.

"They thay you are in charge." he rumbled. He reached up to adjust his tie, and she saw he was missing part of his left little finger.

For supposedly non-violent creatures, they all seemed to have a lot of scars. "Near enough."

"We mutht not thit in these." His head cocked toward the nearest row of wooden folding chairs. "Unleth you need kindling."

"There's, um, I noticed a lounge across the hall with a few armchairs. Could you use those?"

"If we may."

"Sure, I'll get them moved into here."

"I will do it." He stood and nodded. As he headed back toward where the female waited, Ruby let go of a breath she hadn't realized she'd been holding. He probably could carry one armchair in each hand.

A short line had formed at the food tables. Ruby stood behind a tall, pale woman whose skin looked swollen, as if she'd been stung all over by bees. She wore a long, shimmery black dress and smelled like oatmeal.

Raymond Polacek came up to stand behind her. He'd apparently already visited the table once, since he held a dirty plate. "I am too gonna get 'em," he whispered.

"I know," Ruby said, amused. "They can't get away from you."

"You don't believe me, but I know who they are. I saw."

Now Ruby was curious. "You did not."

"Did so! I was supposed to be in bed, but I went for water, and I saw who was with him that night. It was the Skohlars."

"Really? Well, you best not go around telling people. You don't want them to find out you know before you're ready to go after them. You'll lose the element of surprise."

Raymond looked stricken. "You won't tell them?"

"Of course not." Ruby pushed her hair back from her face. "They've got it coming. I won't spoil it for you." She picked up a plate and scanned the trays and bowls, each neatly labeled in English and a couple of other languages. She skipped the pickled slugs and a bowl of lumpy brown objects whose card read, "Blargh (plain)." She filled her plate with cocktail wieners, bread rolls, and crumbly cheese.

"Try the blargh." Raymond reached past her to take three. "It's pretty all right."

"Maybe next time through."

He shrugged. "If there's any left."

Ruby wandered away to find Simon. He'd saved her a seat between himself and Spider, who looked stiff and uncomfortable in a suit too loose and too short for him. She hadn't realized he was still in town. Dr. Fortunato sat on Simon's other side, talking with him.

Ruby tugged on Simon's sleeve, trying to get his attention. "What's a Skohlar?"

Simon stiffened slightly. "Who's talking about them? They have to stop."

Great. Now she was going to get that poor kid into trouble. "I don't know, I just overheard someone."

Simon leaned toward her and lowered his voice. "They're not out."

"What do you mean 'out?'"

"Not everybody knows about them." His gesture encompassed the room.

"Seriously? Even the people here?"

"Most of them don't. If you see whoever was talking about them, please point them out to me."

Should she tell Simon what Raymond had said? He might be jumping to conclusions, thinking the Skohlars had killed his dad. But if they'd hired Polacek for the job that killed him, Simon might need to know.

Captain Urbana showed up in the aisle and squeezed past to sit beside Dr. Fortunato. She leaned forward to hold her hand out to Ruby. "Pleased to meet you," Ruby lied, shaking the officer's hand briefly.

Urbana gave her a long look. "Do I have halitosis, or do you just not like police?"

"Nothing wrong with your breath."

Urbana gave a tiny nod and sat back. Ruby did also and felt Spider's eyes on her. She turned to find him trying to hide a grin. "What?"

"Down with The Man," he murmured, holding out his fist. She bumped it with hers, then turned to look at the podium as the little blue man ascended the steps into the spotlight.

He blinked in the light, looked out over the audience, and placed one hand on the casket. His fingers were long, shading toward red at their tips, which were flat and round. "I knew Alasdair," he said. The cilia around his mouth trembled.

"Use the mic!" someone shouted from the back of the room.

The blue man moved to the podium, pulling the microphone down to his mouth. *"I remember the time we... well, I shouldn't talk about that. One day he... but I can't tell that, either."* He stood for a moment, apparently at a loss for safe things to say, then pulled a magic marker out of one of his many pockets and went to the casket to scrawl *"clever guy"* on the front. "Some days...." he said.

"Mic!"

"Some days," he said into the microphone, waving the marker, *"you are the eater, and some days—one day, anyway—you are the eaten. The idea is to make the ratio of the former to the latter...."*

"Next speaker!" called the heckler.

The blue man made a helpless little gesture, set the marker on the podium, and retired. A large, hairy, black-haired man took his place. The man smoothed his excessive mustache and glared around the room.

"When I meet Polacek first time," he boomed, not bothering with the mic, "I break his nose." He laughed. "Next time, he break my arm." He grabbed up the magic marker and wrote *"TUF"* on the casket. "After that, we friends." He held up a small silver flask on a chain and looped the chain around the handle of one of the daggers, to dangle onto the casket. "Damn shame." He walked off.

Many more came up and left a souvenir on the casket or used the marker. About half of these also spoke briefly.

Polacek's widow stood up last. "Thank you all for coming." Her voice was hoarse. She cleared her throat. "All of you who knew him...." She trailed off, looking at the casket, covered with writing and festooned with enough objects to stock a small garage sale. "So many. It seems so strange without him, though of course"—she gestured out at the audience with a sad little smile—"my life was never this strange before I met him.

"Some of you have asked whether we'll be able to get by. Thank you for your concern, but don't worry. Alasdair had insurance, and we have enough put away—not enough to do the things we dreamed of, but I don't feel like doing those without him, anyway. We'll be okay. I won't carry on the business, but I hope you'll all keep in touch. And now, please, stay and visit for a while. We have the hall for a couple more hours."

Much of the crowd gravitated to the back, with a few conversational clumps dotted elsewhere around the room. Ms. Wheelwright had pulled up a chair next to the piano crate and leaned forward, talking through the gauze to whatever was inside. Ruby couldn't hear any other voices when she walked past, but Ms. Wheelwright paused, listening, then spoke again.

Ruby wandered around eavesdropping for a while, then threaded her way through to the buffet tables. The blargh, as Raymond had predicted, was gone, but there was plenty of other food. She found Simon placing a precise slice of pâté onto a paper plate. "I've got to go soon," she said.

"Very well." He didn't look at her.

"What'd you find out about the missing body?"

He gave her one brief, cold look and turned to take a slice of something green embedded in aspic. "You don't need to know anything about that."

Ruby was a little puzzled. "Are you angry at me?"

He lowered his voice. "Of course I'm angry! You were rude to my friend, Ruby."

"Who? Oh, the captain? Yeah, I guess it was such a beautiful straight line that I took it without thinking."

"To be around these people, you'd best start thinking more before you speak."

"She did ask. Was I supposed to lie to her?"

Simon looked at her incredulously. "If the truth will hurt someone's feelings and a lie won't harm them, yes, of course you're supposed to lie."

Ruby paused. "I'll have to think about that."

"Do."

"I'm sorry."

"I'm not the one you should apologize to."

"All right. I've gotta go now. See you at home?"

"No later than ten." He set down the slicer and walked away.

On her way to the door, Ruby saw Captain Urbana and paused. The captain was sitting backwards on a folding chair, leaning over the back to speak Spanish to a small fruit tree in a wheeled planter. Surprisingly, the tree answered her in the same language. Ruby moved closer and spotted a speaker box resting on the dirt near the plant's trunk. The planter rotated in place, and a branch extended slightly in the captain's direction, a small fruit bobbing on the end of it. It looked like an apricot but deep pink.

"Gracias." Urbana picked the fruit and sat rolling it in her palm while the plant trundled off. Then she looked up at Ruby. "Yes?"

"I wanted to apologize—"

Urbana waved it off. "I'm used to it in my line of work. And I know your history with the police hasn't been exactly cordial."

"What did Simon tell you about me?"

"Take it easy. Nothing recently. But we've known each other for years. Naturally, when his sister was on trial, we talked about it, and your name came up then. I'm guessing not all your experiences with police have been pleasant."

"Yeah. But it's not just that. There are those two detectives who'd like nothing better than to arrest Simon. I've been seeing policemen around every corner recently, none of them friendly."

"Sure. Well, I know better than to think he had anything to do with it. Unfortunately, those guys aren't likely to take my word for it. But there's no evidence against Simon."

Could she get away with asking a few questions? "What happened to Polacek's body?"

"Nobody can figure. The place is kept locked up and has video surveillance, and there's nothing on the tapes. Bodies don't just vanish, you know?"

"Actually, I've seen a body vanish. It wasn't dead," she hastened to add when Urbana's eyebrows went up.

"Well, yeah, with this crowd, there's no telling what's possible. But the Medical Examiner doesn't know that, and he's stuck trying to explain how it left a locked room with cameras in the halls when the biggest opening in the room is a six-inch drainpipe."

"So you think it was some kind of"—Ruby waved her hands— "hocus pocus?"

"Maybe. If it is, whoever's responsible, it could get them in a whole different sort of hot water. Everyone's supposed to keep a low profile with that kind of stuff, or it'll make trouble for us. There are rules, you know, and people to enforce them."

"I've heard you're one of them."

"Right. So, if you hear anything, let me know right away, okay?"

Ruby nodded thoughtfully and took her leave. She collected her backpack and hiked out into the bright afternoon, past the uniformed security guard at the front entrance. There was a car in a parking lot across the street, with someone in the driver's seat. His face was shadowed, but presumably it was a cop. She hesitated and pulled out her phone to check the time. She had a few minutes before her bus, so she crossed the street and approached the car. "Hello again. Aren't you hot in there?"

It was the same detective who'd interviewed her before. He didn't look pleased to see her. "Move along."

Ruby saw a digital camera lying on the passenger seat. "Are you going to photograph people as they leave? You're wasting your time. The ones who came in the rented vans will leave the same way. They're really serious about their privacy."

"You're not kidding. And here I thought the mob was tight. Who are these people?"

"I'm not at liberty to say. Why are you so hot to know who they are, anyway? It's not likely the killer will go to his victims' funeral."

The detective snorted. "You'd be surprised how often they do exactly that. Serial killers aren't rational people."

Ruby tilted her head at him. "I'm really sorry you don't have any better clues than this to be spending your time on. Anyway, I heard it was a large animal that killed him."

"Where did you hear that?"

"Oh, mister suspicious. From Uncle Simon, who heard it from Missus Polacek, who heard it from you guys. Really, if you want to keep a secret, the way is to not tell people."

"It wasn't an animal. Someone just tried to make it look that way. There are no large, invisible predators wandering around Chicago. That's only in Peru."

Ruby opened her mouth to say, "Really?" but realized he was joking and shut it. These days, it was hard to tell.

"Don't you want to see justice done?" he said. "Are you so sure none of these people have anything to do with it?"

Ruby thought about it and was a little surprised to find that she did want to see justice done. From what had been said about him at the funeral, she almost felt she'd known Polacek—was sorry, at least, that she'd never had a chance to know him. She had a little seed of anger for the sake of Netta and Raymond, which was starting to grow into serious indignation.

Someone in the Scene must know something about Polacek's death. Maybe not anyone at the funeral, but what about these Skohlars? Someone definitely needed to talk with them and find out what he'd been doing for them.

She held out a hand. "Give me your card. If I hear anything useful, I'll call."

While waiting for the bus, she looked at the card. Homicide Division, Derek Garbers, Lieutenant. Why had his partner called him

NMI? She had a system for dealing with these, now. She snapped a picture with her phone and tossed the card into a trash bin.

Eleven

"Nice outfit," Marissa stood up from the steps in front of the door. "Is that what you're wearing on the date?"

"Don't be silly. This was for a funeral service. Don't you think I'd be a little overdressed?" Ruby unlocked the door and Marissa followed her in. "I'll go change. Give a yell if they come."

When she returned, in her Black Widow t-shirt and black skirt with pockets, Marissa was leaning up against the door, looking out through the glass. She wore jeans, an unbleached cotton blouse, suede shoes with turquoise beads on the laces, and a matching turquoise pendant and earrings.

"Simple, yet elegant," Ruby commented. "You look very grown up."

"Thanks, that's the effect I was going for. Whose funeral was it? Not a relative, I hope?"

"No. A friend of Uncle Simon's I only met once. I was just logistical support."

"I've only been to one funeral since I was old enough to remember. It was phony and boring."

"This wasn't like that. I know what you mean, though. Both

funerals I went to before this were bogus. When my grandmother died people stood up to say how nice and generous she was, but she was actually pretty terrifying. And my grandfather, you know, not a word about how he tried to cheat his cousins or gambled all his money, though everyone there knew."

"And… and your parents, though?" Marissa said hesitantly. "That would make three funerals, right?"

"Hm? Oh…." Ruby's brain worked furiously. "No, they were the second. The grandparents went within a week of each other, so there was just one service. I guess he just couldn't live without her."

"What was your folks' funeral like? I mean… if you don't mind talking about it."

"Oh, it wasn't so bad, I guess. People just went on and on saying nothing, but they weren't too inaccurate. I wasn't tracking much at the time. It was all pretty awful, you know." She was beginning to feel awful herself, guilty about lying to her friend. "I guess I don't really want to talk about it. Anyway, here are the guys."

Conrad's car was a pale blue, freshly washed convertible. Kirk was in the front passenger seat, but he got out and moved to let Marissa sit in front. He and Ruby swung their legs over the sides to get into the cramped back seat.

"Have you got it?" Kirk asked as soon as they were strapped in and moving. "I want to see it."

"Hi, Kirk. It's nice to see you, too."

"Yeah, yeah, whatever. Give."

Ruby leaned forward to unzip her backpack, which was scrunched between her shins and the front seat. She handed over the metal plaque. Kirk weighed it in his hand, turned it over to scrape the rough back with his thumbnail, with no visible result.

When he pulled out a pocketknife, Ruby stopped him. "No marks. She didn't say I could show it to anyone, so I don't want any damage to explain when I give it back."

"She who?"

"Never mind who."

"Can I borrow it to run a reflectance spectroscopy?"

"A what? No, you can't take it. I don't know when she might come back." Ruby noticed Conrad and Marissa were quiet. Whether listening to them or just too shy to talk to each other, she wasn't sure. They didn't turn around, but Conrad looked at her in the rear-view mirror.

"Are you guys comfortable?"

"No." Ruby glanced at Kirk, whose long legs were scrunched up nearly to his chin. "But it's not far, right? You know," she told Kirk, "you can put your feet over this way. I don't bite unless provoked."

He gave a lopsided grin and shifted so his feet almost touched her calf, which let him stretch out a little. He put his arm along the seat back, again not touching, but so close she could feel the warmth near her shoulder. "What else can you tell me?"

"Ooh!" Marissa turned in her seat. "Tell him about Speck!"

"Speck has to be seen to be believed. Later."

She looked at Kirk's hand, where he was fingering the rough edge of the plaque—perhaps hoping a tiny, unnoticeable bit would break off. His nails were short, a little ragged, not completely clean—maybe auto grease. The fingertips of his left hand had calluses. Much like the ones she was developing, in fact. "Hey! You play guitar. Me, too. I'm just learning."

He looked up. "Not so much guitar—bass mostly. How did you know I play?"

She displayed her own right hand. "Calluses. I'm just starting out, though."

"Do you always look at people's hands?"

"Well... yeah, pretty much. You can tell a lot that way." She leaned forward to tap Marissa's shoulder. "He plays bass."

"Yeah, I got that."

Port Ganymede wasn't too busy, and Ruby was able to grab a ping-pong table right away. Kirk wasn't as fast or coordinated as she was, but his long reach let him hit back enough shots that she barely edged him out, five games to three. Then they looked around for the others and saw them sitting side by side, intent on a road race game.

"Let 'em be," Kirk shouted over the racket in the room. "Hey, are you hungry?"

Ruby let herself be led into the restaurant section inside a large plastic dome with "The Bubble" written in neon above the arched entrance. It was much quieter there, and conversation at normal levels was possible.

"This is nice," he said. "It's not too busy because it's new. In a month, it'll be packed."

Someone had left a half-eaten order of chili cheese fries on another table. "Those look okay." Ruby pointed. "But it's too big. Want to split one?"

Kirk agreed and went to order. Ruby took a book from her pocket while she waited, covertly watching him. He was a bit awkward and unsubtle, but then, for a boy, that was to be expected. He hadn't seemed to mind at all getting beaten at ping-pong, which was a point in his favor. He was older than her—she thought probably seventeen—and had nice hair, curious gray-green eyes, and lots of freckles. He turned his head suddenly, and she looked down at her book, hoping he hadn't caught her looking.

He returned with the food, and she started to put her book away, but he put his finger on the corner and tilted it up to see the cover. "John Steinbeck."

"Not my usual choice. My uncle gave me a summer reading list, and one of them was anything by Steinbeck."

"*The Log from the Sea of Cortez?*"

"It's non-fiction, about marine biology."

"Marissa told me you were interested in biology." Kirk munched a fry. "Don't you think your uncle intended for you to read one of his novels, though?"

"Probably, but what he said was any book by Steinbeck."

Kirk nodded. "What do you want to do next?"

The restaurant floor was a little elevated, so they could look out through the curved plastic at the large room. "What's that big thing over there?"

"*Space Striker.* It's a simulated cockpit of a space warship, two people per team, you have to try to blast the other team's ship to smithereens."

"Perfect. I like smithereens."

"What's perfect?" Marissa said, coming up behind them.

"Oh, hi! We're going to play *Space Striker.*"

"Are you sure? You're not so hot at *Star Raiders.* It won't be so much fun for you if you get creamed."

"It doesn't matter who wins. It'll be fun to play, anyway."

"Hello? Who are you, and what have you done with Ruby?"

"All right, it's really because I know one of the… people who worked on it. I read about it on his blog, so I know a little about it. You and me together, we'll do okay."

"Boys against girls?" Marissa said.

"Is there any other way? Besides, it's not just shoot-em-up. There's strategy involved."

"You *are* pretty sneaky." Marissa looked over her shoulder at Conrad, just coming in. "Are you ready, Conrad? Ruby and I will whip your asses at *Space Striker.*"

The game module was laid out as a high-tech cockpit with two chairs. Marissa took the pilot's position, and Ruby sat in the gunner's chair. They donned helmets with goggles that showed colorful 3-D displays when aimed at blank blue areas on the console and ceiling. Through the tinted Plexiglas windows, they could see the boys settling in across the way. Conrad waved at them from the opposite gunner's chair and turned to face his controls.

They played a couple of practice games against the computer. It seemed the key wasn't reflexes so much as timing and anticipating the enemy. And, of course, hiding and setting ambushes.

The girls discussed strategy until they were interrupted by a rap on the plastic canopy. "Are you guys ever gonna be ready?" Kirk shouted.

"We're ready now," Ruby yelled back. "Right?" she asked Marissa. Marissa gave a thumbs-up. "Bring it on!"

The boys tried to get close enough for a broadside, but Marissa evaded them, ducking behind planets and then adjusting their heading while they were hidden from the other ship's scanners. Occasionally she'd turn the controls over to Ruby, telling her to "keep on the blue line," while she did experimental course plots on a separate screen.

"What are you doing? When do we close with them?" Ruby was itching to test her missile skills.

"Next time." Marissa grinned. "They think they've got our pattern. They'll expect us to turn up-axis when we round that gas giant, so as soon as we're out of sight they'll turn to intercept." She moved the new course to the overhead, a blue line marking their projected path, red for the other ship.

"But we go a different way?"

"Right. Once we're hidden, we'll cut the engines and go ballistic. Use the planet as a gravity slingshot to sneak up behind them." Marissa punched some keys, and the blue course plot moved to curl around the planet and intersect the red line. "Also, when I say 'now,' you launch a bunch of seeker missiles at eighty degrees with a thirty second delay. Their orbits will get the missiles pointed the right way, and it'll make them think we're shooting from that-a-way when we'll really be this-a-way."

"And keep them too busy to look for us. That's fairly brilliant."

"Thank you. Get ready, it's coming up."

Ruby programmed delays on three missile banks and held her fingers over the launch buttons.

"Cutting drive." Marissa punched buttons, and the blurred stars on the forward display snapped into focus. The planet rolled past beneath them, banded blue and green. "Launch!"

Ruby's fingers stabbed down. The whoosh of the missile launch came over her headset, and the status lights on those banks went amber. Ruby imagined crew hurrying to reload them, until they turned green again. "Passive sensors only," Marissa ordered.

Ruby looked around for the red triangle that would mark the boys' position. "Not seeing them. Their engines must be off, too." She glanced across at the other cockpit, where there was some shouting and frantic activity going on. There was a glitter of counter-missile explosions on the tactical monitor. "Spotted them! Ten mark minus five," she read the numbers off the grid.

"Excellent," Marissa muttered, and there was a brief burn of ion thrusters while they adjusted course. "Are they swinging back toward the planet?"

"Not yet." Ruby kept her eye on the tiny bright speck. "There they go, on ions." The red course plot reappeared.

"I've got 'em," There was another burn as the blue line swung to meet the red. "We should pass close enough for lasers. Keep your fingers crossed they don't see us."

Ruby could hear the occasional ping of the other ship's radar, but there were enough asteroids and little moons in the vicinity of the gas giant to hide them. "Be ready to flip over after I launch a broadside, so I can hit them again with the other tubes."

"We're going opposite directions. There's not time for two missile broadsides." Marissa pointed out a countdown timer. "We'll just be in laser range for two seconds after that reaches zero."

Ruby glanced at the other cockpit again. Conrad was leaning back, looking at the long-range sensors, she was glad to see, instead of at his tactical display. He turned to look at her, his expression unreadable behind goggles. She waved and turned back to her board to program the starboard broadside.

With twenty seconds still on the timer, she launched. Marissa turned to her, alarmed. "Too early! They're out of range."

"It's cool." Ruby moved to the controls for the port broadside, whose lights still glowed green. "Flip now."

"It's too early!"

"*Flip,* dammit!"

Marissa made a squeak of outrage and grabbed a control bar. The starfield swung dizzyingly. Ruby's hand hovered over the keys until they settled down, then she ran her finger down the board, launching the tubes in sequence.

"They've spotted us!" Marissa said, and a moment later, "Incoming!"

"I see it." Ruby stabbed at the counter-missile controls, but she was late. Some would get through.

"Laser ready?"

Ruby centered the other ship in the laser sight, thumbed up the magnification, and aimed. Marissa counted down the last three seconds, and Ruby held down the fire button, swinging the stick to draw a line of fire across the rear part of the ship as it whipped past. At the same time, explosions and sirens marked the first hits from incoming missiles. Damage alerts sprang up over her board, and the laser sight went dark. Fine. She was done with it anyway. "Flip!"

"Out of range. We got 'em good." The stars wheeled around them again. "Hang on, they're slowing down. They're coming after us."

"What are they gonna do, bleed on us?"

"Seeing missiles on radar. They're firing? They're way out of range."

Ruby grinned. "Those are ours."

"Ours?"

"The ones I launched early."

"You set them on delay and aimed where they were going to be! Oh! Good hits!"

They waited a few seconds for the explosions to die down. "They're drifting," Ruby said.

"Do we trust that?"

Ruby held down the inter-ship radio button. "Looks like you're toast. Give up?"

"Might as well," Conrad's voice came over the com, sounding bitter. Kirk could be heard in the background saying, "You'll never take us alive!"

All the consoles switched to fireworks and a big "1-0." The girls turned to each other, grinning, and did a high five. "Ready to go again?" Marissa asked.

By the time they headed for home, it was getting dark and raining. Conrad put the top up. Marissa insisted Kirk should sit in front, since he needed the leg room, and she was now leaning forward, happily discussing orbits with him over the drumming of rain on the roof.

Conrad caught Ruby's eye in the rear-view mirror, and she leaned forward. "I didn't know she was an actual rocket scientist," he said, low-voiced.

"This is probably the first time it's been useful for anything, so you can't blame her for getting excited."

"Hm." Something about Conrad's expression seemed to say he'd been a victim of false advertising before, and Ruby suspected this might be Marissa's last date with him. Not, perhaps, the last with Kirk, though. Marissa reached over the seat to grab a calculator from his hand.

By the time they got near Ruby's house, the rain had stopped, and the streets steamed in the last light of day. Conrad let Ruby and Marissa off a couple of blocks from home, so he could get right back on the highway. Kirk got out too and stood awkwardly, hands in his pockets. "I hope I'll get to learn more about that plaque."

"Someday you will, I've been told."

"Come on, we're late!" Conrad called from the car.

Kirk grimaced. "Sorry about that. Gotta go. I'll call you?"

Ruby wasn't sure which of them he was talking to, but she nodded. Then she gave a mischievous little smile, whistled, held up her book in the air, and waggled it around. "Carry home, Speck." The book whipped out of her hand and flew off down the street. "See ya."

"Wh-what? How…."

"Can't stop to explain now, you're late! Good night!" Linking arms with Marissa, she strolled away.

Once they heard the car drive off, Ruby looked around to make sure Kirk had really gone too. She clucked her tongue. "I hope you're not going to make a habit of swiping my dates."

"What? No, I didn't…."

"I understand, you can't help it. It's that fatal glamour you have. Men are powerless against it. Like moths to a flame."

"Cut it out! Kirk was just being nice."

"No, no! Kirk isn't the kind of person who politely pretends to be interested. If he's bored, his eyes glaze over. I saw that twice when I was talking to him."

They passed under a streetlight, and Ruby could see Marissa was blushing furiously.

"You're making me feel rotten, Ruby. He was your date. Anyway, you're the mystery woman with the magical secrets. How could I compete with that?"

"He's interested in the secrets, for sure. Interested in me? Not so sure. Really, it's okay if he likes you."

"I think you're wrong. We're just both interested in space."

"Well, maybe I'm wrong. But if he ends up being your boyfriend, he and I could still be friends, right? That wouldn't bug you?"

Marissa thought it over. "I never had a boyfriend. I don't know. I don't think so. But since it's really you he likes, let's turn it around. Would it be okay with you if I was friends with him?"

"Oh, I don't know." Ruby thought back to the car. How had she felt when he and Marissa had their heads together over the calculator? "Probably. I've never had a boyfriend, either, though, and I'm not sure I want one."

Marissa sighed. "I don't know how I feel about Kirk or Conrad."

"Conrad is a dick. He couldn't drive an extra two blocks to drop us off? And he's a poor loser." She was about to add a couple of other choice observations when they rounded the last corner, and she came to a sudden stop.

"What's up? Who's that on your steps?"

"Could you wait here a minute?" Ruby released Marissa's arm and walked ahead to stand at the bottom of the steps, looking up at the woman seated in front of the door. The door which, she now saw, was open, the lock broken. Her gaze flicked back to the woman's face, whose expression spoke bad news as loudly as any words.

"Captain Urbana." Ruby's heart thudded. "What's going on?"

"I'm sorry, Ruby. Simon is under arrest. They're searching the house."

Twelve

Ruby looked back at Marissa, still standing at the corner, then, helplessly, up at the door again as someone came out. It was the short, burly detective who'd interviewed Simon. He started to pass, then backed up when he recognized Ruby. "Come with me. We need to talk."

Ruby fought down a surge of panic. She had to keep cool and manage things. There was nobody else to do it now. "I'll talk with you after I talk to Captain Urbana for a minute."

"Right now would be better for you. Captain Urbana has no business being here."

Urbana stood. "I'm here as a friend of the accused, not as an officer."

"Funny choice of friends you've got."

"Unless you arrest me, too," Ruby said, "I don't have to go with you right away. I'll stay here and talk to the captain." She stressed the last word, figuring Urbana probably outranked him.

"It's not the captain's case *or* her department." The detective's eyes cast daggers at Urbana. "Anything she tells you about it is a breach of police confidentiality."

"You haven't told me anything," Urbana said, "so I don't know what you expect me to give away. She just wants to be reassured that her uncle's okay. Go away for a minute, Bernard, and she'll come to you in a more cooperative state of mind than if you marched her off right now."

The detective gave them a final suspicious look and went on up the street to his car. He opened the trunk and dug around.

"What's going on here?" Marissa had come up behind Ruby. "Is that a policeman?"

"Yeah," Ruby said. "Simon's been arrested."

"I'm not sure why," Urbana said. "He has a lawyer, so talk to the lawyer before you answer Bernard's questions."

"But what about...." Marissa's eyes darted upwards.

"She's worried about our house guest," Ruby said.

Urbana gave Ruby a hard look. "Who is this, and what have you been telling her? You and I will discuss this later. They won't find Wally. The house protects itself from intruders."

"Protects itself how?"

"In that they won't find anything..." Urbana began, and when she saw the detective returning from his car, "...implicating Simon, since he's innocent."

"Who's this?" The detective looked at Marissa. He had a nylon zipper case tucked under his arm and stood rocking on his heels.

"Marissa, you should probably go on home," Ruby said. "I guess there's no practice tonight."

The detective let Marissa go after taking down her name and address, then jerked his head to show that Ruby should follow him inside.

"I'll wait here," Captain Urbana said. "Alice is on her way, and she'll stay with you. In case anyone talks about calling Child Protective Services, tell them she's in charge of you, and they don't need to. By the way, I think this is yours?" She held out a creased and torn paperback. "Do try to hold onto it. I wouldn't want to have to fight for it again."

Ruby followed the detective into the study, where he gestured Ruby to a chair, then paced back and forth a bit, looking at her.

After a few moments, Ruby said, "I want to talk to Simon's lawyer before I answer any questions."

"You're not under arrest. You don't have a right to an attorney."

"I'm a minor. Not only do I get an attorney, you shouldn't even be talking to me without someone else here. If you want me to answer, you'll get him. Or her."

"Well, you're a little lawyer yourself, aren't you? You're in a great deal of trouble yourself if you don't talk."

Fear rose in Ruby's throat, but she fought it down. "If that's true," she said, her voice shaky, "I'm sure the lawyer will tell me to talk."

"Where does your uncle keep his sword?"

"What sword? I mean, lawyer, please."

"The one that's four feet long and glows. You know, the Chinese kind. Like ninjas use."

"Ninjas are Japanese."

"This sword." The detective handed her a glossy print. It looked like a picture from an outdoor security camera, looking down on Uncle Simon. He looked pale under a streetlight, peering into the darkness, holding ready a long, curved sword, two-handed. A timestamp in the corner showed *11:08 p.m.* the previous night. Oddly, he was wearing sunglasses.

"Lawyer." She handed it back.

"Then we'll have to continue this discussion at the station."

Though her heart raced, Ruby's arms were steady as she held them out. "Slap on the cuffs, then."

"Don't tempt me." He opened the study door and waited for her to precede him out. A uniformed officer followed them out, carrying the sword from the suit of armor. It was straight, so obviously not the one in the picture, but they must be collecting every knife in the house for comparison purposes.

"You take care of that," she called back to him. "It's an antique. I think."

Returning home late, Ruby found the door and lock had been replaced. The new glass was frosted—*about damn time,* she thought—so she couldn't see who was inside, but she could make out light and movement.

Her key didn't fit the new lock, so she pulled the bell rope. After a moment, the door opened to the limit of a chain, and a face peered out—Dr. Fortunato. She looked ready for bed, wearing a fuzzy dressing gown with Simon's initials embroidered on the breast.

"Ah, Ruby."

"Ah, Alice."

The door shut, and there was the jingle of the chain. Ruby turned to the police car at the curb to give a thumbs-up and wave goodbye. Dr. Fortunato tried to give Ruby a hug after she was inside, but Ruby evaded her. "What's up here?"

"It's been pretty quiet. A few people called to see whether they could help."

"Could they?"

"I don't know. I wrote down their numbers for Simon's lawyer. Did you talk to him?"

"The lawyer? For a minute. He just told me not to answer any questions for now. He acts like he's not worried, but I think he is."

"They can't really think he killed all those people."

"Then they're doing a really good imitation of it." Ruby felt impatient. She wanted to be alone and have Alice quit pestering her, but she was also starving. "Is there any food?"

"Don't know. What did they ask?"

"Mainly about last night, what time did Simon leave, come home, where did he go, what did he have with him." Ruby stuck her head in the fridge, looked around, and closed it again, disappointed. "I couldn't have told them much anyway. It's not like I ever know where he's going. What about Wally?"

"He's fine." Dr. Fortunato pointed up. "When the house is in lockdown, you know, it has a different attic."

"No, I didn't know. How would I when nobody tells me anything? I was worried about him. They kept asking about the light in the attic. I figured they hadn't found him, or they would've been asking about the Bat Boy in the attic instead, but they didn't act like they believed me when I said I went up there to practice music."

"No, the other attic is all dust and boxes." Dr. Fortunato settled herself on a stool.

"See the problem with all these secrets?" Ruby got a box of cereal from the pantry. "Is there anything else I should know so I don't make a fool of myself again?"

"The sub-basement isn't accessible during lockdown either…."

"We have a sub-basement? Where?"

"Oh, you know." Dr. Fortunato waved a hand. "Under the basement. Also, the basement holding cells change to a storage room. Oh, your friend Melissa called. You should call her. She says she's freaking out."

"Not Melissa, *Marissa.*" Ruby poured the cereal dry into a bowl and left, leaving the box on the counter.

The lights in the study were out, but a nearly full moon shone through the window. After a moment to let her eyes adapt, she crossed the room to sit in the desk chair, swiveling it around and around.

She ended up facing the desk, frowning at the cereal bowl she'd set on it, and sat there in the dark thinking about her situation.

When she'd come to this house, she'd been thinking of it as just a place to stay for a few years until she was old enough to be on her own. But somehow, without her noticing it, the elegant old house and her odd, fussy uncle had gotten under her skin. The thought of moving yet again, leaving Marissa and Kirk, having no particular excuse to talk to Wally or Seymour or to get to know any of the other exotic people she hadn't had a chance to meet yet.... It gave her a terrible sense of loss, a whole world of fascination slipping out of her fingers.

The idea of Simon possibly spending the rest of his life in prison or worse—well, it just didn't bear thinking of. Why was it that everyone she loved got thrown in jail? Was it something about her?

Where would she even go from here? She knew from her own experience that the courts moved at a glacial pace, so she could hardly stay with Dr. Fortunato until Simon's fate was decided. She didn't think any of the aunts would want her, and the feeling was definitely mutual. Aunt Meg would probably ship her off to a boarding school. She'd threatened it in the past.

Ruby took a couple bites of cereal, then decided she wasn't hungry after all and shoved the bowl across the desk. It clinked against something, and her eyes finally registered what lay before her, shining in the moonlight—a long katana in a dark, polished scabbard. The handle was closely wound with dark cord with a row of diamond-shaped gaps through which shone a pale blue glow. How had the cops missed this? She stood, picked it up by its middle—it was surprisingly heavy—and drew the blade out a few inches. The blade was thin with glowing patterns in the grain of the metal, like overlapping waves, where it had been folded over and hammered flat again.

She drew it the rest of the way from the sheath and found it was too heavy to handle one-handed. It dipped, out of control, and she dropped the sheath to grab at the handle with her other hand, stopping the blade from hitting the floor. But something landed on the rug with a soft thump, and Ruby looked down to discover that she had neatly sliced off the end of the chair's armrest, the interior wood pale against the stained exterior.

"Oops." She hadn't even felt the blade hit the chair. It must be wicked sharp. Well, at least it was a clean cut—maybe she could glue it back on. Holding the sword firmly, she stooped for the sheath, carefully slid it back in, and set it on the desk.

The study door opened, and Dr. Fortunato stuck her head in, groping around for a light switch. Ruby pulled the chain of the desk lamp.

"That's better. Say listen, I got paged. You'll be all right on your own? Ooh! You found the moon sword!"

Ruby looked down at the sword, which seemed a little transparent in the light of the desk lamp. As she watched, it faded further. "This is what the police were looking for."

"Yes, but best not let them have it, I think. They'll set it down somewhere the moon never shines, and nobody will ever find it again."

The sword had faded entirely. Ruby put her hand where the handle had been and could feel nothing. "Right. I'll just leave it here, then. You were saying?"

"Gotta go. I'll see you in the morning, yes?"

"No need. I'll be fine."

Dr. Fortunato looked at her for a few seconds, evaluating. "Mister Kadopolous is an excellent lawyer. I'm sure Simon will be out in a few days."

"I'm sure you're right."

Dr. Fortunato paused again. "I'll look in." She nodded, left, and then leaned back in. "Your new key is on the kitchen counter."

"Bye!"

Ruby turned the light off, and as her eyes adapted to the dark she could once more see the moon reflecting highlights off the polished sheath. On again and watched it fade. This time she rested her fingers on the handle until it vanished completely, and her hand dropped to the desk.

Then the phone rang, and she saw from the caller ID that it was Marissa. "Great." She picked up the receiver. "Hi. Listen…."

"Did you see the ten-o'clock news?" Marissa's voice was tense.

"No, I just got back from the police station."

"My mom saw it, and she had a fit. They had his picture and everything. Wait. What do you mean from the police station? Did they grill you?"

"Sort of, but I didn't really know anything."

"*Yeah, right, you told them everything you know, of course.*" Marissa sounded skeptical.

Ruby paused. "You know very well there are things I could tell them that they're not ready to hear. Look, is there something else going on here? You sound angry."

"*No, not angry. Disappointed that you didn't think you could tell me about your parents.*"

"Shit!" Ruby flopped into the chair, scraping her hand on the sharp edge she'd cut. "Ow. Was that on the news?"

"*No....*"

"How did you find out, then?" Ruby looked at the scrape at the base of her thumb. She squeezed the receiver against her shoulder so she could pick at a bit of loose skin with her other hand.

"*I think we're missing the point, here. Why didn't you tell me?*"

"I just couldn't find the right time."

"*Today, when you apparently forgot about going to their funeral? That would've been the right time.*"

"Well... yeah."

"*Instead you made up another lie. That's what got me wondering, so I googled you when I got home.*"

"I've googled me. You can't get it that way. They left my name out because I'm a minor." Ruby reached across the desk for a tissue to press against her hand.

There was a pause. "*Okay. What are you talking about?*"

"You said you read about it online."

"*I said I searched. I didn't say I found anything. So give.*"

"But then how do you know...." Ruby paused, confused. "Ah. Because I just told you."

"*But that's okay, because you wanted to tell me, anyway, and were just trying to find the right time.*"

"I never knew you were so sarcastic." Ruby took a deep breath.

"Okay. But not on the phone." She was starting to imagine how this conversation might sound to the police if they had the line bugged. "Can you come over tomorrow?"

"No. My mom doesn't want me going over there. She calls it a crime den. That detective took my name down. What if he calls my folks?"

"I can meet you."

"Lunch at the Atrium food court, then, after my soccer game. Will you come watch?"

"I don't know. Maybe. Things are sort of a mess."

"How's Wally?"

"Not on the phone. He's okay."

"And your uncle?"

"I didn't get to see him. He's supposedly got a good lawyer."

"He didn't really do what they said, did he?"

"Marissa!"

"Well, how am I supposed to know? He's barely said three words to me. It's not like you know him all that well either, you know? You've been there what, a month now? It seems like he's always out at night, and you never know where he is."

"Uncle Simon is *not* a serial killer."

"Fine, whatever. Look, I gotta go. Mom's calling me."

Ruby picked up her cereal and crunched it as she went out into the hallway to buzz the all clear for Wally. Going to the kitchen, she dumped the cereal in the trash and tried the fridge again.

Her search was interrupted by a frantic scratching at the back door. She looked at the door, then down the hall—no sign of Wally. Still, she couldn't open the door now. He might show up any second. She turned on the back light, went to the window beside the door, rolled up the shade, and leaned her head against the screen to see who was outside.

What she saw made her gasp. The steps leading up to the door were covered in a moving carpet of dark fur, little black eyes... rats. Rats in tiny vests, carrying things—sticks—and the glint of metal. They milled excitedly, clustering around one of their number that they were holding up… no, they were holding it down, when something unseen would drag it into the air by the scruff of its neck.

"Speck! No! Release! Bad boy!"

The rats who were pulling fell backward as Speck let loose, and the one who'd been held dropped on top of them.

"Crap, crap, crap." Ruby opened the door and stepped back, frightened, as the flood of rats rushed in, their claws ticking on the tiles. Two of them dragged another, limp. Gingerly, Ruby knelt and reached out toward it. Two other rats raised a fork and X-acto knife threateningly, and she backed off. She didn't need to touch it, anyway. She could see its neck was broken, eyes staring blankly.

Great. She'd killed a client.

One who seemed to be in charge stepped forward, holding an opal stickpin like a tiny scepter. It squeaked at her, waving its paws expressively. Ruby heard a noise from the dining room and turned to look. Wally had stopped in the doorway, staring at the furry crowd. "Skohlars," he said with distaste.

"I don't know what to do. Speck killed one of them, and I can't understand them. Should I get the Ouija board?"

"I don't think they can read." Wally pulled out a counter stool and sat, looking on interestedly.

She looked back at the one she had mentally dubbed the king rat. A slim brown rat had come up beside him, unzipping a tiny pink backpack that must have been made for a Barbie doll. She pulled out a small plastic object and held it out. Ruby took it carefully and turned it over in her hands. It was a set of earbuds on a spring-powered reel. The brown rat had gone back into the backpack and now held a small black plastic box. She held it up, not as if she meant Ruby to take it, but to show her the headset plug on one edge.

"Right." Ruby unwound the reel, handed the jack back to be plugged in, and put the earbuds in her ears.

"I'd worry about fleas on those if I was you," Wally commented, which earned him a poisonous look from the king rat.

The brown rat plugged the jack in with some effort, handed the box over to the king, and backed away. The king fiddled with a dial, then chattered into the box. *"Is this on?"* Ruby heard, in a surprisingly deep and resonant voice.

"I can hear you."

"I am Crunchy Bits o' Cheddar." The rat looked at her expectantly.

He was named after a snack food? "Uh, okay. I'm Ruby. Can I call you Crunchy for short?"

"Where is Simon? He said he would meet me, and he did not."

"He's in jail."

"This is not good."

"You're telling me."

There was a pause. Crunchy looked off to the side and down, thinking. Ruby waited, trying to decide what species of rat he was. They all looked like common Norway rats but, she thought, with larger heads and longer limbs. She would've liked to run upstairs and get a book with pictures to compare, but it didn't seem like a good time for it. Most of the crowd had settled down to talk or pick through each other's fur. There seemed to be a few games going on too, one using small dice. She looked nervously at the dead rat, who'd been stripped of his vest and left to lie alone, while two others fought over a small gold earring he'd been wearing. "Look." She pointed. "About, um, him...."

"They're not the sort to care about that," Wally said, and indeed Crunchy, who'd started pacing, waved a paw dismissively.

"You are of Simon's family?"

"He's my uncle."

"You must help us. He said he would solve it. Now you must solve it."

Ruby felt terrible about the one who'd died, but her stomach unclenched a little when she saw there apparently wouldn't be any trouble over it. "What's the matter?"

"One of our creatures escaped. You must capture it."

"Wait. Are we talking about a huge creature with long, sharp teeth, who comes out at night to eat people in the Higsbee neighborhood? And is maybe invisible?"

"What means invisible?"

"You can't see it."

"Not invisible. Hard to see."

"Are you out of your mind? I can't capture that!"

"Simon said he would capture it. You are of his family. His agreements are yours."

Ruby looked at Wally. "Do you know what Simon agreed to do for them?"

Wally shrugged.

"It doesn't matter." She turned back to the king rat. "I don't believe you. He went after it with a big sharp sword. You don't capture things with a sword, you kill them. He's only in jail, you know. I can go there and ask him if I want." Not that he would tell her anything.

Crunchy looked cross but nodded. *"Very well. Kill it, then."*

"How? No, never mind, that doesn't matter. I'm not a monster slayer. You have to go to the Guardians. I'll call Captain Urbana right now."

Crunchy waved his fore-paws agitatedly, and several of the other rats looked up from whatever they were doing, wide-eyed. *"No Guardians! We will be in trouble because it got loose. We are secret people. Everyone will know."*

"The rest of the Scene is bound to hear about you eventually."

"They don't want it to be like this," Wally said. "When they come out, they don't want it to be because they're causing a big problem."

"Well, I'm sorry but… hey! You understand what he's saying?"

Wally flicked one of his pointy ears. "I can hear real high-pitched sounds, remember?"

"I see. Well, any ideas?"

Wally rocked forward and back on his stool a few times. "You could bring Urbana in on it. Maybe she would keep it quiet."

"No, no, no! Urbana will tell them all."

"I'm sorry," Ruby said. "I don't see any other way. I don't know how to kill giant monsters."

"How long until Simon comes back?"

"Maybe never. They think he killed all those people your pet ate."

One of the other rats, a taller one in a long red vest, nudged the king's elbow to get his attention, and they conferred privately for a few seconds. Then Crunchy turned his little black box back on. *"If another one dies, they know he does not do it. He is in the cage, he cannot."*

"Yes, I guess they might let him go then."

"It is well. We wait. When he is free, he will help us."

"You can't do that!"

"No?" Crunchy looked puzzled. *"Why would that not work? There is some risk, yes.…"*

"It's not that it wouldn't work, it's just not right to let someone else get killed."

"This does not concern us."

"All right then, it also won't work because I'll tell Captain Urbana, and she'll put a stop to it."

Crunchy went still, looking at her, at Wally, back at her. He raised the box to his mouth. *"My people are small. We can go anywhere, through drains, inside of walls. Work with us, and we will bring you treasures."*

"By which you mean *steal?*"

"Work against us?" he continued, as if she hadn't spoken. *"My people are small. We can go anywhere. Where can you sleep safe from us?"*

A chill went down Ruby's spine. Wally swore and got down from the stool, but Ruby motioned him to stop. She looked over the fifty or so rats. Some were armed with syringes and what might be blowguns. Crunchy looked back at her silently.

"I'll think about it. You think about this. Speck, who killed your… your subject, he can get your scent from the floor you stand on and track you down anywhere. I can make more like him."

Crunchy looked at the dead rat uncertainly. *"This is not true."*

In fact, Ruby hadn't been able to get Speck to follow people who hadn't fed him. But there was no reason to admit that. "I'll let you know what I decide. How do I get in touch with you?"

Crunchy turned and beckoned. A male rat, small, young, and sleek, came forward. *"Retractable Blade will carry messages."* Another gesture, and another stepped out of the crowd, carrying a drawstring bag over her shoulder. Her muzzle was white, and she blinked at Ruby with clouded eyes. *"Hundreds of Uses knows the creature. She will help you hunt it."*

Fat chance. But she would certainly quiz the old female.

The rats were getting their things together now, putting away their dice, standing. Crunchy handed the black box to the rat with the Barbie backpack, who reached up for the earbuds.

"Wait. How can I talk with them if you take this away?"

"We gave one to Simon," the backpack rat said, her voice soft.

Hundreds of Uses leaned forward and laid a paw on Barbie rat's foreleg, speaking into the box. "I know where it is."

Ruby opened the door, and the rats streamed out into the night, carrying their fallen comrade. It had clouded over, and the air felt heavy. It was thunderstorm weather. She shut and locked the door, then turned to find Wally looking down at the two who remained.

"They can't hang around loose. Is there a birdcage or something?"

"I don't see what difference it makes. Don't you think they can break in anyway if they want?" She turned to Hundreds. "Where's that talkie thing?"

The old rat started off down the hall. Ruby followed, opened the study door for her. Hundreds went to the desk and pointed at one of the drawers.

It was locked. "Right." Which book was that key in? It'd had a tall, grey-green binding. After a minute she located it and shook the key out of the spine.

The device was in the drawer, and Ruby put it on the desktop before taking a moment to look through the other drawers. A tidy stack of notepads, filled with shorthand, and a stack of mini appointment calendars—probably fillers for Simon's black notebook. A pair of sunglasses. A clear plastic box full of shiny bullets. No sign of the gun. Here was a polished wooden box with a stick-on skull and crossbones label. Either poison or pirates. A tall drawer full of hanging files— Ruby riffled through them but didn't find one labeled "Skohlars" or anything else likely to be helpful. Ruby sighed and relocked the desk, keeping the key.

The rain started then, heavy drops beating against the windows and a rumble of thunder. Ruby looked out through the tall study window. Nobody would be out in this, not even whoever was normally stupid enough to be wandering around Higsbee neighborhood at night after how many deaths now? Five, six? She could wait to question Hundreds until the next morning when she'd be more alert.

She found the Skohlars a cardboard box and an old soft towel to line it, then went upstairs. She needed a shower to wash the police station from her hair, and bed. Tired as she was, though, she couldn't sleep. Thoughts raced through her head. Once she began to drift off, but some slight noise made her jerk awake, heart racing, imagining the rats were coming for her. She would have to teach Speck to guard if she were ever to get any sleep.

Finally, she gave up and padded downstairs in her pajamas to check her email. She thought about tweeting. *"Uncle arrested. Getting death threats from rats. Send help."*

She browsed the study shelves, not in the mood for the Sea of Cortez, which in any case was all the way upstairs. The astronomy picture book Teela had been looking at caught her eye. She pulled it out, looked around. There was no decent place to lounge and read downstairs. She made herself as comfortable as she could on a narrow chaise, turned on a floor lamp, and started flipping through pictures of extraterrestrial landscapes.

As she did so, she thought about Teela's parting words. Was this the situation she'd been referring to? Did she know something about it? Too bad there was no way to contact her to ask for details. She could call Captain Urbana and turn the situation over to the Guardians, or she could call Lieutenant Garbers and try to convince him, after she decided whether she believed it herself. Or wait for the creature to kill again and see if that convinced them to let Simon loose. Then he could deal with the problem. She sighed and set the book aside, got up again, and walked to the desk.

She hadn't wanted to look with Hundreds in the room, but now she unlocked the drawers again and pulled the bottom one all the way out. She reached under it to find the edge of a plastic zipper bag taped to the bottom. It was thicker than she'd expected. She pulled it loose and brought it up into the light, dumping several packets of bills onto the desk blotter. She riffled through one, counting. Twenty hundreds. Five packets. "Ho-o-ly crow," she whispered. Her first day Simon had trusted her with the location of ten thousand dollars in cash. She put the packets back into the bag, put everything back the way it was, and went back to the chaise to stare at the ceiling and think.

The dark stairway led up to a perfectly flat plain covered with tiny pebbles, stretching to the horizon in all directions. Tall buildings were visible in the distance all around, but near her there were only mushroom-shaped steel vents poking up from the hard ground. The pebbles crunched under her feet, and she shaded her eyes against bright sunlight that glinted from them. A few pigeons clustered around a dirty plastic bag, pecking at it and trying to pull it away from each other. There was a distant, faint sound of traffic and sirens.

Ruby wandered at random, looking behind and under the vents and satellite dishes that studded the landscape. She couldn't remember what she was looking for but knew it was important.

"Have you got my pick?"

She whirled, startled, and stared at the short man seated on a vent behind her. His ginger-colored hair was long and tangled, hiding his face, and he sat beneath a TV antenna which had an old sheet thrown over it for shade.

"My pick?" He pointed to a guitar propped up beside him. The sheet flapped in the wind.

"Where did you come from? That's my guitar." She leaned in for a closer look, and the head lifted, showing golden eyes and a broad, grinning mouth displaying a familiar set of uneven yellow teeth. "Micah?"

He picked up the guitar and held his hand out. She dug in her pocket, found a guitar pick there, and handed it over. Micah strummed a couple of times, then set the pick down to adjust the tuning, pausing to take a swig from a green bottle which he then set back down on the ground.

"Have you seen a sort of... thing, about this big?" She held her hands out to show the size.

Micah's head came up again, and he looked around briefly before raising one long finger to point.

She hurried off and found a raised wooden skylight with a kind of overhang. Now she remembered. This was where she'd found it before. She leaned over the box, looking through the window into a dusty room filled with crates. She ran her hands under the overhang and felt it—hard, smooth plastic. She pulled it out. A Rolodex. The cover was cracked and scuffed. She flipped it open and riffled through the cards. Some were water damaged but all still legible. She closed it and wandered back to where Micah was playing something soft and ripply.

"'Cha got there?" he said.

"My folks' Rolodex."

"'Cha gonna do with it?"

Ruby shifted uneasily. "I should destroy it, I guess."

"Ya gonna?"

"I don't know. I might give it to the cops, so they could arrest more people."

"Your folks wouldn't like that."

"Exactly." She stepped forward to get into the shade and watched his fingers on the strings.

"Hard to choose."

"What do you think I should do?" She spoke loudly to be heard over some bells.

Micah shrugged. "Flip a coin."

"Isn't that a little… random?"

"Not the way I do it. Ya call it first. Heads for one choice, tails t'other. Ya throw it. And when it's up in the air…." He paused, flattening his hand on the strings.

"Well?"

"Well, right then ya realize how ya want it to come down."

Ruby started to answer, but the bells were getting louder. She turned to see what it was, opening her eyes, and found she was in the study, on the chaise lounge, staring at the skull on the mantle. Her neck ached from sleeping at an odd angle. The phone rang again, and she lurched to her feet.

She didn't recognize the number on the caller ID, but it was local and coming in on the non-business line. "Goodnight residence, Ruby speaking."

"No, put it there." A woman's voice, a little cross, apparently speaking to someone else. *"Just there. That's right. Hello?"*

"Hello." Ruby thought the caller's voice sounded familiar. "Mizz Wheelwright?"

"There you are at last. Napping when there are things to be done."

Ruby checked the clock on the office wall. Eight a.m. "Can I help you with something? Simon's not available."

"Not that one." Ms. Wheelwright again was speaking to someone else. *"The third one."*

Ruby was getting a little annoyed. "Maybe you should call back when you're not so busy."

"No, child, you must come here. Margo! I say, Margo. When am I free?" A pause. *"One-thirty? Do you hear, girl? Be here at one-thirty. For tea. We have much to discuss."*

"Meet you where?"

Someone else came on the line. *"Do you have the address?"* A woman's voice, brisk and efficient-sounding.

"No."

"Write this down."

Ruby scrambled for pen and paper and copied the address. "Wait a minute though. What's this about?"

"Mizz Wheelwright requires your presence."

"Yes, but who died and left her queen?"

"Just a moment, please." There was a pause, and Ms. Wheelwright came back on the line. *"What's this about your refusing to come?"*

"It's not a good time. There's a lot going on."

"Nonsense. That's why you must come. You'll make a hash of things." Ms. Wheelwright lowered her voice. *"The little ones, you know...."*

The Skohlars? "What do you know about them?"

"That's why we must talk. Bring one of them along." There was a *click* and silence.

Last night's visitors were where she'd left them, on the dresser in her bedroom, and they'd finished the food and water she'd left in their box. Ruby let Retractable Blade out into the back yard after calling Speck to remind him to behave.

There was a new note signed *Alice* on the kitchen counter, saying she'd gone out early, giving a phone number, and asking Ruby to pick up dinner for everyone.

While Ruby had breakfast, Hundreds of Uses sat beside the bowl, picking up pieces of cereal from a scattering on the kitchen counter and nibbling them delicately between questions. The old rat's voice, through the earbuds, was high-pitched and hoarse, a little out of breath, as he spoke in short sentences.

"What kind of animal is it? Where did it come from?"

"*We buy. They don't tell where from.*"

"Why did you buy it? What did you want with it?"

"*They fight. We watch. We bet.*"

Ruby had trouble making sense of this for a few seconds. "You make them fight each other so you can bet who wins? There are more of them?"

"*Others are not the same.*"

But the others were fearsome enough to give them a reasonable chance in a fight against that one. "How many others?"

"*It is not your concern. They don't escape.*"

"Why not? This one did."

"*Someone released him. Now we on guard. Not happen again.*"

"*Released* him? Who?"

"*We do not know. Not one of us. But we know his scent. We find him.*" The tone of voice said the perpetrator would be sorry when found.

"Tell me more about this animal. How big is it?"

"*In weight, perhaps....*" Hundreds gave Ruby an evaluating look. "*Perhaps thirty of you. Hard back.*" She tapped the edge of the cereal bowl with the knuckles of her fore-paw.

"A turtle? Solid shell?"

"Shell that bends."

"A giant armadillo?"

"Makes different colors… same like dirt, wall… can't see."

"Camouflage. Like a chameleon."

"Very strong. Very fast. Run, swim. Not climb so good."

Sounded like it would be a lot of fun at parties. "Why doesn't it leave tracks? Does it fly?"

"Ground hard there, most places. Other places, we follow, erase tracks."

"And drag away the bodies, I guess. Hey! You guys must've been the ones who stole Polacek's body."

"I not know about this."

"Yeah, right," Ruby muttered, rolling her eyes. "Why can't you catch this thing yourselves?"

"We try, many times. Lose many good fighters. Too smart, knows we coming. You, though, it not suspect. You look like food."

"What have you been feeding it that I look like food? Never mind, I don't want to know. But how do you control these huge monsters down in your dens or whatever you call them? Not by waving forks at them, I assume?"

"We have machines. Push button, gate open. Wave arm, make poke with big stick." Hundreds paused, wheezing. *"We pay, people build for us."*

"I see." Ruby thought. "It only comes out at night, right? So the idea is, someone goes out there to be bait, and when it comes to eat them, blast it." *Or hit it with a sword,* she thought, remembering the photo of Simon stalking the night. She was almost glad he was in jail—at least he was safe there. "But if they can't see it, how are they supposed to know where to shoot?"

The old rat shrugged. *"Simon said he can see it."*

"But he didn't say how?" Ruby looked at the clock over the stove. "Look, I've got to go out, but later I'll talk with someone about this, and I want you there. Can you come with me now, so I don't have to come back in between?"

"The Cheddar has said I am yours to command."

"Great. I'll fix up a way for you to travel."

Thirteen

Forsberg Garage, which Marissa's team represented on the soccer field, lost badly that morning to the girls sponsored by Tyburn Custom Printing. Marissa had missed two easy goals, and she was in such a dark mood that Ruby decided it would be safer to say nothing until Marissa herself decided to talk. This made for an uncomfortable silence in the van as Marissa's mom drove them to the Atrium, with Marissa glowering out the window and her mom giving Ruby occasional suspicious looks in the rear-view mirror, as if wondering whether homicidal lunacy ran in the family. Ruby considered telling her she was unarmed.

To make matters worse, Hundreds of Uses chose then to get restless, making scrabbling noises. Marissa looked curiously at the backpack, which rested on the seat between them, and Ruby thumped it with her finger. The noises stopped.

How much could she tell Marissa? Her own history, of course, was hers to tell or keep secret. But Captain Urbana had not been happy at how much Marissa already knew about the Scene, and Ruby also had, she began to realize, a duty to protect Simon's reputation for discretion.

If she went around blabbing secrets, even about such unsavory clients as the Skohlars, other clients would stop trusting him with their secrets, and he would lose business. Being put in this situation herself, she could better understand Simon's infuriating habit of keeping secrets from her. She didn't like it any better, but she could see his reasons.

On the other hand, Ruby could really use Marissa's help and believed she could be trusted to keep quiet.

Well, at least Marissa was no longer looking out the window with a scowl that would frighten pedestrians. Now she was watching the backpack instead. "That other team was pretty tough," Ruby said.

"Yeah, I don't care, but Dad's disappointed."

Marissa's dad, Alfonso Gomez, was the coach of the team and owner of Forsberg Garage, which he'd bought from the original owner. Ruby wasn't sure how competitive he was, but she could see the pressure would be on for Marissa to do well, if only to prove to her teammates that she wasn't on the team just because she was the sponsor's daughter. "You're just having an off day."

"I just suck."

"It's not like it was your fault. You guys wouldn't have won with those two points, but you wouldn't have lost if you had a decent goalie."

"It's true. I suck slightly less than Harriet. I'm only the second suckiest player on the team." She was starting to grin a little now. One of the things Ruby liked about Marissa was that she never stayed down for long.

Once at the mall, Ruby started for the food court, but Marissa pulled her into a short side passage with only empty storefronts. "Nobody will bother us down here." Marissa led her to a bench. "Now talk."

"I don't know where to start."

"Your parents."

"Well… all right. You've probably heard of them. Their names are Anton and Reno Looby."

"Sounds familiar…."

"They're in jail for—"

"Wait, wait, I got it! Your parents are *terrorists?*"

"That's a matter of definition."

"But they blew something up."

"A post office."

"OMG, they're famous! But they didn't kill anyone, right?"

"No, they made sure it was empty. Mom calls it an extreme form of civil disobedience. As opposed to terrorism."

Marissa looked as if she was considering arguing the point, but she just shrugged.

"I know. Not a distinction most people care about."

"They're not Islamic?"

"No, anarchists. Everybody at my last school knew all about it."

"That must've been tough."

"Very. So, I didn't want anyone here to know."

"Understandable. But wait, I've seen their pictures, and neither of them are Korean."

"My real dad was Korean, but he died when I was little. Anton's my stepdad."

"So they didn't change your last name when your mom remarried."

"Would *you* name a kid Ruby Looby?"

"I'd be tempted, but no. It'd be cruel. So, Simon is related on your mom's side?"

"He's her half-brother."

"All right, all right, you're making me dizzy. Do the police know they're related?"

"I don't know. I hope not. It can't help his case."

"What's up with that, anyway? Will he get off? Why do they think he did it?"

"I'm not supposed to talk about it. But," Ruby said, as Marissa opened her mouth to object, "seeing as it's you, if you promise not to tell anyone? That includes letting on to Simon that you know."

She got a silent "cross my heart" and zipper across the mouth from Marissa before continuing. "It's all circumstantial. He knew the previous victim, Polacek, and he was in the area when the latest killing happened. With a big sword."

"That's insane! What was he doing?"

"Same as Polacek. Hunting the real killer, which isn't a person but an invisible monster. That's why the police haven't been able to catch it—they've been looking for the wrong thing."

There was a pause. "No, come on. What's the real reason?"

"No kidding. In fact, that ties in to the next thing you were going to ask about, which is, what's in my bag?" Ruby reached for the zipper of her backpack, then paused. "Okay, no screaming, right?"

"When did I ever scream?"

"Some people are funny about rats."

"You have a rat in there? Gross!"

"Be nice. She can understand you." Ruby unzipped the bag and pulled out a short section of thick mailing tube with a fold of towel hanging from the end. A whiskered snout poked out. Ruby reached in for the ear buds. "Sit close so we can each do one ear."

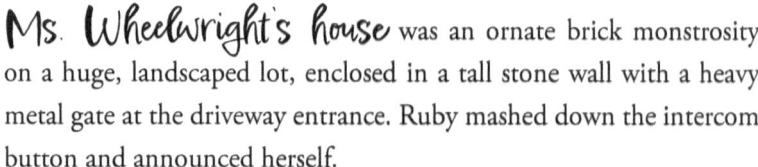

Ms. Wheelwright's house was an ornate brick monstrosity on a huge, landscaped lot, enclosed in a tall stone wall with a heavy metal gate at the driveway entrance. Ruby mashed down the intercom button and announced herself.

"Are you sure it's okay? My coming?" Marissa fidgeted. "She didn't invite me."

"She's the one who wanted to meet. If she's not happy with you being there, we can leave. I don't want to stay long anyway, so I can get to the jail during visiting hours."

The gate swung open and they went in, their shoes crunching on the gravel drive. "She'll probably want to touch your forehead. She does with everybody. It's harmless but better if you're sitting down first."

"Why, will she push me over?"

"It's a rush. Hang on." Ruby pulled out her phone. "It's Kirk. Should I answer?"

"Why not? We've got like five minutes' walk to the house."

"Hello?" Ruby covered her other ear to block the noise from a passing jet. "What's up?"

"I just heard. I mean, I heard last night, but I didn't know he was your uncle until just now. Are you okay?"

"I don't know. Sort of, the shock hasn't worn off yet."

"Did he do it?"

"No, of course he didn't do it! What kind of question is that? Here I thought you were worried about me, but really you just wanted the inside scoop?"

"No, it's not like… I mean, that's not what I meant! Like, it's…." He paused. *"Start over. Look, I've never met him. How do I know what he would and wouldn't do? I was worried about you being in the house with him."*

"Well, don't. I'd feel safer if he was home."

"Are you alone there?"

"Simon's 'friend' is staying over, not that I need her. She's got some entertainment value, but I don't think she'd be much use in a crisis, unless it involved fin rot."

"Fin? She's a veterinarian?"

"Of a sort." They were almost at the house. "Look, I've gotta go."

"Okay, if there's anything I can do to help, will you call?"

Ruby stopped at the base of the front door steps, beside a brick pillar with a stone eagle on top. When there was a crisis, people always volunteered vague help, but Kirk might actually mean it. "I'll give it some thought. Thanks for calling. Talk later."

They were admitted to the house by a pale, pointy, harassed-looking maid in a dusty tan dress and hair net. "I was told to expect one person."

"Sorry. Last minute change of plan."

The maid walked away, apparently expecting them to follow.

The room was large and must once have been a tall, wide hallway running the length of the ground floor, from front to back. However, some walls had been removed and others added at angles, making a large, irregularly shaped room, mostly dark, but with a few floor lamps making islands of light. If there were windows, they were covered.

"Only walk where I walk." The maid led a circuitous route across the room on a floor of polished wood of different types, inlaid with strips of dull metal. They walked past a statue of a sheep made from rusty steel, flat edges crudely welded, steel wool instead of real wool. A round glass case displaying ordinary-looking pebbles. An easel holding a collage of noses cut from magazine photos. A pyramid of cans of olives, all the same brand. Past an open doorway leading into a concrete-floored room, perhaps a large garage, where several young men were building a long boat out of chicken wire on a wooden frame.

They were ushered into a brightly lit room. The ceiling and one wall were made of glass, tinted overhead, looking out onto a stone patio enclosed in geometrically perfect shrubs. The room was humid and overheated, with large concrete planters filled with tropical flora, including some trees reaching almost to the high ceiling.

There were small, round holes in the walls at varying heights—too small for a person. Arching overhead and lining the walls, looping from hole to hole, were dozens of narrow carpeted bridges. A gray cat started to walk out from one hole and ducked back into darkness on seeing them. Another, resting at the peak of a bridge with a leg dangling over, stuck its head over the other side to watch them sleepily.

A cobblestone path led to a stone table with three chairs. "Wait here," the maid said. "Madam will be a few minutes."

The girls sat. "What a weird place," Marissa said when the maid had left. "But I really like the catwalks."

Ruby agreed. If she had cats and a ton of money, she'd copy the idea.

They stopped talking as another maid, this one in a tidy black uniform, came out with a tray and set the table. She set three places, with plates and teacups of delicate cream-colored porcelain, and also put a tiny demitasse cup and a small saucer on a mini placemat. There was no chair at that place, but there was a small speaker and microphone.

Ruby shook her head. "I can't believe she even has a teensy mike stand." She unzipped her backpack and carefully lifted out Hundreds's tube, tilting her out. The old rat was napping and blinked sleepily when let out onto the table.

Marissa had picked up the tiny placemat, which had the same embroidery as the full-sized ones. It didn't look new. "She must get a lot of different kinds of guests."

"All kinds."

They turned to see Ms. Wheelwright standing in the path. Behind her, a tall stiff man dressed in black waited with a tray. She sat, leaning her cane against the chair. The man set down plates of food and a china teapot in a knitted cozy.

"That will do, William. No one is to come unless I ring." She looked at her guests alertly. "You must introduce me to your friends."

"Mizz Wheelwright, this is Hundreds of Uses, and this is Marissa Gomez. She's new to all this, but she wants to help."

"Miss Gomez. Miss Park. Hundreds." Ms. Wheelwright poured a little cream into her cup from a cow-shaped silver creamer, then passed it to Ruby. "Will you be mother?"

"Sorry?"

"That means, please serve the tea. You may help yourselves to food." Using tongs, Ms. Wheelwright placed a small, crustless sandwich and a cookie onto Hundreds's plate, then a few of each on her own.

Ruby gave herself a lot of cream and a lump of sugar. When she reached for another lump, she noticed Ms. Wheelwright stiffening slightly and raised an eyebrow at her.

"One lump for ladies."

Ruby quickly took two more before reaching for the teapot. Hundreds held up a paw to refuse tea but allowed Marissa to fill her small cup with cream.

Once everybody was served, Ms. Wheelwright took a tiny sip. She set her cup down and looked at Hundreds. "Are you comfortable?"

"Yes."

"Then let us begin." She pointed at Ruby with her teaspoon. "I brought you here in part to learn more about you but chiefly to ask a few questions so you could hear the answers. I don't know exactly what's going on, and I don't expect you to tell me. But it has something to do with the Skohlars." She looked at Hundreds. "You expect the Guardians will sanction you."

"What is sanction?"

"Punish your people."

"Yes."

"What will the Cheddar do if that happens? Will he accept such a punishment?"

"I don't understand."

"Imagine someone told you the Cheddar let the Guardians boss him around and take things from the Skohlars."

"When did this happen?"

"Tomorrow."

Hundreds ran a front paw over her head and took a step away from the microphone, then back. *"The others will say he is weak to let them to punish us when we are not to blame. They will kill him."*

Ms. Wheelwright turned back to Ruby. "If the Guardians apply sanctions, the Cheddar will fight back. He has to. It'll mean war." Back to Hundreds. "How many Škohlars does the Cheddar rule?"

"I don't know numbers that big. He rules all of Chicago."

Marissa spoke up. "Are there more Skohlars in Chicago or more people? Humans, I mean."

"I have heard, ten humans for every one of us."

Ruby was shocked. She'd imagined there were a few thousand Skohlars at most and hadn't thought to ask. Now they were talking about hundreds of thousands. The dozen or so local Guardians might have a few tricks, but they couldn't possibly deal with so many alone, scattered all over the city. Any conflict would have to involve many more people. "Oh, my God."

Marissa also hadn't missed the implications. "You'd need an army to go into the sewers with flame throwers, dumping poison."

"Not the sort of thing to escape public notice," Ms. Wheelwright said. "Hundreds, do all the Skohlars live in Chicago?"

"We have many cities."

"Worse and worse," Ruby said. The war would spread. Once they knew they existed, no city would accept super-rats living under its streets.

Ms. Wheelwright leaned back with a satisfied look. "So, there you are then. Miss Gomez, I don't believe I saw you at Mister Polacek's funeral."

"Wait a minute!" Ruby said. "What are you going to do about this?"

"Please don't talk with your mouth full. I never do anything. I just talk to people. What will you two do? Decide, and do it."

Ruby and Marissa looked at each other. Ruby's mouth felt dry. She picked up her teacup, her hand shaking slightly.

"Miss Gomez," Ms. Wheelwright said, "you're very new to the Scene. Whom do you know, besides this Skohlar?"

"Ruby introduced me to Wally... I guess I don't know his last name."

Ruby set her cup down. "It's Boyle. Wally Boyle."

"Ah, yes. What did you think of him?"

Marissa took another little sandwich from the platter. "He, ah, surprised me at first. But I like him. We get together to play music."

"Indeed." Ms. Wheelwright pursed her lips, then leaned to reach across the table for Marissa's forehead. "May I?"

Marissa gave Ruby a nervous look but leaned forward a little so the old woman could reach her.

Seen from the outside, it was nothing spectacular. Marissa just got a dazed look and tilted to one side enough that Ruby grabbed her, afraid she might fall. "You okay?"

Marissa took a deep breath and blinked. "Whoa! That was weird!"

It only then occurred to Ruby that she hadn't heard what she'd expected to hear. Startled, she turned back to Ms. Wheelwright to find her staring at Marissa in shock.

"What?" Ruby said. *"She's the one?"*

"I thought I would know." The old woman sounded dismayed.

Marissa shook her head, maybe trying to clear it. "The one *what?*"

"Hell if I know."

"Please," Ms. Wheelwright said. "Language!"

"So she's *maybe* the one?" Ruby persisted.

Ms. Wheelwright gave a little shrug. "She and I must discuss this."

"Good, because I'd really like to know what that was," Marissa said.

"Later. This is a private matter between us. Will you come again? My secretary will call."

"She's going to tell me anyway after you tell her," Ruby said.

"Perhaps." Ms. Wheelwright pushed her cup back toward Ruby. "Fill it again, please, dear, and tell me what you thought of the memorial service."

Ruby walked down the hall after a corrections officer in a gray uniform. She was a heavy-set woman with a slight limp, whose shoes squeaked on the tile floor. Her hair was a shade of red that only comes from a bottle. She pointed to a bench. "Wait here."

Ruby sat, her back against a cold cinderblock wall, and took out her book.

After a few minutes, a door down the hall opened and Simon's lawyer came out. He was short, dapper, dark-skinned, with a round head and shiny, wavy black hair parted in a precise line. He paused, tucking his briefcase under his arm, and gave a little nod to Ruby. "Miss Park."

"Mister Kadopolous. Did you just talk to Simon?"

"Yes. You will see him now?"

Ruby nodded.

"You should assume the conversation is overheard."

"Yeah, I got that. This isn't my first time doing this, you know."

"Oh, your parents, yes. Do the police know about them yet?"

"Not that they've said."

"They'll find out," Kadopolous said gloomily. "It would be really quite helpful if we could establish an alibi for him for at least some of the killings. But he's not willing to even ask any of the clients he was with at those times."

"You know why, right?"

Kadopolous gave a frustrated shrug. "It would do no harm to ask them. If the police could talk with them and establish he wasn't at the scene, I could perhaps get the charges dropped. They wouldn't need to appear in court."

"Will you have trouble getting him off?"

"Who knows? Objectively, there isn't enough evidence to convict. In practical terms? Juries are unpredictable, and they don't like mysterious characters. The DA needs someone to pin this on because the case is a hot potato. Under the circumstances, it's easy for the police to convince themselves they have the right man. I find myself hoping there's another murder tonight, just to prove he isn't involved. I know that's reprehensible, but there it is."

"Wouldn't that only prove he can't be the only one involved?"

"It would be enough to establish reasonable doubt. Enough to make the police keep looking for another killer. Look, talk to your uncle about this. He knows much more than he's telling me. That's obvious to the police as well, and it's partly why they're so set on him as the perpetrator. I can't help him unless I know what's going on."

"Hm," Ruby said, uncomfortable.

Kadopolous had started to turn away, but now he turned back, eyes narrowed. "You know something."

"I can't tell."

"What *is* it with you people?" Kadopolous, irritated, flapped his briefcase against his leg. "I'm already in on this stuff."

"Maybe not all of it." Seeing he was about to speak again, Ruby added, "It's really complicated. It's a political situation. If there are things he's not telling you, I think you have to assume there are reasons."

Kadopolous huffed. "You're clearly not going to be any use in talking some sense into him. If you don't open up, we may be looking at serious trouble." A door down the hall opened, and Kadopolous turned his head to watch the red-haired corrections officer come out. He turned back to Ruby. "Think about it."

The officer showed her into a tiny white room with a long, shiny table along one wall. Simon was seated at the far end, leaning over some papers, and looked up with a smile as Ruby entered. She started to rush forward, but the officer stopped her with a rough hand on her shoulder. "Stay at this end. No touching. Don't give him anything."

"You guys already searched me. I don't know what you're afraid of."

"Those are the rules."

The wall opposite the table was a window with a bored-looking guard watching them. The woman officer gave him a little wave, then waited until Ruby was seated before leaving. Ruby looked Simon over critically. "Orange is *not* your color."

His eyes twinkled. "Thankfully, Alice sent over a suit for my bail hearing tomorrow."

"Well, get out. Your clients need you. In fact, about fifty of them dropped in last night looking for you. One *big* group."

Simon's eyes darted to the window, where the guard was paying them no attention. "They'll have to wait. I don't want you to try to help them." He paused. "I'm glad you came. Did you water the vegetables?"

"I didn't need to. There was a huge rainstorm. You can water them yourself tomorrow."

"What have you been eating?"

"Oh, you know. Cheerios. Hamburgers. Tea and cucumber-watercress sandwiches. Cookies—only they're apparently called biscuits."

Simon put his head in his hands. "Tell me you haven't been talking with that woman."

"She seems to know a lot."

"She's got several screws loose."

"Maybe, but she knows all about those clients I mentioned. They're impatient. Isn't there someone else I could send them to?"

Simon looked at her without expression.

"Someone who sat next to Alice at the funeral, for instance?" Ruby persisted.

"Definitely not that person."

"Or the one who sat next to me."

"Not him, either. Anyway, he left town. Said to tell you 'bye.'"

"The woman I had tea with, you and her aren't as far apart as you might think."

"You and *she.*"

"You and *she* have a lot in common. She can't resist correcting me, either."

Simon closed his eyes for a moment and pinched the bridge of his nose. "Are you getting along with Alice?"

"She's okay. She's out a lot, so it's almost like having you at home."

"Do what she says, okay? Don't get into trouble?"

"I never go looking for trouble."

"My sources tell me different."

"Idle gossip and slander. I'll just go to my guitar lesson as usual, go to bed early, come to your hearing, then we can go home together."

"Good plan. Say, how did the date go?"

Ruby glanced at the guard. "Maybe later."

"Okay. I think we're out of time, anyway."

Rudy found Marissa waiting outside on the steps, guarding her backpack. "How's Simon?" Marissa asked. "Do you think he'll get bail?"

"Hell no. His lawyer's worried."

"So, what do we do?"

"I don't know. I have to check some things. You have dance class, don't you?"

Marissa gave her a look. "I think the rat apocalypse is a little more important."

"Yeah, but if you cut class and get grounded, you won't be able to come when I need you. I'll call you when there's something for you to do. Keep your phone on."

Fourteen

The outside of the grocery was lined with boxes of fruits and vegetables, tilted for easy access. An air conditioner stuck out over the door, rattling and dripping water onto the pavement. Ruby ducked between drops and pushed through into a dingy store with narrow aisles.

The man behind the counter looked up, swinging a gallon of milk past his scanner. The customer, a large, sweaty woman with straggly blonde hair, had a pile of groceries still to be checked out. Ruby followed the good smells to the back of the store, running her fingers along shelves of cans and bags labeled in Spanish.

There was a little deli counter at the back, the warming trays filled with rice, refried beans, tamales, and sausages.

A withered old woman behind the counter set down a cross-stitch and stood as Ruby leaned on the case to see what was in back. "You want?" she asked.

"Is that chicken mole?" Ruby pointed to something submerged in a dark sauce.

"Jes."

"Is it any good?"

"I make it. It's good."

"Enough for, oh, three people, okay? Rice and beans too."

"Three dinners."

Ruby watched the woman set out Styrofoam boxes. "Is Jimmy or Iggie around?"

The woman paused, a spoon of beans held over one of the boxes. "You a nice kid. What you want with those boys?"

"I'm not all that nice."

"What you want?"

"That's my business."

The old woman plopped beans into one of the boxes. "They out in back."

"Then I want two more dinners."

The old woman scowled. "How much dinners?"

"Five in all."

"Final answer?"

"Final answer."

The two boys were in an alley behind the store, sitting on beat-up metal folding chairs. Iggie played a game on his phone, while Jimmy looked over his shoulder. He looked up and nudged Iggie's shoulder.

"Don't bump me, bro. You'll get your turn."

"Hey, check it out. It's her," Jimmy said. Iggie looked up at Ruby, and his eyes widened.

"I come in peace. No trouble, okay? I want to hire you guys."

The two exchanged a glance. "What for?"

"I'm going to Higsbee, and I want you to come with me."

Iggie snorted. "We don't go way down there. I don't even know who got that territory."

"Look, it's not an invasion, I just want to look around."

"Spike would know who to ask," Jimmy said.

"Ask whoever you have to, but I want you to meet me down there as soon as you can. In fact, see if you can get us a guide who knows the area. I'll pay them, too. A hundred for each of you, plus dinner." She raised the smaller of the two plastic bags she held. "But eat on the train because I'm in a hurry. I want as much time as I can get before dark."

"Shit, that's right," Iggie said. "That's where all those people got killed. I'm not going there!"

"It's perfectly safe now," Ruby said impatiently. "They all happened at night, and the sun won't set until about ten." At least it wouldn't get really dark until then. Almost then.

"Hell no, not for no hundred dollars."

"One-fifty?"

"Three hundred," Iggie countered.

"Feh. What about you?" Ruby asked Jimmy.

"I'll go for one-fifty, but if you're in a hurry, don't take the train. I could drive us down there for another twenty."

"Okay, excellent!"

"That would be twenty each way, of course."

Ruby gave him a hard look and paused before answering. "Of course." It was still less than cab fare. She handed him a dinner. "Make your arrangements and pick me up at my place. No, wait." The house might still be watched, and Dr. Fortunato might be there. "Around the corner on 34th."

"You got a phone, if there's a problem?"

"I'm afraid it might be bugged."

"Just hang tight one minute." Jimmy handed his dinner to Iggie and went through a steel service door into the building.

Iggie seemed uncomfortable to be left alone with her. He didn't meet her eyes but set his phone on the other chair and opened the Styrofoam box to look inside. "Don't I still get one?"

"No. Anyway, isn't that your great-grandma in there or something? From the way she was talking about you I thought you must be related. Doesn't she feed you?"

"She's mean."

"I'll bet if you asked her nice."

Jimmy came bustling out and handed her a phone and a coiled-up charger. They both felt light and cheap. It was nothing fancy, just a plain phone for making calls and not much else. "I already called my phone from there"—he patted his pocket—"so I got your number and you got mine."

"Where did you get this?"

"Oh. You know. Someone gave it to me. Use it for a week and I'll give you another one."

"O-o-o-kay." She dropped it into her pocket. "Thanks. See you in thirty minutes?"

Dr. Fortunato was at the kitchen counter when Ruby ran in and dropped several bags on it. She glanced up from her tea and medical journal.

"I have a class tonight," Ruby announced. "I'll be back around ten."

"Mm-hmm." Dr. Fortunato turned a page. "What class?"

"Japanese," Ruby answered at random.

Dr. Fortunato nodded and gave her a smile and a thumbs up. *"Ganbatte kudasai."*

Ruby headed for the door. "Thanks—uh, I mean *arigato.*" Was that the right answer?

"Oh, hold up a sec!"

Ruby stuck her head back into the kitchen.

"There was a note for you." Dr. Fortunato leaned across the counter to retrieve a folded scrap of paper. "Someone shoved it under the back door."

Ruby took it. It was dirty and looked like a corner torn from a notebook. *Rubby* had been scrawled on the outside in pencil. She unfolded it and found only the word, *Gate.*

"It's for a game. It's a clue."

She could've saved her breath. Dr. Fortunato was already back in her journal. Ruby ran upstairs, quickly changed into jeans and a less-nice shirt, and checked on her passenger. "Are you okay in there?"

Hundreds crawled out onto the bed and walked in a little circle, shaking her legs out and adjusting her vest. She looked the worse for wear. It must be tiring for an old and arthritic rat to be so jostled around. "Sorry." Ruby tied her hair back. "We're not done for the day, but I'll try not to shake you up so much. I have to run down to the office for ten minutes, so rest a while. Do you see my sneakers?"

A little while later, Ruby slipped out the back door, whistled for Speck, and motioned him into a little plastic tube she'd affixed to her knapsack strap. She walked briskly to the gate—not running, to spare her other passenger. As she unlocked it and slipped through, there was a rustling from the weeds alongside the wall. A whiskered face poked out, fixing her with a beady black eye.

Ruby knelt, putting in her earbuds. The Skohlar took the device from her hand. *"The Cheddar asks what you doing about our problem."*

Was this Retractable Blade? The vest was different. "I'm working on it. Hundreds of Uses can tell you I've been running around all day getting information." Looking around to make sure she wasn't observed, she set her pack on the ground and opened it to let the rats converse. She waited, then looked at her watch and at the angle of the sun. "I'm going to Higsbee now. You want to ride along?"

The rat didn't answer, just turned and scuttled down the alley, keeping to cover.

Ruby went the other way. Reaching the street, she looked around. Jimmy waved to her from a beat-up blue compact car. Its rust spots were painted over with almost-matching blue spray paint. She placed her backpack carefully in back, then climbed into the passenger seat, dinner in her lap. "Do you know how to get there?"

"Most of the way. When we get close, be ready to give more

directions." He floored the accelerator to pull out into the street and raced for the highway. Ruby grabbed for the seatbelt as they rounded the first corner.

"I got someone to meet us there. We gotta pick 'er up. I promised eighty dollars, that's okay right?"

"Sure, I said I'd pay a hundred. Hey, we're not in that big a hurry, I'd like to get there alive."

"You sound like my mom," Jimmy grumbled but slowed a little.

"Are you okay with rats?"

"Why do you ask?" Jimmy sounded a little nervous.

"I've got a pet rat in my backpack, and I want to let her out to have dinner. She's tame. And clean."

"Is that, like, your familiar?"

"You know what that is?"

Jimmy looked a bit offended. "I'm not an idiot. I've been reading up about witches."

Ruby wouldn't have guessed he could read but kept that to herself. "I don't have a familiar. She's just a pet." Hearing no objection, Ruby tore off the cover of the dinner box, set a little food on it, and set it on the back seat, before having her own dinner.

She wiped her hands on her jeans and opened a map app to compare with her printout. "Where do we meet her?"

"127th and Yarwood, there's a BP gas station."

As they got near their destination, the buildings got dingier and had more broken windows, the streets had more potholes, the walls and street signs more graffiti.

They pulled up at the gas station, and Jimmy rolled down the passenger-side window to talk to a thin, black-haired girl dressed in black, with pale skin and freckles, leaning against a post by the gas pumps. "You Olga?"

The girl took a last slurp of her giant soda, dropped it into a trash bin, and sauntered over.

She crossed her arms and looked at Ruby. "You the bad-ass witch?"

Ruby turned to Jimmy, exasperated. "You're not supposed to go telling everyone that."

Olga snorted. "Like I care. You got my money?"

"Tour first," Jimmy said. "Money after. Get in. Where's the first place we gotta go?"

Ruby consulted her map. "Up a block and turn left. Slowly. I want to get the feel of the place. And Olga, if you know where there are security cameras, we want to avoid them."

"Smart idea to start out at a gas station, then."

If the surroundings had been grim to that point, after they left the big streets it became positively desolate—crumbling brick warehouses and abandoned factories, giant potholes, weeds growing through sidewalks and parking lots. "Here. Stop." Ruby got out, and the others followed.

"What you looking for?" Olga asked.

"Someone got killed here."

Olga's face grew hard. "Is that what you're here for, a murder tour? I can tell you about the guy who got killed here. He was a friend of mine."

"Hey, back off, girl. She'll put the hoodoo on you."

"You back off!" Olga pushed Jimmy aside and stalked toward Ruby, who backed up a couple of steps.

"Hey, listen," Ruby said.

"You listen! You come around here waving money and wanna see a show, I'll show you something!" Olga yanked her arm loose from Jimmy and shook her fist in Ruby's face. Ruby tried to step back again, but Olga grabbed her shirt and pulled back her fist.

At the same time, Ruby raised her own hand, scraping Olga's wrist with her ring. Olga's grip relaxed, and her face went slack. She took a few stumbling steps back, then shook her head and tried to rally.

Ruby pointed at Olga's stomach. "Speck, whammy!" The other girl doubled over, her breath whooshed out, and she sat on the pavement, gasping.

"I *told* you," Jimmy said.

"Jimmy, shut up." Ruby squatted beside Olga. "Look, I'm not here for fun. I'm trying to solve the killings."

"You are?" Jimmy said.

Olga looked daggers at her. "Yeah, right, you look like a cop."

"Obviously I'm not a cop. I'm a bad-ass witch, as you said yourself. The cops don't know what's going on. They can't help."

"You got that right."

"Look. I'm sorry about what happened to"—she consulted her map—"Marcus. You want to help me get his killer?"

"What'd you do just then? D'ju throw something at me?"

"I threw a whammy. Do you need another one?" Ruby raised her hand to point at the girl's nose.

"One's enough." Olga climbed to her feet, ignoring Jimmy's outstretched hand, and brushed herself off. "You got a big whammy for the monster?"

Spotting Speck still hovering around, she swept him back into his tube. "You already know it's not a person?"

"Everybody around here knows. I was right on this street with Marcus when he got it."

"You saw it?"

"Hell, nobody sees it. I smelled it. I heard it running at us. I heard it… Marcus and me, we both ran. I ran faster." She looked away. "I didn't look back."

"There wasn't anything you could've done," Ruby said quietly.

"I could tell that from… from what I heard."

Jimmy looked around nervously. "Are you sure it's a good idea to be here?"

"It never comes out until full dark… right?" Ruby looked at Olga, who nodded. "Tell me what else you know, while we walk to the next site. Which way did it come from?"

"That way. We could hear it but didn't see nothing, even when it passed under that light. Maybe just a little shimmer, like on the road on a hot day. But we could hear it was big. So, we ran."

"What does it smell like?"

"Like burnt matches, like a sewer, and kind of—kind of sweet, but rotten-like."

"What do other people say they've seen, or smelled, or whatever?"

"Mostly they ain't around to say. We thought it was safe inside at night, but one guy, it got him in his house. He was at the window and it busted through and grabbed him from outside. That was Mister Patel, he on your map? People say they hear it or smell it passing by their place, but they don't go to the window no more to look."

"It didn't cut itself on the broken window?"

"I don't know. There was blood all over the place."

"Didn't the police test whose it was?"

"They don't tell us nothing." Olga paused. "A couple boys said they shot it, but you know, boys say shit. There wasn't any blood on the ground where they said, but how the hell would they know they hit it, anyhow?"

"I hear it's armored." Ruby consulted her map again. "What about tracks? Has anyone tried to follow it?"

"It don't leave no tracks. Just right around the body, not walkin' off."

"No wonder the police don't believe in it." Ruby stopped walking and checked the map. "This is where Randy Thiel died."

"I don't know the name. I heard it was some homeless guy."

"You don't know anything more about this one?"

"Just that someone found him around two in the morning and called the cops."

"Okay. Wait. Found him? His body was still here?"

"Most of it, yeah. At first. When the cops came, it was gone. You know, there's more people who just went missing, which they probably got et, too."

"I have to make a call." Ruby reached behind her shoulder

and grabbed the earbuds, which she'd left hanging out of the bag. "Hundreds, talk to me."

"I am here. But I do not hear well."

"You two, walk ahead a little. Here, take the map. We'll go to this one next." Ruby waited until the others were out of earshot before following. She heard scrabbling and felt a little paw on her shoulder. "Hundreds, where does the beast stay during the day?"

"Many old tunnels below. He goes everywhere."

"But it always hunts around here."

"He wants dark."

So the only reason it didn't head downtown for a late night snack was that it preferred the poor street lights in this neighborhood. "What did you do with the bodies?"

"The monster took some away."

"And the others?"

"We not like to waste food."

Right. Ick. Plus, it would hide the evidence. Ruby shook her head and walked on, envisioning bodies being lifted overhead by a crowd of hundreds of scurrying Skohlars. "How did you get Polacek's body out of the morgue?"

"I not do this—"

"No, but your people did it, didn't they? They can't have chopped him into small enough pieces to get through the drain."

"I'm not to say."

"The Cheddar said to answer all my questions."

Hundreds was quiet for a moment. *"I not there. They say the Cheddar has a thing to do this."* She paused, wheezing a little. *"It made him into water."*

"Into water?!"

"I not see it."

"Why doesn't he use that on the monster, then?"

"Only dead things, it works on."

So much for ever having a proper funeral for Polacek. Ruby started to ask another question, but Jimmy and Olga hurried back around the corner. Hundreds ducked back into the pack, but Olga's eyes widened. "What was that? Do you have a rat in there?"

"That's her familiar," Jimmy said.

"What's a familiar?"

"She's not my familiar. She's a pet. Why did you come back?"

"Cops," Jimmy said. "That way. I thought maybe you don't want to meet them."

"They've been around for a couple days asking around about the monster," Olga said.

"I thought they didn't believe in it."

"It's a different bunch," Olga peeked around the corner. "I think they're looking around on their own. Only two of them are real cops."

"Is one a white woman, about fifty, this tall, muscles, with light brown hair?"

"Yah."

"You're right, I don't want her to see me. But I need to know what they're planning. Do you suppose you could…?"

"Go talk to them?" Olga said.

"Actually, Jimmy should do that. I need you to show me around. Jimmy, if you pretend to be from around here, tell them you're worried about the monster…."

"I *am* worried about the monster."

"It should be easy for you, then. Ask what they're doing about it. Then call me to find out where to meet us."

"Okay." Jimmy looked around the corner again. "They're gone if you want to cross now."

Ruby and Olga hurried across the street, Olga leading. Another block took them to the next site on her map. An unknown person had died here, by an old railroad track. The track was obviously unused, because it started at the curb, crossed the street, and went through an archway blocked off with a heavy, rusty gate, chained and padlocked shut. The tunnel ran through the ground floor of an ancient, thick-walled, sooty building with a similar gate at the other end. Wind blew through the tunnel into her face, pasting up old newspapers and plastic bags against the bars.

"What is this place?"

Olga shrugged. "Nothing now. Used to be a flour mill long ago. I been in there a few times. There's a loose hatch up the street where you can get in. It's huge. There's lots of old machines inside."

Ruby took a flashlight from her backpack and aimed it down the tunnel. There were several brick-walled bays on each side. She could imagine train cars parked here, to be loaded with sacks of flour. "Could the creature get in through the hatch?"

"Nah, it's too big." Olga shifted from foot to foot. "It's getting kind of dark."

Now that it'd been pointed out, Ruby realized it'd been growing darker for some time. It was still an hour to sunset, but heavy, dark clouds had moved in from across the river, and it smelled like rain. "I guess you'd best call Jimmy."

The call made, Olga leaned against the rough wall to wait while Ruby found a seat on a sort of concrete mushroom beside the track. "So, what you think? Can you kill it?"

"I don't know." Ruby had hoped looking around might give her some ideas, but it didn't seem like she was much better off. A powerful creature that could barely be seen, that somehow left no tracks, even after traipsing around in the blood of its victims.... How were you supposed to hunt something like that? "It sounded simpler when I knew less."

"You don't have a magic spell or something?"

"Not for something that size."

"How'd you learn magic, anyway?"

Ruby hesitated. She'd started to like Olga—or at least, to respect her. She didn't want to lie. "I'm not really supposed to talk about it. There are rules."

"But?"

"I don't have powers, just a few tricks people gave me. I have no idea how they work—if it's really magic or weird science or what." The gloom was increasing. Ruby looked up and down the street. "Did Jimmy say how long he'd be?"

"He has to walk back to the car."

"I guess." Ruby waited another minute, flipping her phone in her hand, then redialed Jimmy. "Where are you?"

"Right where you said to go. Could you hurry it up? It's getting dark."

"You're *not* where we said, or we would see you. Hang on." She handed over the phone, so Olga could give him fresh directions.

Ruby had left the top of the backpack a little open for fresh air, and Hundreds climbed back out onto her shoulder at this point to look around.

"...no, it's Pierpont Road," Olga was saying. "Go back two blocks, then right...."

Hundreds's tiny claws suddenly dug into Ruby's flesh. "Ow! Hey!" She craned her head to see the old rat. Hundreds looked around in all directions, sniffing the air. She gave Ruby a frantic look, then dived into the pack.

Ruby could smell it herself now, faintly. Sickly-sweet, slightly rotten, sewery. She grabbed Olga's arm. Olga stopped talking to look at Ruby. Ruby raised a finger to her lips and gave a meaningful sniff.

Olga froze. "Shit! That's all!" she whispered into the phone. "Hurry!" She hung up.

"It's upwind," Ruby murmured. "It can't smell us." But it might have other senses for finding food. She looked at the newspaper still flapping up against the gate. The wind was coming from that direction. "It must be on the other side of the building."

"I can't smell it anymore. I think it left."

"Or it knows we're here and is coming around the building for us. Can we get inside?"

Olga gave a hiss, then turned and took off down the street, running lightly and almost silently. After a startled moment, Ruby took off after her, also trying to go quietly. They ran for about a block, Olga slowly pulling ahead, and then Ruby heard heavy footfalls behind her, quickly getting closer. The tick of claws on pavement. She put on a burst of speed, catching up to Olga for a second, but Olga had heard it too and ran even faster.

Fifteen

Ahead of them, a car rounded the corner, headlights in their faces. Olga ran in front of it, waving her arms, and it screeched to a halt. Olga opened the passenger door and got in, shouting, "Back up! Back up!" Ruby came pounding up, seeing Jimmy's scared face behind the wheel, then Olga slammed the door and the inside of the car went dark.

"Dammit!" Ruby shouted. It was right behind her. No time to get the door open again and get in. She dove, belly down, onto the car, sliding up against the windshield and frantically grabbing the back edge of the hood to keep from falling off as Jimmy stepped on the gas and took off in reverse, tires screeching.

Ruby scrambled for a better position when they stopped at a corner to reverse direction down a side street. They went several blocks, through a red light, and stopped on a brightly lit street in front of a supermarket.

Ruby was caught off guard and slid off the front of the car, scraping her arm and landing on her rump. When she got up, Jimmy was on the sidewalk, tilting his seat forward to let her in to the back seat. "Get in!"

"Where's my shoe?" Several people in the parking lot had turned to look.

"I'll buy you another one if you get in now!"

They were off again before she'd had a chance to take her backpack off and get settled.

"Hey, you're bleeding," Olga said.

"That damn hood ornament got my arm."

"No, it's your foot." Olga reached for the dome light. By the time she figured out how to turn it on, Ruby's foot was starting to let her know that she really had injured it.

The light showed her sock had been neatly sliced open near the heel and was soaked in blood. She gingerly pulled the sock off and used a clean part of it to wipe at her foot, revealing a long, straight cut, welling up with more blood. "Ow, ow." She pressed on it with the sock. She was starting to feel shaky, a little sick.

"It got your shoe," Olga said. "It almost got your foot."

Ruby hadn't had time to feel scared while it was happening, but her heart was still racing, and she felt short of breath. "I need air."

"Where are we going?" Jimmy cranked his window down.

"I don't... I don't know." Ruby leaned toward the window and breathed deeply until she felt a little better. "Olga, can we drop you off?"

"Ha! I don't think I'm going back *there* tonight!"

"Me, neither," Jimmy said. "We're almost to the highway, and I'm getting on it."

"You can stay at my house tonight," Ruby told Olga.

Jimmy looked over his shoulder. "Are you bleeding all over my seat?"

"Your sympathy overwhelms me. I'll try not to ruin the upholstery. And yes, I think I'll survive, thanks for asking. In fact, Alice will probably be tickled pink to have something useful to do for me."

"She must be okay," Olga said. "Her sarcasm is still intact, anyway."

"Then maybe you could turn off the light, so I can see the road."

"Just a second, I have to check on Hundreds." With her free hand,

Ruby pulled the top of the backpack open to peer inside. It was hard to see in the dim light, but there was something scrunched into the bottom of the tube.

Ruby shone a flashlight down, and dark eyes glittered back. The rat was shaking. Ruby could relate. "We're safe now. We'll be home soon."

Ruby sat in the dark for a few minutes, applying pressure to her foot, then remembered something she should do. She dug out her phone and dialed a number from memory.

It was answered on the fourth ring. *"Hello?"*

"Marissa, hi."

"Ruby? S'up? I didn't recognize the number."

"New cell phone. Look, can you get away? I need your help."

"Right now? Shadow Unit is on."

"Record it. I need you to help me plan."

"I mean, me and my folks are watching. I can't get out until they go to bed."

"Oh. When you can, then. And can you call Kirk, too? He'll come if you ask him."

"Okay... um, at your place?"

It would be hard to explain such a late meeting to Dr. Fortunato, who, though easy-going, wasn't an idiot. On the other hand, she couldn't do much walking. "Jimmy, can you drive me somewhere else after this? Revenge of the Bean on Twenty-third?"

"For twenty dollars," Jimmy growled.

Marissa had overheard the question. *"Who are you with? Kirk has a car. I bet we could pick you up."*

"That would be great. Why don't you call back when you know?"

"Aye-aye! Can I tell him what's up?"

"Yeah, we'll have to, anyway."

"Okay, then tell me what's up."

"Oh, God. No time now. Just tell him what you know. And bring your computer!"

After she hung up, she leaned back again and watched the back of Jimmy's head for a few minutes while streetlights flashed past. "Jimmy, you seem unhappy."

"Just a little surprised you didn't mention the man-eating monster part of the business at first. I run into those every other day, of course, but still a guy likes to be warned."

"I see." Ruby paused. She might need Jimmy's help again before she was done—and from their earlier conversations, she had an idea what might soothe him. "I guess I also forgot to mention the hazard pay."

Jimmy thought about this while several more streetlights went by. "How much are we talking about?"

"Oh, say, a hundred?"

"Or one-ten? That would make a nice even total."

"Round numbers are good." She turned to Olga. "For you, too, of course."

"Just kill the thing. That's all I need."

"If I can figure out how." Ruby leaned back, closing her eyes. It would be wonderful to sleep for a while, but there was still a lot to do. Besides, she had to keep applying pressure to her foot. "Jimmy, what did you find out from those people?"

"What people? Oh, them. They say they gonna fix it but looks to me like they don't agree how. They gave me a number to call if I see it, or hear it, whatever. One lady was talking about doing a patrol at night, but some others, they not that crazy."

"Give me that number," Ruby said. Leaning forward to take the card he held up, she bumped her foot on the seat back, and pain shot up her leg. "Ow, ow, dammit! Are we almost there?"

"Almost."

Olga turned around in her seat. "So what's my story when we get there?"

"Let me think about it."

"I use your phone to call my ma?"

Ruby handed it over.

When they pulled up in front of Simon's house, Jimmy helped her out and supported her as she hopped up the stairs. Standing in front of the door, she dug her money out and thumbed off bills for him. "I'll call you in the morning." She turned to Olga, holding out another bill. "Wait out here while I get patched up, then I'll sneak you in."

Olga tucked the money away and sat on the steps.

Dr. Fortunato responded to Ruby's shout and came out of the dining room. When she saw Ruby standing in the hallway on one foot, a bloody sock held to the other one, she immediately became all business, helping Ruby to a chair in the drawing room and going for her bag.

Ruby set her backpack gently down and closed her eyes again until Dr. Fortunato returned, bustling around and setting things out on the floor. "What happened to your shoe?" She wiped away blood and examined the wound.

"I was climbing around on some junk. It got caught on something and got pulled off, and I was off balance, and when my foot came down, this happened. It was some sheet metal, maybe part of a washing machine."

"Have you had a tetanus shot?"

"Last year, when I stepped on a nail."

Dr. Fortunato clucked. "You go to class at night, you're supposed to come right back. You don't go rummaging around in trash piles in the dark. Where's your sense?"

"Sorry. Left it in my other pants."

"Pull up your pants leg." Dr. Fortunato took from her bag a wide, flat metal band with curly lines and characters engraved on it. This hinged open, and she clamped it loosely around Ruby's calf.

The relief was immediate. Ruby's foot went totally numb. Surprised, she squeezed her big toe. It was as if it were someone else's. Dr. Fortunato took Ruby's hand away and laid it on the band. "Hold that while I work."

Fortunato set an enamel bowl on the floor to catch drips and poured alcohol over the cut. Ruby looked away, not wanting to see whatever might be visible inside with the blood washed away.

"Looks clean, at least." Fortunato shook a small spray can, sprayed the wound, and turned to her bag.

Ruby risked a look. The edges of the wound were closed, the cut hardly visible. "Wow! Is that all you have to do?"

Fortunato wiped again with gauze and sprayed something else on it. "No, that's temporary. You still need stitches." Dr. Fortunato took out a curved needle, heavy black thread, and two little red pills. "Before I start, take this for pain." She handed over the pills.

"It doesn't hurt now."

"It will when I take that band off you."

"Couldn't I keep the band?"

"It's not good to use it for long. Take the pills."

"Will they make me drowsy?"

Dr. Fortunato gave her a sharp look. "I hope you're not thinking of staying up after this! Healing sleep, that's what you need!"

"Okay." Ruby raised her hand to her mouth but palmed the pills. She watched the first stitch going in, but that made her stomach turn flips, so she looked away. She'd dissected animals, of course, but this was a little different.

"There you go." Dr. Fortunato unclamped the band, and Ruby hissed a little through her teeth as sensation returned.

"How's that?"

"Not bad," Ruby lied.

"Come on then, we'll get you to bed."

Several minutes later, Ruby opened the front door and came out, finger to her lips, and motioned Olga inside. "Sneak upstairs. My room is straight back. You'll sleep there. I put a 'Do not disturb' sign on the door, but in case she checks, cover up so she'll think it's me. If you're discovered, here's a note to give them."

"What do I do in the morning?"

"I'll be back before then."

Ruby took a silver-headed cane from the umbrella stand near the front door and set it across her lap as she sat on the front steps to wait. There'd been a little rain, and the air was warm and muggy. Despite the throbbing of her foot, she quickly fell into a fitful doze.

She dreamed she was at Polacek's memorial service, up on stage near the casket while people milled around finding seats. The cover was open, and she walked over to look inside. Polacek was in there. He looked cross. "Are you okay?"

"I don't think so. I feel awful. What are all these people here for?"

"They're your friends. They're here for your funeral."

"Let me look." But he didn't move. "I'm having a little trouble sitting up. Don't just stand there, give me a hand."

Ruby reached between his shoulders and the slick satin lining of the casket and pulled him to a semi-sitting position. His head lolled back against her shoulder, and she turned so he could see the room. "Not a bad turnout," he said with something approaching approval. His breath smelled of formaldehyde. "Hey, what are they doing here?"

"Who?"

"The Sasquatches. Wouldn't give me the time of day when I was alive, oh no, but here they are to eat up the free food."

Ruby looked at the pair of Sasquatches, sitting in their armchairs. They weren't eating, though, just sitting with their hands in their laps. They seemed ill at ease among their smaller neighbors. The female's nails were painted red, looking odd on those huge hairy hands.

"And your uncle," Polacek continued bitterly. "Always with the fancy equipment. I used my head instead, and I got along all right."

"Well, until right at the end anyway." Ruby looked at Simon, standing chatting with something lumpy and orange. He reached up to adjust his sunglasses, which had slipped down his nose.

"There you are."

She turned. Lieutenant Garbers had come onto the stage, glaring at Polacek. "We've been looking all over for you."

"Don't blame me. It was your guys' job to keep track of me."

"Hey, who let you in here?" Ruby asked. "You're not supposed to see these people."

The detective scanned the crowd, scowling. "All of these... *things* look suspicious to me."

"Simon's not guilty. Tell him, Polacek." But Polacek's eyes were closed, and he was still.

The detective stared at Simon. "I don't trust a man who wears sunglasses at night. What is he trying to hide?"

"Come on." Ruby shook Polacek's shoulder. "You explain it to him, maybe he'll believe you. Hey, wake up!"

"You wake up," Marissa said, and Ruby's eyes opened to find her friend bending over her. "Hey, you look awful."

"Thanks." Ruby looked around. Kirk was standing a couple of steps lower. "Give me a hand up, will you, Kirk? I've hurt my foot."

Kirk helped her into the car, and she gave him directions to the coffee shop.

"Are you sure they're open?" Marissa asked.

"Yeah, I've seen Simon come in at two in the morning with one of their cups."

"How did you hurt yourself? Is it bad?"

"Later."

There were lights on but few customers. A man with olive skin and graying, curly hair sat behind the counter. He glanced at them as they came in and went back to his book.

"Marissa, we'll need coffee. Lots of coffee. Here, take my pack. Careful, Hundreds is inside."

Ruby chose a table in a cozy, semi-private corner, down two steps and surrounded with a half-wall and artificial plants. Once settled with her coffee, she looked at the expectant faces of her friends.

"Marissa's told you about the monster," she said to Kirk.

"Yes, but I decided to come, anyway. Seriously, an invisible monster? Like in *Predator?*"

"Sorry?"

"He means the movie," Marissa said.

"Whatever. It's nearly invisible, yes, especially at night. I've seen it... er, not seen it myself."

"What?" Marissa sat up. "You went out there? Without me?"

"I had to check it out."

"You could've been *killed!* And *eaten!*" Marissa's eyes narrowed. "How did you hurt your foot?"

"Let me tell it from the beginning."

Kirk munched on a croissant while he listened, looking at her intently. "It sounds pretty fantastic to me," he said when she'd finished. "I don't know what to think."

"You can quiz Hundreds if you like." Ruby reached for her backpack and held it open for Kirk to look inside. "The ear buds will let you hear her."

"Yeah or let me hear someone hiding nearby with a radio transmitter." But he gingerly reached into the pack for the earbuds and put them on. "Could you please wave your right paw? Okay, now the left? Wiggle your ears. Holy crap." He leaned forward, blocking the view from other directions. "How many fingers am I holding up? And now?" Then he was silent for a while. "Can I touch it?"

"Ask her yourself," Ruby said, but Hundreds was already crawling to the edge of the opening, where she held out a paw. Kirk, trembling slightly, reached out one finger, which Hundreds grasped in her little hand. Kirk gulped, pulled his hand away and wiped it on his jeans, and turned to Ruby, eyes wide.

"So, *anyway,*" Ruby said with a sigh, "we need to figure out what to do about this."

Kirk shook himself, looked once more at Hundreds, took a deep breath, then carefully set the backpack aside. "Um, okay. But why not just tell these Guardians what you know? Won't that help them deal with it?"

"Oh, they'll deal with it, all right. They were out there tonight looking for it. But they're so concerned about secrecy that they won't tell anyone about the monster. They'll just kill it and bury it. That leaves Simon on the hook—in fact, it makes it worse for him because they threw him in jail and presto, the killings stop. No, we've got to show the detectives they got it wrong. We have to show them the monster."

"Plus," Marissa said, "Miss W says the Guardians will start a war with the Skohlars."

"Miss W sounds kind of looney tunes," Kirk said, "if you ask me. If they're that concerned about secrecy, they'll be careful not to start a war."

"They might start one without meaning to." Marissa slipped her shoes off and crossed her legs on the couch. "But look, we can't do anything tonight, anyway. Simon will get bail tomorrow, then he can deal with it."

"That would be great." Ruby took a sip of her coffee, which had gone cold. "But he won't get bail. Anyway, we won't know until at least ten thirty in the morning. If he doesn't get out, we have to be ready to act tomorrow night. We can't waste time hoping. We have to be ready. The monster was out hunting tonight. It's hungry already. If it doesn't catch someone tonight, it will tomorrow."

"But by now they must all know to stay inside at night," Marissa said. "That should keep them safe for a while."

"If it doesn't find food, it'll just look elsewhere. Plus, there are homeless people out on the street or even just folks driving through. We can't warn everyone."

"If your uncle isn't released, you want to try to catch it?" Kirk asked.

"Or kill it. If we can figure out how." Ruby sipped her coffee. Still cold. "That's why you're here."

"You'd need heavy ordnance, wouldn't you?" Kirk leaned forward, interested. "You said it's armored."

"But it's hard to shoot what you can't see. Plus, the Guardians mustn't see us. So roaming the streets with RPGs is out, even if we had some."

"Maybe that's why Simon used a sword," Marissa said. "It's quiet."

Ruby set the cup down. "I don't know how he expected to find it. It's a big area."

"Probably it would've found him," Kirk said. "Only it found someone else first. But you still gotta see what you're swinging at. Does Simon have monster-vision goggles or something?"

"No, he...." Ruby paused, then smacked her forehead. *"D'oh!* Yes, he does. They look like sunglasses."

"But," Marissa said, "just the one pair? Well, never mind. Walking around looking for it is way too dangerous anyway."

"Right. I think we can lure it into a trap. I saw a building that might work near one of its kill sites, right where I ran into it. It must go there a lot." Ruby got out a notepad and sketched the layout of the rail tunnel under the flour mill. "Olga says we can get into the building, and there are some second-floor windows where we can watch the street."

"But we need bait," Kirk said.

"Live bait, according to Hundreds," Marissa added.

"We can come up with something. But I need you guys to figure out what to do with it once it's in there."

"Can we just lock it up?" Marissa said. "I don't like to kill it. It must be pretty rare."

"It's rare on this planet, thankfully. I don't know that it's rare wherever it comes from. And wow, that's a place I do not want to visit. Kill it or not, I don't care. So long as I have something to show the police."

Kirk raised a hand. "Will the Guardians let you if they're so hard-ass about secrecy?"

"I don't plan to ask permission. Anyway, it's not like I'm going to the newspapers, just the detectives who are working on the case. Let's fire up the computer and make a plan."

Marissa opened her computer, which was small and pink, and Ruby took the opportunity to grab her cane and head for the restroom and a coffee refill. By the time she returned, Kirk and Marissa were leaning over the screen, intent.

"What'd you find?" Ruby bent to look. "A map of the storm drain system. How did you get this so fast?"

"I know people who go spelunking down there," Kirk said. "Which I'm going to warn them not to do for a while. This is from their website. If it can't climb, it has to be going in and out of the storm drains where they dump into the river, along here. But there are a bunch of them."

"That makes sense. It was barely dark when I ran into it, and I was near the river."

"Where exactly?"

"Right… here. That's the mill."

After a while, Ruby sat back and just watched them, with their heads together over the computer. Marissa found a plan of the mill on the website of a local historical society, who wanted to convert it to a museum. Kirk wore the earbuds, asking Hundreds how wide the monster was, how agile, how strong.

They'll make a nice couple, Ruby thought, with a pang of regret. She watched Kirk's big hands dance over the tiny keyboard. Marissa laughed. Ruby's foot was hurting again—the aspirin she'd taken at home hadn't done much. And she was exhausted. She closed her eyes and leaned back, letting herself doze.

Ruby was startled awake by the clatter of a plate and utensils on the floor. Marissa and Kirk looked up at the sound, too. The man

behind the counter dropped out of sight to pick the stuff up. Ruby edged over to see what they were doing, rubbing her fingers through her hair to chase the clouds away. "Where are we?"

"Stuck," Marissa said. "We could tempt it in there and lock it in. Hundreds says they have a bell they used to use to call it to dinner, and I bet if we rang that bell, and actually had some food for it, it would come. But then what? Hundreds doesn't think the bars will hold it for long. We'd have to kill it. But how?"

"I was thinking poison," Kirk said. "Like we could poison the bait."

Ruby checked her cup. Empty. "You didn't get the memo about live bait, then?"

He stuck out his tongue. "We could put the poison in a balloon and make it swallow the balloon whole?"

"Will someone get me more coffee while I think about that?"

Marissa picked up the cup and left.

Ruby thought, then shook her head. "Most large predators don't eat the stomach contents of their prey. We couldn't count on it."

Kirk raised his eyebrows. "It's so cool you know that off the top of your head. Poison gas?"

"Too open, the wind blows right through. We'd have to find a different place to set the trap." Noticing a short, rumpled bald man at a nearby table looking at them curiously through the fake plants, Ruby added, "No, we'd need at least a level five Paladin with a magic sword to make that work. I have the sword, but our Paladin is in the dungeon." The bald man went back to his book, curiosity satisfied. Ruby lowered her voice as Marissa returned with three cups. "Thank you, thank you, you've saved my life. I think something like a landmine would be better. Its underside is its weak point."

"Ruby, no!" Marissa whispered. "No explosives."

"Could you get something like that?" Kirk asked.

"I have… contacts." Ruby was thinking of her parents' Rolodex in her dresser drawer. "We'd need something to set it off, like a trip wire."

"Ruby!"

"What kind of explosives would we need, and how much?"

"Let me check." Kirk turned back to the computer.

Marissa waved her hands between them, whispering furiously. "Just a minute. Just a minute. That's crazy talk! Hello! Don't you look up that stuff on my machine, the government tracks that kind of thing."

Kirk withdrew his fingers as Marissa pushed down the cover of the computer. "I know that," he said. "I was gonna use an anonymizer."

"Can we talk privately for a minute?" Marissa asked Ruby.

"I don't want to get up."

Kirk stood. "I'll go." He ducked under a low-hanging light as he walked to a small table in another corner, pulling a small tablet from his pocket.

"Listen," Marissa said urgently. "Explosives. Bad idea."

"Got a better one?"

"I've got plenty—"

"Not bothering with any of the options I already said no to?"

Marissa shut her mouth. Blew her breath out. "Ask Miss W to find someone else. This is too big for us. Unless what you really want is to complete the set by joining the rest of your family in prison."

"That's unkind."

"Reality is unkind. I'm honest." Marissa reached for her phone. "I'm calling her."

"Right now? It's after midnight."

"She hardly sleeps at all, just little naps. She said call anytime."

"I don't remember that."

"When I went back there this afternoon."

"What? When were you going to tell me about this?"

"I had to find out about that 'The One' business. I called you after, but I guess you were out monster hunting and didn't answer."

"What'd you learn? No, tell me later." Ruby waved at Kirk, beckoned him over.

Marissa dialed and waited. "Hello? It's Marissa. That's right, 'The One.' I need to talk with Mizz Wheelwright. No, I can't talk louder."

Kirk sat down next to Ruby. "What's up?"

"Calling Miss W for assistance."

"Okay, thanks." Marissa set her phone down. Her paper was still blank. "She told them I'd call. She told them when I'd call. How'd she know?"

"What'd she say?" Kirk said.

"She said, quote, 'No, there's nobody else.'"

"Well, that's okay," Kirk said cheerfully. "I thought of another way to kill the beast. No landmines. I have everything I need, except a crate of tomato paste."

"Tomato paste? You know we're making a death trap, right?" Ruby said. "Not monster marinara."

Marissa jumped as her phone, still in her hand, began to vibrate. She looked at the display. "Oh, shit. It's my folks."

"Don't answer."

"Why, I'm not in enough trouble?" Marissa swiped the screen. "Hello?" She paused for a considerable time, during which Ruby heard faint squawks from the phone. "It's a little complicated. No, I'm fine, nothing's wrong. Uh-huh. Uh-huh. I'm with Ruby." Marissa closed her eyes, covered the mic, and gave her head a little shake. "She didn't like that," she muttered. "No," she said into the phone, "she needed to talk because she's upset about her uncle. No, it's just us. Okay. Yeah, right away. No, you don't have to come get me. No, really…. Look, my battery's almost dead. I'll be right there." She hung up. "Damn." She looked at Kirk. "I don't suppose you could give me a ride home."

Kirk looked at Ruby, who shrugged. "I'm pretty much done in. Drop me off, too, and we can pick up early in the morning."

"Okay. I'll explain my idea on the way."

"Just let me run to the little girl's room." Marissa stood, slipping her computer back into its bag.

"Help you to the car?" Kirk held out his hand.

"First, hand me that cup." Ruby unfolded a tissue she'd taken from her pocket, revealing the two tiny pills Alice had given her. She washed them down with a swig of coffee.

"Hand up." Kirk pulled her easily to her feet, and she stumbled a little and bumped into him.

"Ow," she said.

"Sorry. Here's your cane."

Ruby, overcome with exhaustion, rested her head against his shoulder for a moment. He smelled of boy and laundry detergent and shellac. She stepped away and took the cane, trembling a little.

It had begun raining while they were inside, big warm drops, and Ruby waited at an outdoor table under the awning while he ran for the car. Marissa came out and stood nearby, flapping her computer bag against her thighs. "You have to promise me no explosives."

"I don't know if I can do that."

"Then don't tell me what the plan is. My folks will ground me for sure, anyway, so it's not like I'll be able to help. If they ask later whether I knew what you were up to, I want to be able to say no."

They drove toward Marissa's apartment building in silence. The windows had fogged from humidity, and Ruby wiped off a peephole. They passed a laundromat with a large, discouraged-looking man folding clothes inside. A couple walking together, huddled under an umbrella. She closed her eyes.

She started awake when Marissa slammed the car door. Ruby sat up and watched her run for the lit entrance of her apartment building, holding the computer bag over her head. They pulled away from the curb, and Kirk asked, "You okay?"

"Yeah, no problem. Hey, you're not gonna be in trouble for sneaking out, are you?"

"Nah, I didn't have to sneak. My dad doesn't care."

"That's sad, yet convenient." Ruby rolled down her window a crack to let in the cool night air and only a little rain. She stuck her hand out to get it wet, then rubbed her face with the cool water. "So, tell me this plan of yours."

When they pulled up in front of the house, Kirk got out and walked around, but Ruby opened her own door and stood, facing into a refreshing breeze. She felt dizzy—those pills of Dr. Fortunato's were strong stuff. Kirk helped her up the stairs, and they stood at the door, awkwardly. "Well... good night."

"Okay. Take care." Kirk paused for a moment and seemed about to say something else, but he just nodded and left.

After he drove off, Ruby knelt to open her backpack. Hundreds uncurled, stretched, and looked up at her. "Go on home. I'll meet you in the gazebo in the morning. Bring the dinner bell. Okay?"

Hundreds ran down the slanted surface beside the stairs and vanished down a storm sewer that rainwater was still trickling into.

"I'll take that as a yes." She slipped inside as quietly as she could. She'd hidden her pajamas under a couch cushion in the study when she went out. Leaving the light off, she changed into them, hiding her clothes under the same cushion.

The moon sword caught her eye, and it occurred to her she should do something with it now in case Simon did get out and wanted it tomorrow night. Earlier, she'd noticed a long box leaning against the wall. Opening it, she found a velvet-lined, sword-shaped recess. She placed the sword inside, shut it, and waited until the box felt lighter. Then she moved it, opened it, and after a few seconds the sword reappeared inside. So, she had a way to carry it where no moonlight shone. Was the box special, or could it be carried in any kind of container? If her hand could pass through the space it occupied, why didn't it fall through the desk, through the floor, through the earth, when it was vanished?

Well, she'd worry about that some other time. She headed up to bed. Halfway up the stairs, she got frustrated with the cane and did the rest backwards, on her butt. At the top she paused, listening. She could hear Alice, snoring gently in Simon's room. There was a whisper of movement from the attic stairs. "Wally?" she whispered.

A rustle, and he appeared in the doorway, darkness against shadows. "Where you been?"

"Just downstairs for a glass of water."

He came out to squat down near her. "For three hours? And who's your friend?"

"What friend?" She wished she could see his face.

"In your bed. Saw her in the hallway when she came in."

"Oh, her. She just needed a place to stay. It wasn't safe for her to go home."

Wally was silent for a moment. "Missed you the last few nights. You and Marissa."

"I know, sorry. It's been awful. I keep hoping I'll wake up and it's a dream."

"Alice told me how you got hurt."

"Yeah, dumb, huh?"

"Yeah." Wally paused again. "I've known Simon a long time. Can't go out in public, but if you hear of anything I can do to help…."

He knew she was trying to help Simon. Of course he knew. And he wasn't going to rat her out. She felt a release of tension. "Of course."

"How's the foot? Need help?"

"I can do it." Grabbing the stair rail, she got to her feet and used the wall for support. She paused at the door and looked back. "Good night."

"Be careful, Ruby," Wally whispered from the shadows. "Really, *really* careful."

Ruby nodded and slipped into her room. She found Olga sprawled across the bed and poked her half awake. "Make room," Ruby said and slipped between the sheets—the cool, heavenly sheets.

Sixteen

The dream picked up where it had left off. She stood on the endless, sunny roof, under the makeshift shelter, heat rising around her. Micah had the Rolodex in his hands, flipping through the cards. "Who would they arrest?"

"Whoever sold them the explosives. I don't know."

"Lots of cards here. How would they know who it was?"

"They could figure it out. They'll investigate them all."

Micah snapped the cover shut and handed it back. "Would that be a good thing, then?"

"I can't decide." The canopy flapped in the wind, and a beam of sunlight shone through a hole into Ruby's eyes. She covered her face and sat up in bed, pushing back the covers. She limped to the sink to splash water on her face, then shook Olga. "Come on. Come on, wake up."

Olga pulled the covers over her head. "May wild dogs eat your liver."

"We have to get you out before Doctor Fortunato wakes up. And I need you do something else for me."

Olga pulled the covers down to look at her. "What?"

"Find out whether our friend with the claws had dinner last night."

Olga grimaced. "I won't have to find out. I'll hear about it. Give me your number."

A crowd of reporters waited outside the courtroom, but Ruby and Dr. Fortunato were able to edge through unrecognized. They waited down the hall, near a row of beat-up pay phones.

When Kadopolous came out, the reporters mobbed him. He answered, "No comment," to most of their questions, and eventually they gave up and went away.

Seeing Dr. Fortunato's wave, Kadopolous came over to talk with them. "So, no bond," Fortunato said. "What now? Do we have a good case? Can you get him off?"

Kadopolous ran a hand through his slicked-back hair. "It's hard to know. Their case is circumstantial, but you know how it is. Too many dead, and people are scared. Juries and judges are people, too. They want it to be over. Solved. If the real killer is smart enough to quit now, or even move to a different city and change their M.O., Simon's chances are pretty iffy. Of course, if there's another killing, it would throw things into doubt. But even then, the police might just assume Simon has an accomplice. Either way, this will drag on for months. We should see about a more formal custody arrangement for the child."

"Hey!" Ruby said. "No more aunts! I'm managing just fine, thanks, anyway."

Dr. Fortunato gave her a dubious look. "I can look after you for a time, but Simon isn't technically your legal guardian, is he?"

"No, Aunt Meg is."

"We should write to ask what she wants to do with you, then," Kadopolous said.

"I'll take care of that when we get home." Dr. Fortunato put a hand on Ruby's shoulder. "If you need to reach us, we'll be at Simon's."

Kadopolous said his goodbyes, and Dr. Fortunato went off in search of a restroom. Ruby wandered out to the front of the courthouse and sat on the sun-warmed steps, off to one side and out of the way. She pulled out her burner and dialed Marissa's number. "Hey. I got your text, but I don't know how to answer it on this phone yet."

"What's the verdict?"

"No bail."

"Oh. Well, you expected it."

"Yeah." Ruby paused. "What's up, did you catch hell last night?"

"It was a little hard to understand there at the end, but I think I'm grounded until I'm twenty-five. Maybe thirty."

"I feel like this is my fault."

"Well yeah. No... I'm kidding. Sneaking out was only part of it. Being bad at soccer entered into the discussion, lying, not talking to them about anything, and generally being rebellious, and, let me think... oh, yes, intentional use of irony."

"Rebellious? *You?*"

"Was that irony?"

"No! You're the best-behaved girl I know."

"Great, explain that to my dad."

"Yeah, he'd believe it from me. Look, was this what you wanted to talk about? I have to figure out what to do. Do you still not want to know the plan?"

"Absolutely not." A pause. *"But if you run into trouble, call me and I'll see what I can do."*

"Okay." Ruby saw Dr. Fortunato come out and look around for her. "Thanks. Gotta go. Call you later."

As they rode home in the cab, Ruby leaned back and stared up out the back window, watching power lines pass by overhead. She sighed. Things had been going great for a while there, but now her life was right back in the crapper, as per usual. And there it would stay, apparently, unless she did something fairly drastic. Not to mention the potential rat apocalypse. That would be hell for everyone.

She rolled her head over to look at Dr. Fortunato. "Do you have a coin?"

"Ah… yes, here." Dr. Fortunato handed over a quarter.

Ruby considered the coin in her palm, then flipped it into the air, catching it on the way down. She held her closed hand out to Dr. Fortunato.

"Aren't you going to look at it?"

"No."

Dr. Fortunato took the coin and dropped it back into her purse, looking amused. "Micah used to do that. You never met him, did you?"

Ruby shook her head. "Not in this world."

When she got home, Ruby went straight to the back yard. Whatever Dr. Fortunato had put on her foot seemed to be helping. It hurt less this morning and only gave her a little trouble walking around. Thank goodness for small miracles.

She found a Skohlar at the gazebo but not Hundreds. It was a young male, sitting on the railing looking alert. The wind ruffled his fur, showing light brown under the black tips of the hairs. A small bronze bell rested on the rail beside him—it must be the monster dinner bell. Ruby picked it up as she passed and sat where the clematis would shield her from view of the house. She patted the bench beside her and got out the earbuds.

"Where's Hundreds of Uses?"

"You tired her." The young Skohlar's voice was gravelly. *"She is old, almost seven. And she fears the beast. I am Fat Free. I will carry messages."*

Ruby suppressed a smile. "You're not afraid of the monster?"

"I fear nothing."

"All right. Well, make yourself comfortable. I have to make a few calls." She pulled out her cell phone.

When Jimmy answered, he said, *"Yeah?"* a little warily.

"I've got another job for you. Is it safe to talk?"

"Just a sec." There was the sound of a door closing, shutting off music in the background. *"What's up?"*

"I have a shopping list."

They spoke for a few minutes, then Ruby hung up and called Kirk. "How's it going? Do you have everything you need? The gunpowder wasn't a problem?"

"Yeah, so far so good. There's no electricity in the building, right?"

Fat Free had gone instantly to sleep, his sequined vest barely moving with his breath. Ruby wondered whether he might like to be scratched between the ears. He might be offended, she decided. The Skohlars all seemed very proud. "I'd be amazed if there was."

"Right, I'll bring the emergency generator, then. How exact do you think that building plan is? As far as the dimensions of the rooms? Well, never mind. There'll be enough time to adjust things if I need to. I was going to pack everything in the pickup and go over right after lunch. When will you arrive?"

"Around four, I think. I don't want to stretch my excuse too thin."

"You'll bring the sword? I'd really like to see it."

"I'll bring it." Ruby felt oddly light, detached. They were really doing this. Her heart was beating faster as she hung up. She dialed again.

"Yeah, hey." Marissa sounded distracted.

"Hay is for horses, ninny."

"Neigh, neigh. Hay for all, hay for the masses. It's cheap, it's grassy, it's nutritious. What's up? I'm on the bus, so nothing too weird. They're already looking at me funny."

"I didn't force you to suggest feeding people hay. I need a favor. I have to get away for a while, maybe overnight. Can I tell Doctor Fortunato I'm spending the night at your place?"

"I guess. What do I do if she calls and wants to talk with you?"

Ruby had already thought about that. "Make sure you're the one who answers. Tell her I'm in the bathroom, tell her another call's coming in, put her on hold and conference me in. Do you know how to do that?"

"I'll look it up when I get home." Marissa lowered her voice. *"Look, I'd really like you to reconsider whatever rash plan you two have cooked up. There has to be a better way."*

"If I could think of it, I'd do it. Don't you know I'm scared out of my mind?"

"No, you're not. If you were really as scared as you should be, you'd be looking harder for other ways. Last night you were scared, when the thing attacked you, and you're doing this dumb-ass thing to prove you can beat it because it almost got you. Kirk, on the other hand, is doing it because he's a boy and, I'm assuming, the plan involves explosives and magic swords. Maybe it's also to please you."

"Not that. But those other things might be a factor." She was silent for a time. "Maybe you're right. Maybe I do want to get back at the thing. But it's still the only answer I have to save Simon. Maybe there's something I haven't thought of. Tell you what. That can be your job, to think of a better plan. If you can really come up with one, we'll do that, I promise. But it has to be tonight, and meanwhile I have to keep going on this one because I don't have time to spare. It's a good thing there's no overcast. We might need every minute of daylight."

"Deal. But this is such a bad idea. I'm almost to Scouts. I'll call you."

Seventeen

Jimmy parked near the railroad gate of the old mill on the side she hadn't visited before. Ruby got out to study the building across the street. As Olga had promised, part of the building was only one story tall with a flat roof. A doorway let out onto the roof from the other part of the building, which was two stories. She took the guitar and sword case from the trunk, since it wasn't the safest neighborhood, but left the ice chest. Jimmy carried a crate of supplies and led the two goats from the back seat on a rope lead.

Ruby pointed at their stakeout roof. "Do we have to climb up there, or can we get in through that door?"

"Olga got a key somehow," Jimmy said. "I ain't askin' how."

The gate into the train tunnel looked locked from a distance, but up close she could see the lock had been cut and was just hooked over the chain. From inside came a purr she assumed was the generator. As they walked down the dim passageway, a power-tool whine started up, echoing loudly in the narrow space.

The side room Kirk had chosen to set the trap in was lit with halogen lights strung along the walls.

Kirk looked up, grinning from behind his goggles, took off hearing protectors, and set his circular saw on the sheet of plywood he'd been cutting.

"Where you want these guys tied up?" Jimmy held up the goat rope.

Kirk pointed. "Olga just went out for burgers. If you guys want anything, call her."

Ruby pulled out her cell. "I didn't think she had a phone."

"She said she was going to the K-Bar Diner. I guess you could call and tell them what you want."

Jimmy set the crate down, outside the goats' reach. "Nothing for me. I'll set stuff up across the street."

"I could have something." Ruby pulled out her phone. "No signal. Jimmy, could you call from outside? Chili dog if they have it, cheeseburger otherwise. Pepsi or Coke. Thanks."

"Right. Catch you later."

Kirk watched him leave. "Where did he find the goats?"

"I wondered that, too. Craigslist."

"Really?"

"So he says." Ruby looked around at Kirk's work. This room was identical to the others lining the tracks on both sides. It was an open-ended rectangle. A metal door at the far end stood open. It must lead to a hallway connecting the rooms at the back. The generator sound came from there, and everything electric was plugged into a thick power cord that ran through the doorway. In front of the door, a low platform covered the floor from side to side, except for a cutout to let the door swing outward into the room. Judging by the amount of unused lumber lying around, the platform was about half complete.

Ruby opened the flaps on the box Jimmy had carried in and took out a battery-powered boombox. She looked around, then set it near the bars. "Can I walk on the platform?"

"Sure. The charges aren't in place yet. But what's that for? If you brought tunes, we won't hear them over the power tools."

"It's a recording of that dinner bell, on a loop."

"Ah. I'd wondered how you were going to set it up to ring."

"Yeah, at first I figured I'd stand in here shaking it and waiting for the monster, but then I thought, maybe not."

"Probably better this way. Will it be able to hear that from far away?"

"Hundreds said it has excellent hearing. If it passes by, it'll hear."

The top of the platform was thick, rough plywood with a pattern of widely-spaced holes. Ruby knelt to look into the holes. Each contained a small tomato paste can, open at the top and empty except for a small loop of shiny wire dimly visible at the bottom. "Shouldn't they be closer together?"

"I'd need more, and I'm not sure I'd have enough current to fire them all. Don't worry, from what Hundreds said about the thing's size, it'll be over at least five of them when they go off, and the shot will ricochet off its armor on the inside, doing more damage. It'll be enough."

"How do you know how to do this?"

"Model rocketry. My rocketry club has a big spool of igniter wire, and I borrowed the black powder from them, too. I tested one at home. They work."

"Won't the cans blow apart?"

"Probably, but I wrapped them with duct tape so most of the force goes upwards. Did you know, about the only thing duct tape isn't good for is ducts?"

"How can I help?"

"Wrap more cans, nice and thick like those two I did there. Then you can put ball bearings into those little plastic bags, maybe fifteen in each. Those will go in on top of the black powder, just like a giant shotgun shell. But I'll take care of that part." He held up the saw. "I have to do more cutting, sorry. There's a spare pair of hearing protectors over there. Then I'll do the gate."

Kirk doing a last bit of welding on the gate, had curtly refused offers for help. Everything else was ready, so Ruby and Olga were on the roof across the street, playing cards. "Heads up!" Kirk called from the ground. A half-brick sailed up over the edge, trailing clothesline.

A minute later, Kirk came pounding up the stairs and out onto the roof.

"Where's Jimmy?" Ruby said.

"He left. He said no way he's staying after dark."

"That coward. It's perfectly safe up here. I tell you. It's just impossible to get good minions anymore."

Kirk nodded. "Back in the old country, you could put an ad in the paper, and in the morning, there would be twenty, thirty prime hunchbacks in line at the castle gate."

"Exactly—oh, an eight? Nice." Ruby picked up the card Olga had just laid down. "People are so quick to leap to judgment now, too. One little mistake and it's hoy, Martha, fetch me my pitchfork!"

Kirk tied the clothesline to a protruding pipe.

"Ha! Gin!" Ruby said. "Let's see your cards."

"Curse you. May your headphones catch on every door handle."

"Your deal. Kirk, you wanna play?"

"What are the stakes?"

"Ten thousand dollars a point. Olga owes me, let's see, three hundred forty thousand."

"Too rich for my blood. Anyway, I have to test the gate. Come see."

The girls came to the edge of the roof. The clothesline ran across above the street, over a rusty hook that had perhaps once supported a sign, and down to the railroad gate. The gate was open, flat against the outside wall, opposite a heavy iron bar with bright spots of recent welding. Kirk pulled the cord, releasing the gate. With a screech, it swung closed. As it slammed, the iron bar dropped with a clang, falling into newly added brackets.

Kirk frowned. "A little slow, but it'll have to do."

"Good. Go reopen it, and hurry. It's almost sunset. Don't forget to reset the flag! And start the bell recording. Then you can get cleaned up." The building, though empty, fortunately had a working bathroom on the ground floor.

Olga looked down at the gate, watching Kirk hurry back across. "I thought you were going to kill it. Are you planning to trap it now?"

"That's a backup in case killing it doesn't work."

"You sure it couldn't get through that? Can't it just lift up that bar?"

"No. There's another bit to hold it in place once it falls."

"What if it's strong enough to just pull it loose?"

"Let's hope we don't find out. Look, don't worry. We're safe up here, anyway. Your deal."

After a few more minutes, Kirk was back on the roof, looking like he'd dunked his head in the sink. He roughed up his hair, scattering drops of water.

"Relax," Ruby said. "Drinks in the cooler."

"Oh, yeah," Kirk said, flopping into a folding chair. He rummaged in the ice chest, opened a root beer, and moved the ice chest to use as a footstool. He looked at the stuff scattered across the rooftop— table, chairs, a bag of books, a small battery-powered lamp, a rat in a beaded vest sleeping on a folded towel, an air mattress. "Hey, is that your guitar?"

"Yeah, I've missed a lot of practice the last couple days."

"That rat's not Hundreds."

"She wasn't feeling well, so she sent a substitute. Is it my play?"

"Yes," Olga said impatiently.

"Where's the sword?" Kirk stood near the long box. "Is it in here?"

"Yes, but there's nothing to see until moonrise."

"Are you playing or talking?"

Ruby looked at the sky. "Actually, I think it's time to get ready to start watches."

Olga set down her cards. "It's not dark yet."

"No, but I don't like to leave the open entrance to our death trap unwatched. Someone could get hurt. Olga, you and I have first watch."

"Okay, what do I do?"

"Look for people coming from that direction and watch the flag." Ruby pointed to a white rag draped over the middle bar of the gate. It was tied to strands of fishing line across the gate opening, so it would fall if anything invisible passed that way.

"I thought you'd be able to see it with the sunglasses."

"I hope so. I tried them in a dark room at home, and they work great, but I didn't have anything invisible to try them on." Except Speck, who hadn't looked any different, but then he had no edges for the glasses to outline.

"What's my job?" Kirk asked.

"Sleep until your watch." Ruby listened carefully and could barely hear the bell across the street. Loud enough, if Hundreds was right about the thing's hearing. Ruby picked up her guitar and earphones.

As the last light began to fade, Ruby put on the sunglasses. They made everything purple, but every edge was sharply visible. She kept an eye out toward the river, while Olga watched the other way.

It was dark enough. The monster was probably out hunting. Ruby found it hard to focus on her playing when every movement in the corner of her eye distracted her. Olga seemed twitchy, too. After an alarm over a pigeon, Ruby set the guitar aside and just watched.

Olga had borrowed a book light, which she clamped to a tablet, so she could draw. After a while, Ruby leaned over to get a better look. It was a sketch of people leaning out the windows of a brick building, yelling and throwing things at each other. Olga was filling in detail of an old man lying unconscious on a fire escape with pieces of flowerpot scattered around him. "That's pretty good," Ruby said.

"We got a painting contest at my school every year. Last year I came third. So, I look for ideas for the next one."

"What gave you this idea?"

"Our neighbors, what you think? Oh, hey." Olga snapped off the light. "Someone's coming."

At first Ruby saw nothing where Olga was pointing, but then thought to look over the tops of the glasses. From a side street, a spotlight shone across their road, playing on the side of a building. She couldn't see light through the glasses, only shapes.

A few seconds later, a pickup turned the corner, driving away from them. The truck bed held three spotlights on stands, with people standing behind them, beaming around in all directions. The girls ducked behind the side wall as one of the lights swept towards them, then Ruby leaned out again to watch.

"What are they doing?" Olga asked. "I can't see for all the lights."

Ruby raised the glasses again. "I think they're hunting. They work the lights with one hand, and they've each got some kind of weapon in the other." The weapons were complicated, heavy-looking things that the people in the truck let hang beside them, their hands hidden inside a curving shield.

"Guardians?"

"Probably. They sure look unofficial." Ruby ducked back as the beam passed again. "I guess they think they can see it if they get it in the spotlight."

"But it hates light. It'll just avoid them."

"Maybe they don't know that. Well, who knows. They might catch it by surprise."

The truck turned off down a side street. Kirk came up behind them, yawning. "What time is it?"

Ruby lifted the glasses to check her watch. "A little early, but why don't we change now? Olga, your turn to sleep."

Kirk used a flashlight to look in the ice chest. "Hey, anything here with caffeine?"

"Dig around, there are a few little cans of iced coffee. Can you grab me one, too?"

Kirk sat beside her, shaking water off a can, and tossed another over her way.

"Oh, good." Ruby looked pointedly at Kirk's legs dangling over the edge of the roof. "More bait."

Kirk switched to a cross-legged position. "Do I get to try the sunglasses now?"

Ruby passed them over.

"Whoa. It's not infrared, is it? But I can see everything. The army would love to have some of these. Where did they come from?"

"No idea."

There were no working streetlights nearby, but there were some distant lights across the river and the usual big-city night sky glow. That was enough for Ruby to see him looking around. "Where'd your rat go?" he asked.

"He gets huffy if you call him a rat. He's a Skohlar. And, he's not *my* rat. He's off reporting to his ratty boss."

"How can you tell he's male?"

Ruby was glad the glasses only showed shapes, not the color in her cheeks. "Um. The difference is fairly obvious if you know where to look." She looked away, then picked up her guitar and ran through some scales, then played a couple of pieces.

"I thought you just started taking lessons," Kirk said when she'd finished. "It looks like you actually sort of know what you're doing with that thing."

"Oh, well, thanks. I've been spending a lot of time on it, I guess, and I have two teachers who are both tough. To hear them tell it, it sounds like I'm playing with mittens on."

"No, not mittens. Gloves, maybe."

"Oh, la, stop it, sir. You'll turn my head with your flattery. Hang on, here they come again. Get back." The spotlight truck was back, or one like it, but farther away than before. This time it just crossed the road without turning.

They returned to the edge of the roof, Kirk this time bringing two folding chairs. "My legs went to sleep."

"Not for me, thanks. The arms get in the way of the guitar."

"Okay. So, when do I get to see what's in the box?"

"Oh, you can look now." Ruby clipped an electronic tuner to the head of the guitar.

Kirk went to look. "It's empty."

"Right. Look again in…"—Ruby consulted her watch—"… ninety-five minutes."

"What happens then?"

"Moonrise." Ruby bent over the guitar and tried "Blackbird," going repeatedly over the difficult fingerpicking section until it was almost satisfactory. Then she did some exercises. Boring but necessary.

She looked up at Kirk in his chair. He sat quietly, his head turned partly away to watch towards the river, the lights reflecting off the sunglasses. He started to turn towards her, and she quickly looked away. She should be keeping watch in the other direction anyway.

He stood. "Is there anything to eat?"

"Now that you mention it, I am kind of starving. Hand me that flashlight, will you?"

Ruby set up a chair for herself and dragged the table over. "I didn't have much time to shop, so I mostly raided Simon's cupboard. Sorry it's weird stuff." She pointed. "There's dolmades, shortbread cookies, mushroom paté, French bread, some kind of hard cheese, sardines in fancy sauce, and this which I don't know what it is."

Kirk picked up the jar. "Pickled something. Got a knife?"

They chatted while they ate, keeping a half-hearted watch on the street. Ruby set some of everything aside for Olga for later, knowing from experience with her cousins that teenage boys didn't tend to leave much food on the table. The cheese was really good, and at one point she was obliged to defend her share with the knife. "Watch it, mister. Don't get between me and my cheese."

"That would make a good song title." He withdrew his hand. "Something along the lines of 'Blue Suede Shoes,' you know? Do what you like but leave my cheese alone."

"If you write the lyrics, Marissa could do the music. She's good at that. Oh, are you getting up? I could use a crappy orange soda."

But Kirk wasn't paying attention. He stood motionless, hands on the table, staring down at the street. Ruby twisted to look but saw nothing. But then the wind shifted, and she could smell it.

She drew in her breath with a hiss. "Give me the glasses, Kirk." she said urgently.

With the sunglasses on, she could see it as clearly as anything else. She'd been expecting something like a giant armadillo, and this was a little like that in general shape, but instead of layers of shell, it had bony-looking scales with concentric ridges. Then, of course, there were the large, sharp claws and the flat, crocodile-like head.

"My God," Kirk breathed. "I didn't really believe it."

Ruby looked at him sharply. He'd done an awful lot of work for someone who didn't believe, and she had to wonder why. She hoped he'd done it well, anyway.

The creature had seen them, or scented them, or whatever. It was looking straight at them, anyway. It ambled over to sniff around at the base of the wall below them. Ruby's heart was beating a mile a minute. The beast raised its head as far as it could on that thick, short neck and stared at her with one blank, reptilian eye.

"For Pete's sake, what's it doing now? Come away from that edge."

"It can't get up here," Ruby wished her voice wouldn't shake quite so much.

It was trying to climb, though. It raised a forefoot, hooked the tips of its claws in a gap between bricks, and pulled itself up a couple of feet. Then it reached higher with the other foot and lunged up a little more. Its tongue, like a snake's tongue, darted out. Ruby stared down, standing her ground, and shook Kirk off when he took her arm to pull her away. When she wouldn't move, he stood beside her and looked for himself, aiming the flashlight down.

"You're gonna pay," she told the monster, feeling anger rise within her, not understanding why.

It opened its mouth, revealing multiple rows of serrated teeth, and hissed.

Kirk choked, and Ruby coughed and took a step back. "Oh, good lord. I'll never complain about puppy breath again."

"What's it doing?"

"It couldn't reach the top," Ruby said with relief. "It dropped back down."

"Give me the glasses now. I have to get another look."

"Can't you see it at all?" She exchanged glasses for flashlight. "Tell me what it does."

"It's trying the alley, but it's too wide to fit." Kirk pointed, and Ruby knelt at the edge to aim the light down. Knowing where to look, she could see something there, but it was like Olga had described—just a slight wavering and distortion. The thing's camouflage was nearly perfect.

Where was Olga, anyway? Surely, she couldn't be sleeping through this. She looked around, and saw Olga sitting upright on the air mattress. Turning the flashlight on her, she saw the girl was frozen, wide-eyed, clutching the sheet to her chest.

"We're safe up here, Come look."

Olga shook her head.

"It's looking down the tunnel," Kirk said. A few seconds later, "It's going across. It's sniffing around the gate. This is fantastic! What is that thing? Where did it come from?"

"My turn."

The creature nosed around the gate for a couple of minutes, while Ruby kept mentally urging it to go in. Either it wasn't telepathic, or it was in a contrary mood because it gave another look back at them, then moved off down the street, its claws clicking on the pavement.

"Come back!" Ruby called. "Fresh, tasty goat! Dammit!"

"Maybe it doesn't like goat," Kirk suggested.

"Young and tender!" But it rounded the corner and was gone. Ruby sighed. "I think it suspects. Hundreds said it's pretty smart."

"It might come back. We'll wait."

Ruby snorted. "We'll wait in any case. I'm not going down there before dawn."

"Was it a dinosaur?"

"Not a kind I recognized."

"There were no invisible dinosaurs, were there?"

"Think a minute about whether that's an intelligent question."

"Oh, right. You couldn't tell from a fossil. But how is it possible we can't see it? It couldn't really be transparent. If it ate something, wouldn't we see what it ate?"

"No, I think it's just a really good active camouflage ability. Like, have you seen videos of octopuses blending with their background?" Ruby went over to Olga, who'd lain down again and covered herself completely. "As long as you're awake, do you want something to eat? Hey." She twitched the sheet down to uncover Olga's face, but Olga pulled it right back up.

"What's up with her?" Kirk asked when Ruby returned to the table.

Ruby decided not to mention the tears on Olga's face. "She needs some time alone. So tell me, where'd you learn to weld?"

Kirk gave an uncertain glance back toward Olga. "Um, my dad's in the ornamental ironwork business. I help out." He lowered his voice. "Shouldn't we talk to her?"

"Leave it."

"All right." Kirk ran his hand through his hair. "Marissa seems to think your band needs a bass player."

"We don't really have a band. It's just three of us who get together to practice."

"You and her and…?"

"Uh, someone who's serious about his privacy. We haven't had a chance yet to talk to him about you."

"What do you mean? Is he a celebrity?"

"In a sense. I don't know how long he's going to—*shit!*" Ruby leaped to her feet, got her leg tangled in her chair, and went down in a tangle of aluminum, scrambling back from the edge.

"What? What?" Kirk stood up and waved the flashlight around.

Hearing footsteps coming up behind her, Ruby rolled to the side to avoid getting trampled, at the same time trying to get a better look at what she'd seen coming up over the edge of the roof near her foot.

"It's okay!" Ruby shouted. Olga staggered past, waving a glass pop bottle, and Ruby grabbed her shirt to keep her from blundering into the table or going over the edge. Olga shrieked and made a wild swing with the bottle, connecting to Ruby's wrist with a glancing blow. "It's okay! Sorry, false alarm. It's just the rat. Ow." Ruby cradled her wrist in her other hand.

"Jeez!" Kirk sat down. "You gave me a heart attack."

Olga sobbed and dropped to her knees, letting the bottle fall. It rolled over the edge and smashed on the pavement below.

Ruby glared at the Skohlar. "Next time, maybe a squeak or something to let us know you're coming?"

Fat Free—Ruby thought it must be since he wore the same beaded vest—scurried away across the roof.

"Did he climb right up the wall?" Kirk asked.

"Apparently." Ruby watched Fat Free delve into her backpack for the rat-speaker, which he brought back to her. She put on the earbuds and watched him fumble with the controls in the dark for a second, then gently took it from his paws and used her fingernail to press the "on" button.

"I watch from below." He must have been hiding in a storm drain, since he would hardly sit out on the street as a handy monster-snack. *"You failed."*

"The night is young. Who knows?" Ruby watched as Kirk gently helped Olga to her feet and sat her in his chair. She pulled her leg loose from her own chair to let him set it upright, feeling a twinge from her injured foot. She hoped she hadn't pulled any stitches loose. She looked at Fat Free, who seemed puzzled. "Wait until morning to decide it didn't work," she clarified. She waved away Kirk's offered hand, patting the roof to indicate she was happy there for the moment. He nodded and walked away to patrol the far corner.

"The Cheddar will be angry. I must go, report now."

"Did it catch someone tonight?" Maybe it hadn't gone for the goats because it was already full.

"I do not know."

"If it's hungry, it'll come back. Just stay here and wait with us."

Fat Free considered. *"I smell cheese."*

Ruby wondered what Simon would think of the uses to which she was putting his expensive cheese, but she got up to cut a small piece. Fat Free took it and retired to his towel.

Ruby sat and took off her shoe and sock to check on the cut. The gauze still felt dry, and gentle probing didn't cause any more pain than before, so she decided it was okay.

"I'm sorry," Olga whispered from across the table. "Did I hurt you?"

"Just a bruise. For future reference, though, if the monster comes back, I don't think a bottle will bother it much."

Olga gave a low laugh. "I had it under the covers with me. I know it's stupid, but it made me feel safer."

"Why'd you come rushing out?"

"I don't know. I was so ashamed that I froze up before, and I was going over it in my head, thinking what I oughta done, and then you yelled, and…." She shrugged.

"It's perfectly understandable—"

"Oh, don't give me that. You and Kirk were right there dancing on the edge making fun of the thing."

"Yeah, but then again, neither of us had a friend eaten by it while we... listened."

Olga shivered.

"Anyway, thanks for coming to my defense. That was brave."

Olga snorted. "Or brainless."

"Why don't you go lie down again? It's almost an hour yet till your watch."

"Are you kidding? I'm too keyed up to sleep now."

"Then I will. You take the glasses. Hey Kirk, I'm turning in. Wake me if anything happens."

"Yeah, okay. But what about the long box?"

"Open it when I said. But be careful, it's heavy and really sharp. And don't set it down where the moon can't shine on it."

Ruby was awakened by someone shaking her shoulder. "Wha—?" she said.

Olga was leaning over her. "Shh. There's a cop down there."

Ruby crawled to the edge to see. There was an unmarked car parked across the street, headlights on. A man in a suit stood next to the gate, his back to them, looking at the fresh welds on the locking bar.

"Glasses," Ruby whispered, and Olga handed them over.

The policeman, if that's what he was, leaned over to touch the white rag hanging over the bars. "Where's Kirk?"

"Bathroom."

The man might have heard some sound because he looked around. Ruby recognized his face. "Garbers. What's he doing out here? He already got his man."

The detective stepped up to the gateway, shone a flashlight around inside, and started to step through.

"Hey!" Ruby yelled.

"Shit!" Olga muttered.

"Hey, don't go in there!" Ruby ducked back as the flashlight swung in her direction. "It's booby-trapped!"

There was a pause, and Ruby risked a peek over the edge, ducking back as the light pointed right at her.

"Who's up there? Miss Park? Is that you?"

"Crap."

"Come down here and explain what's going on. Did you break into this building?"

"I'll gladly explain in the morning. But right now, you have to get off the street. You're in danger!"

"I think I can handle myself." Garbers sounded amused. "I've got a gun."

Olga had been bobbing up to look. "He's going in!" she hissed.

Ruby looked and saw him pick up the rag from the ground inside the archway and hold it up. "Nice booby-trap!" he said, then turned and went further in.

"That's not the trap! Damn you!" She ripped off the sunglasses and held them out to Olga. "Yell if the thing comes back."

"What do you mean? What are you doing?"

"I'm going down there to keep him from getting killed!"

"Ruby, no!"

But she was already at the door, slamming it against the wall. "What's going on?" Kirk called out as she started down the stairs. Halfway down, she realized she should've grabbed a flashlight, but there wasn't time to go back. She felt her way down a short hall to the street door and bumped it open, stumbling out, and ran across to the gateway, yelling, "Lieutenant, stop!"

She paused when she got to the opening. The moon was up, lighting the street, but inside the tunnel was completely black. The detective's flashlight pointed at her, and she hurried inside, stumbling over something on the floor. "Wait up! I can't see!"

She picked her way toward him. He beamed the light at her feet, which helped.

"Ruby?" Kirk called from across the street. "What the hell are you doing down there? Come back!"

"Stay up there! I'll only be a minute."

She could hear him swearing, but it didn't sound like he was coming down. She caught up with Garbers, who stood near the entrance to their trap. "There's a tripwire in there," she said, pointing. She grabbed his flashlight hand to illuminate the wire. "See? It's rigged with explosives."

"What the hell—"

"It's a trap to kill the monster. It could come back any minute, so we have to get out of here right now."

"You're not going anywhere, young lady." He grabbed her arm firmly. "You're under arrest."

Olga's voice came echoing faintly down the corridor. "It's coming! It's coming, get out!"

Ruby twisted and pulled desperately toward the street, managing to drag Garbers a couple of steps before he got his footing. They engaged in a furious silent struggle which ended up with her hanging from his arm, looking hopelessly at the street, while he dragged her upright. It was with a sense of unreality that she saw Kirk run out in front of the gateway, limned in moonlight, wearing the sunglasses, sword held high over his shoulder. He took a fighting stance, waiting.

"Let me go!" Ruby screamed. "It'll kill him! Let go!"

Garbers dropped the flashlight and drew a gun, dragging her over the rough floor toward the opening. "So that's what became of that sword."

Helpless, Ruby watched as Kirk dodged to the side, swinging the sword. He fell, and the sword went flying. *"Kirk!"* she screamed, then there was a terrific bellow from the street.

Garbers stopped. "What the…?"

Ruby couldn't speak but watched with relief as Kirk stumbled to his feet, ran to the gate, and reached for the release cord. The gate started to swing shut, and Kirk tugged on it to speed it up, looking over his shoulder.

Ruby found her voice. "Inside! Get inside, Kirk!"

Finally, he slipped around the end of the gate and pulled it shut with a *clang,* then danced back. There was a second, louder clang and another bellow. The gate rattled in its frame, and Kirk ran down the passage toward them.

"Freeze!" Garbers yelled. He let Ruby go to grab for the flashlight.

"Stop it! Kirk, get down!" She grabbed Garbers's hand, and the gun went off, ricocheting into the darkness. "Stop, you idiot! You'll kill someone! If you have to shoot something, shoot that!"

"There's nothing there!"

There was a terrific screech, and the bars of the gate bent out a few inches.

"All right, then what did that?"

Garbers fired four shots at the gate, then his gun clicked, empty or jammed. Kirk limped up to them. Ruby hadn't seen him silhouetted against the entrance, so he must have been keeping to the edge to stay out of the line of fire. "We have to get out of here," he panted. "That way." He pointed into the booby-trapped room.

"What *is* that thing?" Garbers shouted. The gate gave another screech and bent down several more inches.

"Later!" Ruby hurried ahead. "Come on. Watch the trip wire!"

The gate gave way with a crash. Ruby rolled under the wire. The men stepped carefully over it, which put her ahead of them. She fumbled with the door handle in the dancing light of Garbers's flashlight. The goats' leashes were tied to the handle. They bumped against her, bleating panic, and nearly knocked her down, but she got it unlatched, and the goats pulled it open with desperate lunges. Ruby tripped over the row of car batteries as the men crowded through after her, the grit on the concrete floor grinding into her palms. The monster sounded close. Garbers was last through. He thrust the light into Kirk's hands and struggled to pull the door shut. The goats bleated. The detective swore.

"Leave it!" Kirk shouted and grabbed Garbers's arm to pull him clear of the doorway. There was a tremendous rolling thunder, too loud to even be a sound, like a blow to her whole body. Then, darkness.

Eighteen

Ruby woke to darkness, silence, and a terrific headache. "What happened?" she tried to say but couldn't hear her own voice. She reached up, and another hand found hers, holding it tightly. She squeezed back and tried to sit up, but someone held her down. A light came on, waving around. It looked like a keychain flashlight. Kirk shone it on his own face. He still wore the sunglasses, with a crack across one of the lenses. He was shirtless, covered with gray dust, and had a long scratch on one cheek. *"Don't move,"* he mouthed.

Ruby lay still, except to reach out to wipe blood from his cheek. Kirk jerked his head back, then touched his own face, gingerly. "What happened?" Weird not to hear herself talking.

"It's dead, I think." Kirk looked back over his shoulder and pointed. "He's unconscious." He pointed the light at Garbers lying on a rubble-strewn floor, limbs askew. His head was wrapped in a blue band that, on more careful inspection. turned out to be his tie, holding in place a blood-soaked pad that had enjoyed a former life as Kirk's Dr. McNinja t-shirt. "I think a ball bearing hit his head, but it's just a graze."

Ruby touched her own head and found a bump but no blood.

"Ow." There was a ringing in her ears, which gave her some hope her hearing would return. Pushing Kirk's hand aside, she sat up, then paused to recover from dizziness before crawling to the fallen detective to check his pulse and respiration. She took the flashlight and used it to check the dilation of his pupils because she'd seen that on TV. The same on both sides, as best she could tell, which was probably a good sign—not that there was anything she could do about it anyway. She turned her head, so Kirk could see her lips. "Did you call 911?"

In answer, Kirk punched a button on his cell phone and held it up for her to see the lighted display. No signal. "Then go outside," Ruby said impatiently.

Kirk shook his head. "Can't," she thought he said. "Trapped."

"Show me."

Kirk gave her an exasperated look, then stood, holding out his hand. She took it, and he hauled her to her feet. She winced, hopped on one foot as she pointed the light down at the other. Her sock was bloody. She had for sure pulled stitches loose this time.

Kirk shivered as her arm went around his bare back. He walked her carefully the few steps to the metal door. The door was dented, as if something had hit it hard from the other side. It would only open a little way.

"Too narrow for me." Kirk pointed up and down the hall. "Doors all locked."

How had he gotten this door open in the first place? Presumably using tools that were now in the building across the street. Ruby shoved at the door, and Kirk leaned over her to help. It grated and opened another fraction of an inch. Ruby stuck her head through the gap and beamed the light around.

The room where they'd set their trap was a mess. The goats had been torn to nauseating, bloody pieces. The wooden platform was splintered, and big chunks of stone, concrete and masonry littered the room. Twisted, rusty rebar poked out here and there. The railroad track at the far end of the room was buried under the pile. The monster was there, too, under the debris, visible now that it was dead. It was pinned under a slab of floor and part of a large machine, which must have fallen on it from the second floor. Only its snout and one ruined eye poked out of the mess. Thick, pinkish blood dripped from its open mouth, and the thing's sweet-sewery smell filled the room.

Where had all this rubble come from? Ruby aimed the light into a huge open space above the room. The floor and walls above had fallen in, and part of at least one higher floor, making a void filled with twisted metal, hanging cables, splintered beams, and slow streamers of falling dust. The weak beam of the keychain light couldn't reach the far side of that opening. One side wall on this level had collapsed also, and the adjoining room was full of rubble. They were lucky the hallway hadn't fallen in, burying them under tons of rock.

Ruby pulled back and looked at Kirk. "Too much gunpowder?"

Kirk shrugged. "The walls must've been weak," he shouted. She could hear him a little, now. "I think it was more the creature thrashing that brought it down. Can you get through there?"

Ruby ducked under the door handle and squirmed through the narrow opening, glad for once to be flat-chested. Once through, she picked up a loose piece of board and used it to lever away a couple of the stones from in front of the door, while Kirk shoved it open enough to get through. He looked around, grimacing at the goats. A fist-sized stone fell out of the darkness to land on the rubble pile, rolling down to end at his feet.

"The whole track must be buried. I don't see a way through." He went to the monster and touched the scaly snout. Then he looked up at the debris pile, tested a couple of chunks for stability, and started climbing into the darkness.

He had the sunglasses, so he didn't need her little light. Ruby went back into the hallway and looked around more carefully. She found several ball bearings, the detective's flashlight—broken—and a quantity of grit. She swept a bit of floor relatively clean with the edge of her shoe and sat near Garbers, her back against the cold wall. She turned the light off to save the battery.

The wait, in darkness and silence, seemed like forever. Her backpack was still up on the roof, but Speck usually stuck pretty close. She called his name softly and turned the light on to find a little shimmer hovering before her. She couldn't think of a use for him at the moment, but at least she wasn't totally alone. "Stay." She aimed the light at Garbers to assure herself he was still breathing.

After a while, she sensed movement and turned the light on again to find Garbers looking at her. He covered his eyes. "Ow."

"Are you all right?"

"What?"

She raised her voice and repeated.

Garbers shook his head and winced. "Why are we in the dark?"

"Do you remember the invisible monster chasing us in here?"

"Oh. Yeah. That."

He remembered. Finally, something going right. "Part of the building collapsed, and we're stuck. Kir—um, my friend went to look for an exit." It might be better not to use Kirk's name, under the circumstances. "Can you get up?"

"Do I have to?"

"Are you that comfortable there? I need to show you something."

Garbers struggled to his feet, putting a hand against the wall for support. "Where's my light? What hit me? Where's my gun? "

"Light's broken, and I don't know. We can look for the gun out here." Ruby went back out into what she'd begun thinking of as the monster chamber and handed the detective the light after he squeezed through after her. She pointed. "Here's your killer."

The light played over the exposed snout. "The hell?" Garbers went over to touch the monster. "What *is* this thing?"

"Invisible river monster." No need to mention the Skohlars or the sewers. "It was coming up out of the river and eating people."

"Jesus." Garbers peeled up the thing's lip to look at its teeth, then wiped his hand on his pants.

"So, you see, it wasn't Simon. He was trying to kill it."

"With a goddamn sword?"

"It's an excellent sword."

"Why would he do that himself? Why not tell the authorities?"

"Lots of people in this neighborhood told the authorities. Did anyone believe them?"

"Even so." Garbers looked up, then stepped back, as a chunk of masonry rolled down the slope, followed by Kirk. "Now who the hell are you?"

Kirk held out a hand. "Kirk Donnell, sir. Are you all right?"

Ruby sighed. So much for keeping him anonymous.

The detective ignored Kirk's hand. "Is there a way out?"

"Not that I could find."

"You think maybe you'd have better luck if you used a light?"

Kirk took off the sunglasses and turned them so Garbers could see the insides of the lenses, glowing with purple light. "Feel free to look around yourself, officer."

Garbers put on the glasses, tentatively, and looked around the room. "Where did you get these?"

"They're a prototype from a defense project. Classified. Please don't tell anyone about them, or you'll get my dad in trouble."

"You people are so full of shit." Garbers handed Kirk the little light and scrambled up the slope and away.

Kirk looked again at the monster. "You think Olga will phone for help?"

"Let's go in the hallway. It's less stinky." Ruby led the way. "Olga has no phone. And she can't know the creature's dead, so I don't think she'll come down before morning. But she might shout to the

Guardians if they pass by again. Or, maybe not. I was pretty definite about not wanting them to find us." Ruby sat and patted the floor beside her.

Kirk sat, put his head against the wall, and sighed. "We're safe enough until morning. Didn't look like the rest of the building was likely to collapse." He turned out the light.

They sat quietly for a couple of minutes. Ruby worried about publicity. She'd hoped to contain the situation, to show the corpse to a select group of people. But, if rescue workers came to dig them out, the TV stations would come, too. The monster would be in the news. Simon would. She would. The Guardians would be pissed.

Someone would find out who her parents were. That was surely too good a story to pass up. Girl joins the family business of blowing up buildings. So much for making a fresh start in a new place.

Something touched her hand, and Ruby squeaked and pulled away before realizing it was just Kirk. She reached back out, found a forearm, and worked her way down to his hand. "You startled me."

"Sorry. Is this okay?"

Ruby slid her fingers between his. His hand was large, slightly callused. It was a hand that did stuff.

He squeezed slightly. "Are you scared of the dark?"

"Not usually. But it is awfully dark."

"We have to save the battery."

"Yeah."

They sat quietly for a minute. "Hey, can I ask you something?" Kirk asked.

"Something else? Sure."

"How did you do that trick with the book?"

What he was talking about? "Sorry, what?"

"When Conrad dropped you off after our date."

"Oh, that." That night seemed as if it was part of another life, and the thing with the book was the last moment before everything came crashing down into ruin and disaster. She was embarrassed now to think of it. She'd been showing off, ignoring the rules. "I shouldn't have shown you that."

"It's a little late to start worrying about what I know or don't know, isn't it?"

True enough. He already knew about the Skohlars, so if he couldn't keep a secret, she was already screwed. "Fine. Turn on the light and shine it here." She held her free hand out, palm upwards. "Speck, home!"

The shimmer raced out of the darkness to float above her hand, tickling her palm. Kirk took a sharp breath and moved away a little, letting go of her other hand.

"It's a spectral dog. It's okay, he doesn't bite. Bounce, boy." Speck bounced. "He can fetch, too. Fly through walls. I got him because he could always find Simon, but just now I know exactly where Simon is anyway, so that doesn't help us."

"Where did you get him?"

"Payment from a client. The one you helped with those equations, in fact, so I guess he should be part yours."

"Could he carry a message? Get us help?"

"I thought about that. He can...." Speck hovered, awaiting commands. "He could F-I-N-D Marissa, but she's already in enough trouble without rushing out here in the middle of the night when she's grounded. It's not like there's anything she can do."

Kirk passed his hand through the space Speck occupied. Then he was silent for a long time, and Ruby was afraid she'd scared him off.

"You're a strange girl." He settled down again next to her, turning the light off. She was conscious of the heat of his bare arm near hers, and she could smell his sweat a little—though the monster was still the predominant scent in the area.

They were quiet for a while, sitting in the dark. Suddenly, Ruby thought of something. "Hey, where'd you learn to use a sword? *Quelle heroic,* by the way."

"Hm? Oh, I'm in SCA."

"Sorry what?"

"Society for Creative Anachronism. My character is an Irish knight from the fifteenth century, so I practice with a broadsword. Not exactly like a katana but close enough."

"So, LARPing?"

"Not exactly. There aren't quests. We study old time crafts and everything. We do the Bristol Renaissance Fair."

Great. Trapped in the dark with a history geek. "How did you get down so fast?"

"What do you mean?"

"From the roof. You were up there yelling at me, then like five seconds later, you were on the ground waving that sword around like a wild man. How?"

"Oh, that." Ruby could hear the grin in his voice. "I jumped."

"You jumped off the roof with a sword in your hands, and you didn't stab yourself or break your leg? What are you, Spiderman?"

"I'd like to let you think that, but you'll find out the truth from Olga. I held the air mattress in front of me and jumped flat. Still a hard landing, but it cushioned my fall just enough. And the sword was sheathed."

"That's ingenious."

"Thank you."

"In kind of a brainless way."

Kirk laughed. "What's that mean?"

"You could've just pulled the cord to shut the gate from up there."

"Oh." A pause. "Actually, I didn't think of that. Not that it would've kept the thing out, as we saw."

"It was enough to give us time to escape. But no, you thought, I'll just leap down and battle that huge monster with my little sword." Though she was glad of his company, Ruby was also, now, piqued that he was in here, instead of outside calling someone to dig them out. She was so ready for a cold drink, aspirin, and a bath. In that order. And for Garbers to call the people who'd need to see the monster.

Plus, she felt a little terrified in retrospect. He could so easily have been killed. "I didn't know you were such a caveman." Her voice was a little sharp.

There was a long pause. "I guess I lost my head." His voice was almost too low for her to hear. "I saw you were in danger, and the only thing I could think was... I can't lose her."

"What?" Ruby said, shocked. She thought he might not have heard. Her heart seemed to have moved up into her throat, her fingers went cold, and she felt as if she were watching herself from a great distance.

"I couldn't stand to lose you." He cleared his own throat. "I like you. I really like you," he added, apparently by way of clarification.

Ruby swallowed, took a breath. "But... but you like Marissa."

"Um, I like her as a friend."

"No, I've seen you together. You two talk a mile a minute the whole time, and you hardly say a word to me."

"Well... she's easy to talk with. She doesn't intimidate me."

Ruby took another deep breath, determined not to stammer. "I *intimidate* you?"

There was another pause, and Ruby so wished she could see his face. When he spoke again, the words came out in a rush. "Marissa's nice and all and really smart and has a good sense of humor, and I'm sure someone will like her—maybe even Conrad if he gets his head out of his butt. But she's not right for me. I mean, she reads *Teen Vogue*. She says 'BRB' when she goes to the bathroom."

"I did warn her about that. And by the way, *I* read *Teen Vogue*. You might be surprised what's in there."

"She has a pink computer. When I tease her, she sits there worrying whether I mean something by it instead of teasing back. She's perky. For God's sake, she's a cheerleader!"

"Ex-cheerleader, actually." Ruby felt a strange hilarity bubble up. "She's cast aside the cheerleading lifestyle to hang out with us."

Kirk drove on, seeming determined to get it all out at once. "Whereas you… well, you're dark and strange and mysterious and playful and a little dangerous. All right, given the situation here, I'd have to say a *lot* dangerous. Everything that happens with you is out of the ordinary. Every minute I'm around you is an adventure. That's what I want. That's what I need."

This romantic vision of her was so out of tune with her own ideas of herself that she felt a perverse desire to laugh. "Kirk, you hardly know me. How much time have we actually spent together? I'm not mysterious. I'm just introverted. Strange, okay. I'll grant you my life has gotten a little weird lately. But that's not me, just my situation. Believe me, I'd like nothing better than to have a normal, unexciting life." She laid her hand on his arm, which was damp with perspiration.

"Well… I haven't known you long, that's true. But actually, no. I don't believe you. Maybe your life was fairly normal until recently. But you don't want it to be normal again. I've been watching you as we set up this trap, and you've been having a blast. Up on the roof, when the creature showed up? Anyone with an ounce of sense would be cowering away like Olga did. But not you. You looked slavering death in the eye and yelled threats at it. You're not terrified by all the weird shit that happens to you. You get this light of fierce joy in your eye and leap right in."

"So, you're saying you want a woman who hasn't an ounce of sense? Okay, I probably qualify there. But you were right there with me at the edge of the roof."

"Exactly. I was there because you were there. I couldn't let you do me one better. You challenge me to step up."

"My, sir. What a way you have with words." Despite her light tone, Ruby was all confusion inside. She was stalling. And he sat there waiting, knowing she was stalling.

Could she really never go back to a normal life? Would she be bored? He was probably right. With that realization, she felt she'd lost something. Nothing could ever be easy anymore. She couldn't run away from trouble and weirdness. Ruby swallowed and wiped at her eyes. "I don't know how to deal with this. I need time to think."

"Take all the time you need. But while you're thinking—let me hang around, okay?"

"Yeah. Yeah, of course. Friends, okay? At least for now."

Somehow, he must've sensed that she'd stupidly stuck her hand out in the pitch black, because he found it and grasped it in both of his. "Okay."

A little way down the hall, someone cleared his throat, and both of them jumped. "Much as I hate to interrupt this moment," Garbers said, "there's something you need to see."

"Shit! How long have you been standing there?" Ruby asked.

"Never mind that. Come quick, it may not last long." She could hear him moving off down the hall.

"Where's the light?" Embarrassed, she used the wall to stand and accepted Kirk's help to hobble along, though she felt horribly self-conscious putting her arm around his bare torso. Everything had changed with his little revelation.

"In here," Garbers called. "Quickly!"

They followed his voice into the trap room. The monster odor was stronger here, of course, and different from before. More pungent.

"Look at the creature." The detective pointed. "It's… slumping."

Kirk played the flashlight over the small part of the carcass that was visible. It did, indeed, seem to be more formless, mushy—like a tomato left out far too long. A translucent green liquid flowed sluggishly over the surface of the jaw, dripping down to pollute the pool of blood it was lying in.

Kirk knelt next to the disgusting thing. "Has it gotten smaller?"

He was right. Even the teeth seemed smaller than before.

"I think it's melting," Kirk said.

Suddenly she realized what was happening. "Of course it's melting! Those *fuckers!* Those rat-bastards! They're getting rid of the evidence!" She yelled up at the rubble pile. "Stop it, you idiots! I had it all solved! Come out here and talk to me!"

"Who is she yelling at?" Garbers asked Kirk.

"Um… I can't tell you, or she'll have to kill you?"

"I'm going to need a better answer than that." Garbers prodded the softening tip of the snout with his shoe. "Is this thing even real? How can it just melt away?"

Ruby turned on the detective. "This is how they stole the body from your morgue. They liquidated it, like the Wicked Witch of the West." She turned back to yell at the rubble pile. "Do you hear that? I'm not keeping your secrets anymore, you screw-ups! This is stupid, what you're doing! It's rats," she told Garbers. "Intelligent rats if that's not using the word too loosely. This was their pet, but it got away. They claim someone else let it loose. Come out, you cowards!"

But there was no response. She sat on a medium-sized chunk of concrete and started to cry. Kirk patted her back awkwardly, and she buried her head in her hands. "I worked so hard."

"I know. But look, Garbers saw it, he knows now that Simon's innocent now."

"Pfft. That doesn't do any good." She wiped at her eyes with the hem of her shirt.

"She's right," Garbers said. "I already didn't think Simon did it. That's why I was out there looking around. But I can't tell anyone about this. Not only will they not believe me, they'll arrest you two for blowing up the building. It's not up to me whether to prosecute her uncle. It's out of my hands."

"If you didn't think he was guilty," Kirk said hotly, "why'd you arrest him?"

"Chief's orders."

"Well, that's just great." Kirk danced back as the head of the creature partly collapsed, starting a small landslide and splashing a few drops of repulsive glop on his pants. "We'd better get out of here before the whole pile comes down on us."

They retreated to the hallway, then farther down in case an avalanche should cave in the wall. Ruby brushed a bit of floor clear of rubble and sat.

Kirk slid down the wall to sit beside her. "So now what? What can we do for Simon?"

"I don't know." Ruby said. "Why do I have to make all the plans? I'm just tired."

"Actually, I was asking the Lieutenant here."

"It'll be tough. He was at the scene, caught on tape prowling around with a weapon, no good alibis for any of the killings. He won't talk, and it's not clear how he makes his living. He does a lot of his business at night, he says, but he won't name the people he does business with, so we can't ask them to confirm where he was when."

Ruby laughed. "That would sure make an interesting scene in the courtroom."

"What would convince them to drop the charges?"

"Not much at this point. It's received a huge amount of publicity, so they can't just let their only suspect go. They'd look like fools. A convincing confession from someone else is about the only thing that might do it."

"I don't think the monster will confess at this point," Kirk said. "But what do you mean, a convincing confession?"

"Giving details only the killer could know."

"What, people can't just admit they're guilty? They have to prove it?"

"Sometimes people who didn't do it will confess, just for the all the attention."

"You know those details," Ruby said. "If you're convinced now that he's innocent, will you tell us?"

Garbers didn't answer for a while. "That's asking an awful lot. An anonymous letter won't do. They have to be able to actually lay hands on the culprit. Let me think about it."

"I don't hear any more falling rocks," Kirk said.

They all paused to listen. "Let's see whether things have shifted enough to dig our way out." Garbers made standing-up sounds.

"Can we have a minute here first?" Kirk said.

No! Ruby thought. She wasn't anywhere near ready to talk more.

"Sure." Garbers sounded amused. "When I come back I'll make some noise." The door scraped open and shut again, and they were alone.

"Snoop," Kirk muttered.

"Look." Ruby hurried to speak before he could. "You kind of sprang this on me."

"I guess my timing could've been better. I really hadn't planned to say anything."

"Kirk, if you add up all the time we've spent together, it's less than twelve hours total. A lot of that time, we weren't even talking."

"Well, no, but I've been observing. You could say I've been thinking about you for years. I just didn't know who you were."

"See, that's just what scares me. You think I'm some amazing mystery girl you've been fantasizing about. When you get to know the real me, you'll be disappointed. I'm nothing special."

"I beg to differ, but anyway it seems to me that's my problem." Kirk paused. "Look, I know it was probably way too early for me to say anything. It's just, well, it was the answer to your question, and I didn't know if I'd ever be able to… to get the courage to say it if I backed down then."

Ruby reached down to sweep a pebble out from under her butt and rocked a little in the darkness. "You sure talk bold for a shy boy."

Kirk gave a shaky laugh. "If there were light, you could see I'm sitting here trembling."

"Actually, turn on the light for a second. I want to make sure

Garbers isn't lurking." After she was sure the coast was clear, she went on. "There are some things you should know about me. I was going to tell you anyway because Marissa convinced me it wasn't a good secret to keep from friends."

"This sounds serious."

"It's about my parents."

"I heard you were an orphan."

"That might be easier, but no." She explained the situation, then continued, "I have four aunts, and I stayed with each of them, but I'm so much trouble that they each got rid of me and that's how I ended up with Simon."

"What kind of trouble?"

"Oh, you know. Lots of stuff. Not fitting in. Not being properly ashamed for what my parents did. Why should I be? It wasn't my fault. Refusing to go to church. Telling Aunt Martha she wasn't British. Shaming someone into paying a mentally disabled boy a reasonable amount for painting his boat—it took him two days, and he did a really good job, and the bastard wanted to give him five dollars. Can you believe that? I picketed his house. There was other stuff. Oh, I chased the neighbor boy up a tree with a toy gun."

"Dare I ask why?"

"He offended my virtue, so watch yourself, buddy." Ruby's eyes narrowed at a note she thought she'd picked up in Kirk's voice. "Are you laughing at me?"

"I'm sor—" Kirk snorted. "I can't help it. Yes, I can see I was mistaken. You're totally normal, and your life before here was completely uneventful."

"Cut that out." Ruby punched at him, aiming for the arm and hitting something. "No making fun of me. You have to tell me something about you now."

"Let me think. I might not have anything to match that."

"Wait." Ruby put a hand on his knee. "I hear something."

It was a sort of hoarse squeaking noise, and Ruby had a horrified vision of Garbers, collapsed on the floor, making that horrible sound while he finally succumbed to a brain hemorrhage from his head wound. But it wasn't coming from the direction of the monster chamber.

Kirk pointed the flashlight at the sound. The Skohlar, Fat Free, blinked in the beam. He ran forward on three feet, holding the talking box and coiled earbud cable in the other. Reaching Ruby's feet, he held this up, and she took it.

"What's up? And why'd you make that ghastly sound?"

"You said to make big sound when I come." The little Skohlar sounded puzzled.

"Yeah, okay, maybe I did. Well, I never thought I'd say this, but I'm sure glad to see you. Is anyone out there trying to dig us out?"

"There is a way out. I show you soon."

"A way that we'll fit through?"

"Yes."

"Super." She turned to Kirk. "He says there's a way out."

"Ask him why they melted the monster."

"You can believe I was about to get to that."

"The Cheddar is pleased. We pay as we agreed. Look under the gazebo."

"No, we're not done. Simon's still in jail."

Fat Free pondered this for a while, brushing at his whiskers with his free paw. *"I do not understand why this is a problem for us."*

"It's a problem you caused by melting the monster. You destroyed the proof that would've freed him. How could you do this without talking to me? That wasn't part of the plan!"

"The Cheddar makes his own plan. He doesn't say why. Only 'do this, don't do that.' But I think he will say we did not agree what happens to the kraal *after it dies."*

"This isn't about agreements—it's about common decency. It was your project that got Simon in trouble, and you need to help get him out. Fair is fair."

"I don't understand all your words. I tell the Cheddar your request."

Ruby sighed. "Okay, fine, if that's the best you can do for now. Where do we get out?"

"That way." Fat Free pointed. *"But there is a man there. He must not see me."*

"It's in the monster chamber. Help me up."

They found Garbers in a corner, throwing bricks back into the room from atop the pile. "I think we can get through here now! You, boy, help me shift this chunk."

The collapse of the monster's carcass had caused the debris to shift so it was lower on that side. Kirk scrambled up beside the Lieutenant and grabbed hold of a piece of rebar to pull. Soon they were out of sight around the edge of the wall, except Ruby could see the light from the little flash now and then.

"Ruby, it's clear!" Kirk shouted. "Do you need some help getting through, or are you good?"

"I can manage." Favoring her injured foot, Ruby climbed to the opening and pulled herself through, the flashlight shining in her face. The detective caught her on the other side—there was plenty of space in the adjacent bay. The gap past the next wall was wider, and Kirk was there to help her down. After that, they could walk on the track, though the ground was still littered with little stones and covered with pale grit.

As they approached the twisted gate, two silhouettes appeared against the moonlit street. "Ruby, are you in there?" Marissa's voice echoed down the tunnel.

Marissa, here? "We're okay! The monster's dead!"

Garbers slid down the final slope. "Who's out there?"

"Friends," said Kirk.

When Ruby came out onto the street, Marissa grabbed her, hugging her and laughing.

"What are you doing here?" Ruby said. "Did you sneak out? Did nobody call the fire department or anything?"

"Wow!" Olga said. "There was like this bang and a big cloud of smoke and dust came out."

Marissa held up her phone. "I called you and it went right to voice mail. Kirk's, too. Nobody called back, and for like an hour, I lay there imagining what might have happened to you. Then I couldn't stand it anymore, so yeah, I snuck out and came to look."

"Are you nuts? You could've been eaten!"

"No, I knew where you were doing your lookout, so I drove right to the door and ran inside. But there was nobody there."

"Because I was down here!" Olga said. "I came in but couldn't see nothing."

"Where'd you get a car?" Ruby asked Marissa.

"It's Dad's."

"You're not even legal! We have to get you home before your folks notice. I still don't know whether the rescue squad is about to show up."

"I didn't think I should call them." Olga's face was flushed, and she seemed proud. "I waited a while and then came down to look."

"That was brave," Kirk said.

"Talking about brave," Olga said animatedly, turning to Ruby. "Wow! Did you see how he jumped off the roof and stood there waiting for the thing with that sword?"

"Yes. I was terrified for him."

"But he's really good with a sword!" Olga looked admiringly at Kirk.

Ruby felt a flash of annoyance, quickly suppressed. "I saw. I'm beginning to wonder whether there's anything he can't do." Great, good way to not encourage him.

"I'm not that good. I think I only nicked him."

"Who are you two?" Garbers asked. "What's your part in all this?"

Ruby turned to face him. "They helped you with your case, Lieutenant. You're not planning to arrest anyone, are you? They're anonymous benefactors." She looked at Marissa. "Where did you park?"

"Right out there. Come on. Oh, you're bleeding!"

"Nothing new. Just give me a hand to the car."

There was a huge fan of dust from the tunnel mouth on the street covering Garbers's car. He got an ice scraper and brush combination from the trunk and started to brush it off.

Kirk trotted down the street to retrieve the sword, then paused on the way back to pick up something near the curb. He held it out to Ruby—long, dark, curved, wickedly pointed, glistening, and slightly translucent.

"You cut off one of its claws." She rubbed her thumb over the flat end where it had been cut, then handed it back. "Your souvenir."

"Couldn't you use it as evidence?"

"Of what? That something once had a big claw? If we need it I'll let you know. Hey, be careful with that sword, it's really sharp. Will you go get its box? Everything else can wait until later. No, don't take the sword inside. Set it down and bring the box. Look, the scabbard's over there. And bring my backpack. And a plastic bag!" She turned to Marissa. "I don't guess you have aspirin."

"Maybe in the glove box. Get in."

"Just a second." She turned to Olga, who was shaking out and rolling up the deflated air mattress. "Do you need a ride home?"

Olga shook her head and smiled. "It's safe to walk now. Well, as much as it ever was."

"Come here." Ruby held out her hand. Olga came and took it, then moved in for a hug. "We make a good team. Keep in touch, okay?"

Olga grinned, then saluted and walked away, air mattress tucked under her arm.

"What are you going to do with that?" Ruby called after her.

"Throw it in the dumpster down here. It's bust up."

Ruby turned to find Kirk, sword box under his arm, guitar case in one hand, and a bottle of water and an empty plastic bag held out in the other. "Bless you," she said, taking the water. "Marissa, you should tie this bag around my foot, so I don't leave bloodstains in your dad's car."

"If Marissa's in a hurry to get home, you should ride with me. I'm parked around the corner. The bag's still a good idea, though." Kirk set the things on the curb and ran off.

"Aspirin." Marissa handed it over. "Stick your foot out. So, when do I get the whole story?"

Ruby took a long slug of water. "Call me when you get home and I'll fill you in. We still have a problem, and I need your help to figure it out."

"So long as the new plan doesn't involve explosives."

"Not if I can avoid it, but please note the explosives did 'git 'er done.'" She took another sip. "Thanks for coming out. I hope you don't get in trouble."

Marissa leaned against the car beside Ruby and watched the detective drive away. "What's up with you and Kirk?"

"Um...."

"I saw the way he looked at you. And then when Olga complimented him, you were jealous."

"I wasn't.... all right, I guess I was a little. But it's not like that!"

"What is it like?" Marissa's voice had a definite edge. "I thought you weren't interested in him."

"I said I didn't know. I thought he wasn't interested in me."

"Which was wrong, apparently."

"I still don't know how I feel about him." She watched Kirk's car pull up, unable to meet Marissa's eyes. Kirk leaned across the passenger seat to open the door. "We'll have to talk about this more later."

"Yeah." Marissa stood, noticed she'd left a faint butt-print on the car, and brushed dust from her pants seat. "I guess the dust didn't all settle before I got here." She walked around to the driver's side.

"I'll have to find an all-night car wash." She slammed the door and started the engine.

"I'm sorry." Kirk had started to get out, but when Ruby plopped her butt in the seat, he sat back down and closed his door. "I thought she would help you get in."

"Me, too." Ruby buckled up.

"Is everything okay?"

"Just drive."

Kirk drove. A few times, he looked at her still face in the passing streetlights. "You make me nervous when you're like this."

"When else have I been like this?"

"That's partly why I'm nervous. I somehow think all hell is about to break loose. Are you mad at me?"

"Yes. No. Not exactly. I'm just thinking."

The silence stretched on. "I have to stop for gas."

When he got back into the car, he put a bottle of water in the cup holder and passed another to Ruby. "Wash the dust down."

"Thanks." She opened it and took a sip. "We shouldn't have left that stuff on the roof. If someone sees the dust on the street...."

"I hauled it all inside and locked the street door."

"Good thinking."

"How's your foot?"

"Hurts. Have to get it re-stitched."

"What'll you tell the doc?"

"The truth, I guess. I have to tell the Guardians anyway, so they'll stop hunting the thing." Ruby pulled down the sun visor to check her reflection. Every bit as frightful as she'd feared. She bugged her reddened eyes out at the mirror. "Too bad it's not Halloween."

When they got to the house, Kirk saw her to the door, carrying her things. "We have to stop parting this way." He looked like he wanted to hug her, and she did her best to look unsafe to hug. "Call me tomorrow?"

She nodded and slipped inside.

The house was quiet.

"Is anybody home?"

"Here!" Wally trotted out from the kitchen. "Wow, you look like hell, Ruby."

"You're sweet. Where's Alice?"

"Since you were gone to a friend's overnight, she went home." His eyes went to the bag-wrapped foot she was holding off the floor. "Need her for something?"

"Don't give me a hard time, Wally. I've had a really bad day. Can you get her?"

"Sorry. If it's nothing too serious, I can help you."

"I think I'll need to be re-stitched."

"I can do that. Just let me get the kit while you get cleaned up."

"Help me up the stairs, okay? I didn't know you knew first aid."

"Second aid, too. Who do you think takes care of me if I hurt myself when I'm at home?" He sounded a little bitter.

Nineteen

The sun was high when the phone in the upstairs hallway woke Ruby. She covered her head with the pillow and muttered, "Go away." It stopped, then started again, and at the same time, there was a banging from the attic. "Oh, for... okay, I'll get it."

She shambled, zombie-like, to the hall table and blinked at the caller ID. Marissa. "Oh, God," she moaned. She picked it up.

"All right," Marissa said. *"I'm waiting."*

"I'm really sorry. I got home, and Wally patched me up and gave me dopy pills, and I just forgot to call you."

"You forgot, or you were afraid to?"

"Look, I swear I didn't do anything to encourage Kirk."

"Nothing?"

"Not before he started it. It was all his idea."

"And then what happened?"

"We just talked.... I tried to discourage him."

"But not real hard."

"What am I supposed to do, M? I can't make him like you. The whole thing was so upsetting. I can't stand to have you mad at me, too."

"Learn to live with it." There was a *click.*

"Hello? Hello?" Silence. Ruby hung up and stood by the hall table for a moment. At least, she reflected, things could hardly get any worse. With any luck, the Guardians would be satisfied the thing was dead and wouldn't be able to trace it back to the Skohlars.

Ruby threw on some clothes and went downstairs. There didn't seem to be anyone around, but a note on the counter told her Dr. Fortunato had already left, promising to return with lunch. Evidently she hadn't heard about last night yet but surely would by lunchtime. That would be an unpleasant conversation. Ruby started some coffee, looked for something to eat, and decided she didn't want cereal.

She picked fresh rosemary and garlic chives from outside and made herself a fancy omelet, à la Simon. She took it into the drawing room to see what was on TV. Flipping through channels of toddler shows and soaps, she sipped coffee and ate a few bites. Hearing a car door, she glanced out the window. Another unmarked cop car—Detective Garbers got out of the passenger side, his head now neatly bandaged, and Captain Urbana stood up from the driver's seat.

"Oh, hell." Ruby hurried out to press the lockdown button on the staircase, feeling the slight vibration underfoot that told her it was working. She got to the door just as Captain Urbana rang the bell.

"Miss Park." Urbana sailed past her.

"Come in."

"We need to talk." Urbana pushed into the study. Garbers grimaced apologetically as he edged by.

The captain leaned against Simon's desk. Ruby took the couch and looked at her expectantly.

"I feel you must not have understood me before. You're not to go telling all our secrets to anyone you feel like."

Ruby looked at Garbers, then innocently back at Urbana. "This is in reference to what, exactly?"

"In reference to the events of last night," Urbana said dryly. "In particular, to your idea of showing everybody the dead monster to prove your uncle's innocence."

"I didn't do that."

"No, but it wasn't for want of trying. And you brought him into it without checking with anyone." Urbana pointed at Garbers.

"You're right, I absolutely should've let the monster eat him instead. What was I thinking? What's your plan for getting Simon loose?"

"I understand some intelligent rats made the monster dissolve."

"Some *what?* Where did you hear that?"

"That's what you told Detective Garbers."

Ruby had thought better of that revelation in the cold light of morning. "We couldn't see who was doing the melting. I called them all sorts of names. I guess rat might have been one of them. But I didn't mean it *literally.*"

Urbana drummed her nails on the edge of the desk. "Very amusing. What do the Skohlars have to do with this? Garbers says you said the creature belonged to them."

"He had a pretty good wallop on the head. He might be misremembering. What are Skohlars?"

Urbana smacked the desk with her palm, making Ruby jump. "Cut the crap, kid! This isn't your and Simon's business any longer. The Guardians need to know what's going on here, so *we* can police the community."

"You'd have to ask Simon about that. If someone hired him to hunt that monster, you know he's never going to tell his clients' secrets, and he wouldn't want me to either. If I even knew anything."

"You knew enough to trap it and kill it."

"Which, by the way, I have yet to hear one word of congratulations for, even though I managed to beat your people to it, with their stupid lights that scared it off. As they'd have known if they'd bothered to talk to the locals, like I did."

"Congratulations." Garbers sounded amused.

"Thanks. I was starting to worry the blow to the head had damaged your speech centers."

Garbers turned to Urbana, who'd gone red. "You know, she has a point. I was disoriented and watching the monster melt distracted me while she was talking. I'm not certain I got it right what she said. I don't remember her mentioning Skohlars or whatever. You're the only person who's used that word."

"Yeah," Ruby said. "You know, Captain, if these Skohlars are a secret, which I guess they must be since nobody's told me about them, maybe you shouldn't talk about them in front of the mundane." She cocked her head in Garbers's direction.

Urbana, jaw set, stalked to the study door and jerked it open. "If you happen to talk with Simon's client, you can tell them we're going to find out who's responsible for this disaster. And when we do, there will be sanctions."

"Okay."

"You can also consider yourself under house arrest. You stay right here. We'll deal with you later. In the meantime, I'd advise you to shut the hell up. Any further disclosures will be disastrous for you... and for whoever the hell else you tell them to." Urbana looked at Garbers. "Are you coming?" When he made no answer, she slammed the door and left.

"There goes your ride." Ruby tried to sound nonchalant, but she was shaking inside. Were the Guardians going to do something to Marissa and Kirk? What could that be?

Garbers had gone to the window to watch Urbana drive off. "That's okay. I was starting to dislike her attitude, anyway. What was that you called me? A mundane?"

"Oh, you're part of the in-crowd now, I expect. Baptism by fire. They can always use more friends in the police, so I doubt you have anything to worry about. Don't expect them to tell you everything, though. There are layers and layers of secrets."

Garbers looked uneasy. "There's more? Where did that creature come from, anyway?"

"Nobody knows—or they're not saying, at least. I wish you hadn't gone to her. It looks like I'm in some big trouble now."

"Sorry. I didn't know, and anyway she came to me. When I was leaving the scene last night, I ran into a truckload of her vigilantes, and I guess someone took down my license number. Who are these people, anyway? What gives them the right to punish you?"

"I'm sure they believe they're dealing with stuff that would freak out the regular police."

"They might be right, but I don't like it. Where's the oversight?" Garbers looked at his watch. "I need to get gone, or I'll be late."

"First, I think you have something that belongs to us."

The detective gave a sheepish grin, pulled Simon's sunglasses out of his suit pocket, and handed them over. "Besides seeing in the dark, these make excellent sunglasses, provided you don't have to read any signs. You're not going to do anything else crazy, right?"

"You heard the woman. I'm under house arrest. What kind of trouble can I get into here?"

Ruby went back to the drawing room, finished her cold omelet, and put her feet up on the coffee table, rocking her chair onto its back legs to look at the ceiling. The more she thought about Captain Urbana's vague threat to "deal with" her and her friends, the more alarming it sounded. What could that mean? Turn them into toads? Banish them to another dimension? Use some otherworldly gadget to erase her memory of the last few weeks and pack her off to an aunt?

That last seemed particularly horrible. She let the chair thump down, her head still leaning over the back, and looked out the window. Everything had gone wrong so quickly. Just four days ago, things had been... well, not normal, but going along as usual. Their regular Sasquatch visitor, early for his appointment as always, had been sitting awkwardly right there on the window seat. Now, she might never see one of those gentle monsters again, or Wally or Seymour. Maybe not even Marissa or Kirk.

The window seat wasn't nearly high or deep enough for a Sasquatch. Like those undersized armchairs at Polacek's memorial service.

What had those two Sasquatches been doing there? Polacek hadn't known either of them—no, wait, she'd only *dreamed* him saying that. But he had told her he never got any Sasquatch business. Why had those two attended?

Suppose the Skohlars were telling the truth. What if someone had released their pet? Lieutenant Garbers thought a murderer was likely to attend his victim's funeral. Had one of those Sasquatches let the monster loose and attended the service from guilt at indirectly causing Polacek's death and others? But if so, how could she prove it? And what good would it do, anyway? The Guardians wouldn't let the police arrest a Sasquatch. But maybe once they knew the whole story, they'd put some effort into freeing Simon. It would at least take the heat off the Skohlars and prevent the war Ms. Wheelwright predicted.

She sighed, stood, and went out back to see whether the Skohlars had brought her payment yet. When she looked under the gazebo, a pair of glittering black eyes stared back, and a Skohlar came out. He wore a red vest embroidered with gold thread and a tiny camo backpack, and dragged a cotton drawstring bag that jingled.

Ruby opened the bag. It contained a jumble of rings, earrings, tie tacks, a few tiny old coins that looked like they'd been stamped out by hand. It was mostly gold, and the bag was heavy.

She took the earbuds the Skohlar held out to her. "Retractable Blade?" she guessed.

"The Cheddar sends greetings and reply to your request."

What request, she wondered, then remembered—she'd asked for help getting Simon out of jail.

"He asks what assistance you need and what you offer in return."

"Well, I like that! How about this? Simon can't do any more work for them while he's locked up and neither will I. And Polacek is dead, so where will you go when you need something?"

Retractable Blade looked off to the side, thinking. *"I will tell him...."* He sounded doubtful.

"I'll tell you what." Ruby paused. She was in plenty of trouble with the Guardians already. She had a feeling that violating Urbana's house arrest order wouldn't make them any happier with her. On the other hand, there was nothing more she could do from home, and if she quit now, it would be disaster for everyone, herself and Simon included. She took a deep breath and took the plunge. "Suppose I find out who let your monster loose."

"You can do this?"

"Sure can." Ruby tried to sound confident. "I'll need you guys' help, though."

"This might interest the Cheddar."

"It should. I just talked to Captain Urbana, and she said she'd find out who caused the problem, to punish them."

Retractable Blade's eyes narrowed. *"Then why should we pay you to do the same?"*

"She already suspects it's your monster. When she knows for sure, she'll stop there. She won't believe someone else did it unless you can prove it. She'll make trouble for you."

"How will you make proof? The scent is long gone."

"Wait, what?" Did he really mean a scent, or was that code for something else? But the Skohlars weren't big on metaphor. "You know what the person smells like? Some of your people would recognize the scent?" Come to think of it, Hundreds had said something about that.

"Yes, many did. I would know him."

"What did it smell like? Was it a person? A human, I mean?"

"Not human. Male. Stronger smelling than a human, musky, some leaf mold...."

Ruby felt a stirring of hope. That totally sounded like it could be a Sasquatch. "You'd recognize it if you smelled it again? Wait here a minute." Ruby hurried inside and returned with the cushion from the window seat. "Smell this."

Retractable Blade sniffed, then grabbed the cushion to sniff again. He started chattering, and Ruby donned the earbuds. *"This is very like! What is it?"*

"The same person?"

"No. But close."

Same species, then. "You're sure you'd recognize him, just by scent?"

"Yes. But the Guardians will not believe it."

"Let *me* worry about that part. My question is, what will the Cheddar pay if I can catch him?"

"What kind of creature is it?"

"That's all you're getting for free. Tell the Cheddar what I said."

"You can get proof for the Guardians?"

"Maybe."

"What payment do you want?"

"Do you still have the remains of the people the monster killed?"

"Some skulls, I think, some bones. Some we made into water."

"All right then, here's the deal. I want those remains, all of them you have left. That's just for searching." Their families deserved to get them back, whatever else happened. And they might be useful somehow. "I need some Skohlars who'll recognize the scent to help me search. If I find him, this much again." Ruby jingled the cloth bag. "But nothing stolen, understand? Only things you've found." She was damned if she was going back to any of the aunts or to foster care. She wanted a decent stake to run away with in case it came to that. "If I can prove to the Guardians who's guilty… then I will."

"I will carry your offer. Is that all?"

"Yes, go." Ruby stood and brushed off her knees, watching him scurry away. Walking to the house, she shook the bag gently to hear the solid-sounding chink of its contents. Maybe she'd have time to give

Octavian a call, to see what the stuff would bring. But she had a lot to do to put her new plan in motion.

The dolly with its stack of boxes would never fit through the turnstile. Ruby steered to the wide lane near the ticket booth. She had an explanation ready if she were stopped, but the attendant, disappointingly, just took her money and nodded her through.

She passed a skinny Asian man playing a saxophone and went to the far end of the subway platform where tracks emerged from a tunnel. A few people waited near the middle of the platform, but there was nobody at this end. Ruby leaned against the chilly tile wall, took out her current paperback, and waited.

After a few minutes, a stream of Skohlars came single file out of the tunnel, walking alongside the tracks. Crunchy Bits O' Cheddar led the file, his opal pin of office stuck through his vest to leave his paws free for walking. The Cheddar scaled the drop-off to the platform as easily as if he'd been walking on level floor. The same female attendant as before followed him up, with her pink backpack, then a crowd of twenty or so others in camouflage vests, male and female. They all gathered on the platform, where the dolly and its stack of file boxes would hide them.

Ruby took earbuds from the attendant. "I said no weapons." She waved her hand at the rat brigade, who bristled with polished sticks, pointed objects, and some things she didn't recognize but might be weapons. These looked much more efficient and technical than the miscellany of pencils and plastic swords the Skohlars had carried when she first met them. Perhaps those had been their casual equipment, and these were for when they meant business.

"You expect them to face the enemy unarmed?" asked the Cheddar.

"They're not going to face the enemy. This is a reconnaissance mission. Anyone seeing them is supposed to think they're ordinary rats. No weapons, and no clothes, so off with the vests and jewelry, too."

This last request caused unrest among the troops, but the Cheddar signaled them, and they scrambled back into the tunnel.

"There are Guardians in our tunnels asking questions. Will you finish this today?"

"I don't know. I hope to have a name for you today."

"And then we will kill him."

"You will *not* kill him." Ruby unstacked the boxes and set them on their sides with their covers off. "If you do, I might not be able to get the proof you want." The first of the troops came back, and Ruby was amused to see the Cheddar's attendant look away so as not to see them unclothed as they got into the boxes. "These are all ones who can recognize the scent, right?"

"Not all. All who are fit."

Ruby covered the boxes and stacked them back on the dolly, securing them with bungee cords. The earbuds got in the way of this, so she handed them back. "You should get Bluetooth. There, all set to go. I'll drop them off here, after. You guys keep still in there."

Ruby rolled the dolly back up the platform and sat on a bench near the musician, who had his own folding chair. She threw a couple of dollars into his case, and he nodded thanks.

When he finished a number, the saxophonist set his instrument in his lap and looked at Ruby over the top of his dark glasses. "Who you talk to over there?" His voice was pitched low so only she could hear.

"I was on the phone."

"Nah, you look down all the time. You talking to the dark things of the earth."

"All right. You caught me. It was the dark things."

"I see them before. You don't wanna mess with them."

"I know. I told them to go away."

His dark eyes rested briefly on the stack of boxes, but he just leaned back, licked his lips, and started another song. After a minute, the train came, and Ruby gladly got on.

Relying on the Skohlars was starting to seem like a bad idea. They did follow orders reasonably well, if a touch literally, but they seemed impulsive. At least they stuck to their agreements. Perhaps she could use that to keep them in line.

After several stops, she got off and rolled the dolly out of the station, now at ground level. She paused on the sidewalk to consult street signs and the map program on her phone. She walked several blocks to where the way was walled off by a tall, serious-looking wall. A road led into the compound through a gate, past an air-conditioned guard shack containing an alert-looking guard.

All the local Sasquatches lived in there. What she could see through the gate looked more like a forest than a housing development. There were no green lawns, but one narrow road curving off between walls of thick plant life. Tall wild grasses, native plants, and lots of trees hid whatever houses might be in there. The stone wall was tall and topped with razor wire, but the Skohlars should have no trouble getting over it. She crossed the street to a park and found a shady bench to sit on. This early, the park was fairly empty. Some children ran around in a small playground, and the few adults around were watching them.

"Where's Retractable Blade?" Ruby asked.

A dark snout protruded from the carry hole at the end of the middle box. Ruby pointed. "I need you guys to get over that wall."

Retractable Blade took the talking box. *"Someone may see us."*

"Well, yes, but we have to get you inside somehow."

"Don't they have storm drains?"

"Fine. Get inside however you like. You're in command of this patrol. Once you get in, spread out. Check the doors and yards of every house and see whether you can pick up the enemy's scent. Do you all know how to read house numbers and street signs?"

"Some do."

"Find the house and remember exactly where it is so you can tell me. There's lots of tall grass, so it's easy to keep out of sight. If someone does see you, what do you do?"

"Hide and pretend to be dumb rats." Retractable Blade's reply sounded reluctant.

"I know it's not dignified, but it's necessary. Remember, the Cheddar's agreed you'll follow my orders exactly. He won't be happy with anyone who ruins the agreement."

"I will make them understand."

"Don't stop looking the first time you pick up the scent. I need to know which house he lives in. Check all the houses to see where the scent is strongest. Okay?"

"Okay."

"Ready to go?"

"Ready."

Ruby rolled, following the wall until she found a storm drain that was sheltered from view. "We'll meet here when you're done. If I'm not here, wait." She watched the Skohlars stream down the opening in the curb, then re-stacked her boxes and headed for the station. She'd noticed a Burger Barn across the street from there, and she was starving. Maybe they would have peanut butter ice cream.

She took an outside table. While waiting for her order, she put away her regular phone and dialed Marissa's number on her new burner.

"House of Blue Things," Marissa answered. *"Your source for all things blue."*

"Say what?"

"Oh, it's you. What's with the new number?"

"My old phone broke and I got a new one from Jimmy. What's this House of Blue Things?"

"I plan to start a business online. What do you think?"

This was how she answered strange numbers? And she called *Ruby* weird? "You'll only sell blue things?"

"Blue towels, blue stationery, blue shoes, the movie Blue *on Blu-ray...."*

"B. B. King?"

"Is he blue?"

"He *sings* the blues."

"Close enough."

"What if someone asks whether you have this blouse in green?"

"I've got my niche, and I'm sticking to it. What do you think?"

"I think captivity has driven you bonkers." Ruby paused. "Are you still mad at me?"

"Yes. No. I don't know. I guess it's not really your fault, but you're the one who made me think there was something there. I don't know. Yeah, I guess I'm still steamed. I wanted to talk before. Why don't you ever answer your cell?"

"Which phone did you call? The one that broke?"

"Oh. I guess that would explain it."

The waitress came out, and Ruby thought it might be her food, but the plates went to another table. "I might need your help, though."

"With what? Why don't you get your boyfriend to help?"

"Marissa, come on. He's not my boyfriend. I'd feel uncomfortable asking him for anything."

There was a pause. Ruby shifted in her chair and felt something hard in her skirt pocket. Simon's sunglasses, which she'd stuck in there and forgotten about after Garbers returned them. She set them on the table.

"Well, help with what?"

"I haven't figured that out yet."

"Then update me, and I'll help you figure out a plan that doesn't involve more explosives."

Ruby paused. "Captain Urbana is steamed about how much I've told you already. She says I'm under house arrest. But there are no explosives. Just talking to people."

"You're grounded, too? But it kind of sounds like you're outside."

"I *am* outside. Having a burger." Ruby watched the waitress emerge again. "In fact, here it comes now."

"O-o-kay, so you're defying the captain. What will she do to you when she finds out?"

"I'm not going back until this is all over, one way or the other, so she'd have to find me first."

"What do you mean exactly, one way or the other?"

"I don't think I should say more."

"Because of the captain?"

Well, yes. But not in the way Marissa meant. Should she say that Urbana had threatened consequences for Marissa as well?

"Hello?"

"Partly because of the captain," Ruby said at last. "Partly because it involves some other clients of Simon's. I don't think you'd cause them any problems, but they haven't given me permission to talk with anyone about them."

"Seriously, you're starting to worry about that now?"

"That's exactly what Kirk said. Yeah, I have to think about that. If Simon does get off, I don't want him to get home only to find I've wrecked his business while he was gone."

"Well, fine, but ask them if it's okay. I want to meet more of these people. So what kind of help do you need that I can give without knowing what's going on?"

"Well, if I need anything blue, I'll come to you, of course. But also, I'll probably need to get past a guard or something. I need to look older and businesslike."

"Okay, interesting problem. Like, what business would you be in?"

"Simon's business. Sharp but practical. Can you help with clothes and makeup?"

"Yes and hair. I've been meaning to speak to you about yours. If you want to look professional, the frizzy ponytail has got to go. You need a total salon makeover."

"I've been dragged to salons. It always ends up looking like a birds' nest in my hair. Nobody knows how to cut it."

"At school there's a half-black, half-Chinese girl who likes Van Cleef. Try them. Seriously, they can only improve on the situation. They do nails too and maybe makeup. Ask them to do something about your eyebrows. Call ahead to make sure you can get in."

"Thanks… I think." Ruby flipped the receipt that had come with her burger to take notes on the back.

"If Van Cleef don't do makeup, try Laura Black. They did a nice job for my cousin's wedding. For businesslike attire, let me think. I haven't shopped for that. But at least you can buy off the shelf. I'd think you could find something acceptable at Nordstrom's. Text me a picture, and I'll answer thumbs-up or down."

Ruby made a note. "Mm-hmm."

"And get a two sizes larger bra and stuff it. If the guard is a man, that'll distract him. Shoes are a problem. You've never worn heels, right?"

"No."

"Me, neither. Too bad. You could use a couple extra inches, but you won't fool anyone if you don't know how to walk in them."

Even if she'd been used to heels, she needed shoes she could run in, just in case. But she didn't say that, not wanting to worry Marissa any more. "I have some black suede with little silver buckles." Also rubberized soles.

"Oh yeah, I was with you when you got those. They should be okay."

Ruby took a bite of her burger. "You remember where we bought them? I didn't bring them from home."

"Not Cole Hahn but the next place we went after that, I think. Don't eat with your mouth full. I mean don't talk."

"Ha ha. That reminds me—do I ever get to hear what's up with you and Miss W?"

"Sometime. It's all mystical, and I'd have trouble explaining it on the phone. Can't you tell me anything about what you're up to? Don't be like

those people in mystery stories who say they know who the killer is and then turn up dead and nobody knows what they knew."

"I think I have a line on the person who let the monster loose. I'm trying to prove it, so the Guardians will let the Skohlars off the hook and we don't have that war. Don't worry, dozens of people will know who the suspect is before I do." She supposed Skohlars counted as people. "He, or she, can't escape justice by murdering me."

"How will you prove it? Did he leave fingerprints in the Skohlars' caves?"

"Maybe. Though I don't know how long they'd last in the damp."

"Too bad they didn't have a security camera down there."

"Yeah," Ruby said. "Yeah," she said thoughtfully. "Too bad."

They threw around some more ideas, then Marissa signed off, saying she had soccer practice but promising to think about the problem. Ruby took her time with lunch, finishing her book and winding down with coffee ice cream—they didn't have peanut butter. She browsed the second-hand section in the bookstore next door and found the fourth book in a series of which she'd read the first three—*The Universal Pantograph* by Alexei Panshin. She took it to the park, sat on a file box within view of the storm drain, and read while she waited.

In the middle of the fourth chapter, something popped up in the storm drain, then again. She went over to squat nearby, dangling the speaking box through the grate.

"We have found him."

"You're sure you have the right place? You checked all the houses?"

"All, yes. Scent is strong there."

"How many live in that house?"

"Two. The other is female."

"Okay. Get back in the boxes, then you can tell me where."

Ruby left the U-Spy store on Fullerton with one more bag than she'd had going in. She found a bus stop bench and took inventory. Clothes, check. Shoes, check. Stockings, check. Briefcase, okay. Her coiffure and makeup had gotten her some weird looks in combination with her usual clothes, but she hadn't wanted to risk getting the new suit dirty or rumpled by putting it on before she needed to. It was still in its protective hanging bag.

She pulled out her phone. This part would be tricky. She pressed the key combination to call anonymously, then dialed Dr. Fortunato's cell. When it was answered, she cautiously said hello.

"Ruby, where are you? I get home, and you're not here."

"I had some shopping to do."

"You should be staying off that foot."

"I'm taking it easy."

"Why is Captain Urbana over here threatening you with 'extreme measures?' What's this about you killing a monster? What have you been doing?" Dr. Fortunato's voice was calm, as usual, but Ruby heard a definite undertone of tension.

"I was going to tell you all about it when I saw you."

"You can tell me now. The phone's been ringing non-stop. I've heard four different versions of the story, each one more wildly unlikely than the last."

Ruby outlined recent events briefly, leaving the Skohlars out of it. Dr. Fortunato asked a few questions at the beginning but shut up when it became obvious they would only delay things.

"Well," Dr. Fortunato said at last. *"That's… remarkable. And the thing just melted, you say?"*

"It was weird! Lieutenant Garbers saw it too, though—just ask Captain Urbana, he told her all about it. I guess that's just what happens to creatures like that when they die."

"All right, but I still don't understand why you're not at home."

"I'm not home because Simon's still in jail. I'm still working on it."

"Dear, there's no question of your doing any such thing. You'd best return immediately. Susan is furious. She's camped out on the doorstep this minute."

"Who's Susan?"

"Captain Urbana."

"Oh, right. What the hell gives her the right? No, if I come home, she'll lock me in a room or something."

"I should lock you in a room. When Simon hears of this... well, I don't know how I can explain it. He asked me to take charge of you, but really, this goes so far beyond anything I know how to deal with... really, going out in the middle of the night and blowing things up.... It just leaves me speechless."

Not speechless enough. "Look, Alice, I'm sorry, but it's impossible for me to quit now. I have a chance to get Simon out of trouble. So far, I've only gotten myself in trouble without helping him. Don't you want me to get him loose?"

"Well of course, dear. We all want him freed. But you can't do that by yourself. Come and tell Susan what you know, and she'll take it from there. She's Simon's friend, you know."

"Ask her how her investigation's going. I think she's already made up her mind. She won't go after someone else on my say-so." Especially based on second-paw information from a generally unreliable source.

"She wants to talk with you."

"No! I'll hang up if you put her on. I want to talk to Wally."

Ruby could hear Dr. Fortunato in the background saying, *"She won't talk to you."* She strained to hear Urbana's response but heard nothing, which seemed ominous.

"If Wally says I should come in, then I will." Ruby's voice went higher than she liked.

"I'll get him," Dr. Fortunato said.

There was a long wait before Wally came on the line. *"What is it? I was sleeping."*

"Sorry to bother you. I'm sure they've told you to convince me to go home. But Urbana will lock me up, at a minimum, and I think I'm Simon's only chance at this point. You said before you wanted to help. Do you still?"

"What? I... yes."

"It's a little thing, but kind of important, and you have to not let them know where I'm going."

"I can do that."

"I need the name, address, and, if you can get it, phone number, of any client of Simon's who lives in Yetitown. One of them is named Ureen Ka-something, and I'm sure I saw a letter from him in the pile of mail on Simon's desk. But it can be anyone inside the fence. If you can get more than one, that would be better. Can you look it up and email it to me?"

"Yes."

"Good. Now, since they're waiting, you should tell me whether you think I should come home or stay free to help Simon."

"Of course you should go help Simon. Good luck! And stay safe."

"You're a peach! A fuzzy one! Ta!" Ruby hung up.

Twenty

Shadows were lengthening as Ruby finished preparing for the next phase of the operation. She'd returned to the same cafe for dinner, but her stomach was too knotted up to eat anything. She'd called the number Wally sent her and made an appointment with the gruff-sounding Sasquatch on the other end of the line. She had no intention of keeping that appointment, though—it was just to get her through the gate.

She changed in the cafe's restroom, then stood in front of the mirror at the orange-stained sink, seeing an exotic stranger. The oval halo of black hair, coming to points at her jawline, held with just a little gel. The elegant, arched eyebrows. Cheekbones enhanced with a little careful shading. Plum-colored lipstick—striking but not too showy.

She'd be amazed if anyone could recognize her. She looked nothing like her idea of herself, nothing like her mother. She could be twenty or twenty-one. She opened the bag from U-Spy, took out the brooch, set it on the counter. She tore open the clamshell pack of tiny batteries, managing not to draw blood, and set them out beside the brooch.

She closed her eyes and took a deep breath. Was this really a good idea? Sasquatches were supposedly peaceful, but what about those scars? If she was right about this one, he'd deliberately caused trouble of a fatal variety. He might not have intended for the monster to eat people, but he surely meant to expose the Skohlars to get the Guardians to punish them, and she suspected the punishment wouldn't be gentle.

It wouldn't be in his best interest to hurt her, since the Skohlars knew where she was going. She couldn't tell him that, but she'd have to somehow let him know that killing her wouldn't solve anything. She had to get him off balance enough to make mistakes but not enough to get violent.

She could do that. She had a lot of experience annoying adults to the verge of violence. She'd just have to watch her step.

She finished her preparations, took a last look at the stranger in the mirror, stuffed the empty bags into the trash, and went outside. She didn't have to wait long. The cab she'd called for pulled up, and she got in for the three-block ride to the Yetitown gate.

She had two reasons for riding the short distance. She'd been staying off her injured foot as much as possible, but she also wanted the guard to see her arriving by taxi. It was part of the professional image she was trying to project.

Also, by sending the taxi away before asking for admittance, she hoped the guard would be more likely to take pity on her and let her in. She exaggerated her limp a little as she walked to the booth, the guard's eyes on her. He was a white man, fortyish, short, stocky, with acne scars.

"Ureen Kanardee, please." She patted her satchel. "I have some papers for him."

The guard tore his gaze from her chest to glance at a clipboard hanging on the wall. "I don't know you."

Ruby dug into her satchel for a business card, made fresh that afternoon at a copy store. "Ruby Park, Goodnight Agency." She'd managed to duplicate the logo rather nicely.

"I'll let him know you're here."

Ruby lifted her phone. "No need, I'll call him."

"You know the way?"

She didn't, but she was going to a different house anyway. "I'll be fine. Please open the gate now."

"I didn't know Mister Goodnight had an assistant. Isn't he in jail?"

"Yes, that's why I'm here. He's unable to do this work for Mister Kanardee's project himself, and I don't know how. I'm returning the papers, so he can find someone else to help him."

The guard pressed a button, and the gate swung open. "Say, I get off at seven. Want to get a drink?"

Ruby was taken aback. "Um, what? No."

"Got something else to do?" There was an edge to his voice now.

Ruby flushed. Who did this idiot think he was? "Do I need to have something else to do to tell you no?"

"I asked you nice. You didn't have to be a bitch about it."

Had her "no" been rude? She'd been startled and afraid at the invitation and answered without even thinking about politeness. But he was being rude now.

It would be lovely to tell him so, but then he'd probably find some excuse to make her wait. She forced herself to smile. "Sorry, you just caught me by surprise. As it happens, I do have another appointment after this." She pulled held up her phone, open the calendar application, which she'd filled in with fictional appointments, just in case. "But I'm free Friday night. You have my card, right?"

He tucked the card into his pocket, tapped it, and winked at her. "I'll give you a buzz."

"Great!" Ruby smiled again, waggled her fingers, and turned away, seething inside. He was, she suspected, watching her ass as she limped away. She felt humiliated, dirty. She wanted to sic Speck on him. She wanted to turn and tell him, "By the way, I'm sixteen, and I've been recording this conversation." She hadn't been, but let him sweat.

That would have to wait. She walked down the curving road until she was out of his sight, behind a stand of trees. Then she took out the map Retractable Blade had drawn, turning it to match the direction she was facing.

Her hand was shaking. She let it drop to her side, her other hand on her stomach. She felt like she might throw up or cry or scream. She fought all those things down, closed her eyes, and focused on breathing, listened to her heartbeat. She couldn't go in like this, or she would lose. Cool as a cucumber was where she needed to be.

Cool as a cucumber was nowhere near where she was.

She had enough. With the payment the Skohlars had given her already, plus the money from under Uncle Simon's drawer, she could be away from here. Hide out, get a job, make the money stretch until she was eighteen.

But then who would save Simon?

Who would prevent the war?

Who would avenge Polacek for the sake of his wife and kid?

Ruby remembered Netta Polacek at the memorial service, talking brokenly about her wrecked dreams. She remembered Raymond turning away, so people couldn't see him cry. Cold fury accomplished what her attempt to relax had not. She took another deep breath and looked again at the map. Her hand was steady now.

The house marked with an "X" on the map was modern-looking with lots of large mirrored plate-glass windows, built on a slope and mostly hidden by plantings artificially placed to look natural. A pebble walk led to the door. She looked around and found a gray snout poking out from a stand of sword grass, black eyes gleaming at her. "Is he still there?"

The Skohlar nodded.

"Still alone?"

Another nod.

"Give me ten minutes inside. Then go for help."

Ruby paused at the door. Her heart was still racing, but waiting wouldn't help. She arranged herself, trying to look calm and steely-eyed, and pressed the buzzer.

She then waited what seemed like forever. Finally, she heard the lock, the door opened, and she looked up into the face of the killer.

He was large, so much larger up close than he'd seemed before—if it was the same one from Polacek's service. He had the same relatively pale hair, the same arresting blue eyes. She looked into those eyes. "We need to talk about the Skohlars."

Did that huge hand tense a little, as if it wanted to form a fist? Did the brow furrow for a second? He took just a little too long before replying. "I have neffer heard of these."

"Perhaps I should come inside?"

The giant paused another long moment, then wordlessly stepped aside. To walk into his reach and past him, looking unafraid, was perhaps the hardest thing she'd ever done. He wouldn't touch her, she told herself, not until he knew exactly what she knew and who else she might have told.

She passed through the hall into a wide, white living room filled with oversized, overstuffed furniture. A wall of outward-slanting windows looked out, down a slope into a flower-filled glen. A comfortable room but a little austere. She took a seat at the edge of an armchair she could easily have shared with a friend and waited for the Sasquatch to sit. She looked at him thoughtfully as he waited for her to speak. Did he look wary? Afraid at all? She couldn't read him.

"You probably didn't realize, there are security cameras in the Skohlars' dens."

There. He had *definitely* stiffened slightly.

"Simon set it up for them a few months ago. They store video onto a private server over the internet."

"You lie."

"And yet, I knew to come to you. Did you have a different theory about how I found you?" Don't give him time to think about that one. Keep talking. "The problem is, Simon didn't give the Skohlars a copy of the video with you on it. I think he meant to, but he got arrested before he could. The Cheddar's at my house nearly every day demanding I give it to him. I've been putting him off by telling him I don't know the password. But really, I do know it, so I've seen the video, and I found Simon's notes with your name. I wasn't sure he had it right until I saw you, but yeah—the shape of your head, that scar next to your ear—those show up on the video. It's definitely you. By the way, I gave the password to a friend of mine. To use in case she doesn't hear from me again."

"What do you want?" The Sasquatch showed his teeth a little.

Ruby managed not to shiver. "I need to understand why Simon didn't give them that video right away. If I don't turn it over to the Guardians, there'll be a big dustup between them and the Skohlars. Maybe he was waiting to get the monster taken care of first. Maybe he never meant for anyone to see it. I can't ask him right now because I'm sure the police are listening when I visit him. So, I have to decide for myself. That's why I need you to explain why you did it."

"There ith no fideo. It wath dark—" The Sasquatch stopped.

Gotcha.

"Simon's got lenses that can see in the dark. He was using them to hunt the kraal, in fact." She took the sunglasses out of her satchel and tossed them onto the coffee table between them.

"You lie."

"So, you're not going to explain?" Ruby stood and patted her satchel. "All right, then this goes to Captain Urbana." She took a step toward the door.

The Sasquatch moved amazingly fast for something of that size. Suddenly, he was between her and the door, holding out a hand. "Gif it to me."

Ruby swallowed. "Look, the Skohlars are nobody's favorite species. They're furry little dirty liars. I'm half inclined to erase this video anyway and let them take their medicine. But you have to talk with me or it's no deal. Simon's lawyer says he can get him off, but it might take quite a while. He'll be out a lot faster with the Guardians on his side."

"They are fermin," the Sasquatch snarled. "Breeding and multiplying in the dark. They breed for intelligenth, you know. Thmarter with efery generation. They will oferrun us unless we wipe them out now. There mutht be war, before they are too thtrong to defeat."

"But it'll pull in the humans, too. You're blowing everyone's cover."

"We need their rethourthes to win. The human people we can deal with. The Thkohlars are too therious a threat."

"Who else is in on this plot?"

"Thimon knows. He agreed with me. You mutht thee my cauthe is jutht. Gif me the fideo."

Ruby paused. She remembered Simon, in the garden, talking about how he hated rodents. Could he really have approved this plan? "I have to go away and think about it."

The Sasquatch's hand flashed out and grabbed the satchel.

"You know, there's still one archived online."

"I haf a computer. You will erathe it now."

"Stay away!" Ruby ducked behind the chair.

The Sasquatch didn't bother to chase her around the chair. He lunged forward, planting one huge foot in the middle of the cushion. He was fast! Ruby stumbled back, raising her palm in front of her. "No!" she screamed into a muffled blue zone of dead air. The Sasquatch was slammed back and fell awkwardly. The entire wall of windows shattered and blew out onto the deck. Tiles fell from the ceiling. The floor bucked, and Ruby ended up sitting on the floor, gasping.

The ceiling creaked, and she looked up at it. Would it collapse without the windows supporting it? She hurried out onto the deck. Hearing a sound, she looked behind her.

He climbed to his feet, looking stunned, blood running from his ears and nose. He used the chair back for support and stood upright, glaring at her. She ran to the deck railing—it was a long way down.

He came lumbering out onto the deck, walking unsteadily, bits of glass crunching underfoot.

Higher frequencies have more energy, Ruby remembered. She raised her hand again, took a deep breath, and screamed as high and loud as she could. The Sasquatch fell immediately, and the brick wall across the living room collapsed. The roof crashed down, but Ruby kept screaming until her voice came back no longer muffled. She leaned over, hands on her knees, panting.

He didn't move again. Was he dead? She wasn't about to go over and check. No. No, he was still breathing but showed no sign of stirring. Ruby gave a sigh of relief. He was a tough cookie.

The deck gave a lurch, and Ruby reeled over to the railing. She waited, clutching the rail, but it didn't collapse. She sat with her back against the railing and took off the brooch. She took a mini USB cable from her attaché case and plugged it into a tiny port on the brooch and the other end into her phone.

"Hello?" someone called from below. Ruby looked over the edge. A Sasquatch—female, she guessed—in an orange tracksuit stared up at her. A couple of others were just rounding the corner of the house, staring at the wreckage.

"Hi. I think I'll need help getting down. Is there a ladder?" The phone found the video file on the brooch, and she touched the button to start copying it.

"What wath that horrible thound? Ith eferyone ok?"

"There's a Sasquatch up here who's hurt, but I think not badly."

"But what happened?"

"Please call whoever's in charge around here. I'll talk with them about it." The file finished copying. She opened it and fast forwarded to the important part. The picture was clear enough—the sound tinny but comprehensible. Good thing, since it didn't look like she'd get to do a second take. She laughed. With a few more clicks, she emailed the video to Captain Urbana.

Twenty-One

Confined to the house for real this time, Ruby wandered around restlessly. She opened the front door, leaned against the solid air that trapped her inside. She looked up and down the empty street, a hot wind blowing past her from outside.

They should've been here half an hour ago. She went to the study and picked up her guitar again, practicing the new song Marissa had emailed her—Kirk's lyrics, Marissa's music. But she kept looking at the clock. When she finally heard a car door close out front, immediately followed by two others, she set the guitar down and went to the hallway. She leaned against the wall and tried to look nonchalant.

The first person through the front door was Dr. Fortunato, with Mr. Kadopolous close behind. Ruby had a moment's fear that they hadn't managed to come back with Simon after all, but then she heard his voice. A second later he showed up in the doorway, his head turned to talk to someone. He looked in and their eyes met. Ruby gave a careful little nod of greeting. Simon, looking amused, nodded back, hanging up the suit coat he'd been carrying over his arm. Behind him came a few more people—Captain Urbana, an older-looking Sasquatch, and a tall Asian man she didn't recognize.

Dr. Fortunato stepped ahead of the others, blocking their view, and holding out a small black rectangle where only Ruby could see it. She waggled the object as she approached, signaling with her eyes for Ruby to take it. She did, as Dr. Fortunato sailed past in a whirl of colorful silk, heading for the kitchen. Ruby palmed the object—a thin leather wallet the size of a playing card, slightly worn—and tucked it into her pocket.

"Who's for beer?" Dr. Fortunato called. "I'm about to dry up and blow away."

Ruby eyed the doctor's bulk from behind. She was far from blowing away.

"One for me," Simon said.

"I'd like to get started." Captain Urbana sounded cross. "I've got other things to do." She looked at Ruby and gestured toward the study. Ruby preceded her inside. Urbana looked around at the arrangement of the furnishings and pointed at a chair a little away from the others. Ruby sat, hands shaking, a lump forming in her throat. Urbana and the Asian man sat on a couch facing her. Kadapolous pulled up a chair beside Ruby, and Simon went to his desk and leaned against it, arms crossed. Noticing his pile of mail, he reached down to sort through it until the Sasquatch got settled on the end of the settee. He looked like the same one who'd come to take charge of the situation in the compound.

Dr. Fortunato returned with two beers, handing a bottle to Simon and pulling the desk chair around beside him. Her eyebrows went up when she saw the sheared-off end of the chair arm, which Ruby had forgotten to repair. She looked at Ruby, and Ruby shrugged. It was the least of her problems at the moment.

The Asian man reached into his suit coat for an envelope, opened it, and removed a sheet of shiny yellow plastic. This, he unfolded into a circle two feet wide, which he set on the floor beside the couch. It instantly shot up into three dimensions, taking on the shape of a seated woman. The figure leaned forward and turned her head toward Urbana, speaking in a whispery voice. "Will you read the charges?"

Urbana was ready with an envelope of her own, shaking out a paper and reading crisply. "The defendant, Ruby Park, is charged with unauthorized revelation, three occurrences of further unauthorized revelation following a warning, interfering with and obstructing an official investigation, and violation of house arrest. Sitting in judgment, Susan Urbana, Doctor Reginald Sin, Hezphaia Biri Phoon."

Ruby, counting in her head the people she'd roped in to help her, thought they'd missed an unauthorized revelation or two but decided not to bring it up. Heads turned as Wally stumbled in, looking sleepy, then Urbana looked at Kadopolous. "Do you represent the accused?"

"Yes, and I think we can clear this up in short order." He sounded confident. He opened a leather notebook which he'd set in his lap, folding it back to refer to his notes. "To begin with, I have a procedural point. It appears one of the judges in the case is also a complainant." He looked at Captain Urbana. "As you were conducting the investigation with which Miss Park is alleged to have interfered, I request you recuse yourself."

"It's a good point." Dr. Sin had a cultured British accent.

Captain Urbana looked cross. "It's nothing but a delaying tactic. I want to get this wrapped up. If we have to find another judge, we'll have to reschedule."

Kadopoulos pointed. "Actually, as a Sasquatch elder, Ren'ha Otto is qualified to sit. Sir, are you willing to serve?"

"I wondered what he was doing here!" Urbana said. "You invited a sympathetic judge to replace me!"

"Are you suggethting I am biathed?" Otto rumbled.

Dr. Sin and Hezphaia had put their heads together to confer, and now Dr. Sin turned to Urbana. "We believe the point is valid. Will you withdraw in favor of Mister Otto?"

"Very well," Urbana huffed. "It won't matter. The facts speak for themselves." She didn't rise from her seat but crossed her arms and leaned back.

"In regard to the first charge," Kadopolous said, "the case of Marissa Gomez, I have here the signed statement of Wallace Boyle." He pointed to Wally, then half-stood, passing a paper to Dr. Sin. "It states that the original revelation was his. I assume the panel doesn't dispute Mister Boyle's right to choose his own friends. Given that Miss Gomez already had entrée to our community by way of him, any further information she happened to pick up in the course of that association can hardly be laid at Miss Park's door."

Dr. Sin and Hezphaia glanced over the statement, then he passed it to the Sasquatch.

Urbana was visibly fuming. "You can't deny that bringing in the others was her decision, after she'd been warned!"

"As to…"—Kadopolous consulted his notes—"Kirk Donnell and Olga Gregoiovich, in that case Miss Park was acting under instruction, in her capacity as an employee of the Goodnight Agency."

"An employee! Nonsense! What instructions?" Urbana turned to the judges. "Simon was in *jail!* Every conversation they had was overheard!"

"We communicated by means of secret signals," Simon said calmly.

"What signals?"

"*Secret* signals."

"Bull." Urbana leaned back and crossed her arms again. "She's not an employee. Prove it."

"Is Miss Urbana still a part of this proceeding?" Kadopolous said mildly. "She seems to be asking all the questions."

"Susan, please leave or be silent," Dr. Sin said. "However, it's a good question." He turned to Simon. "Can you prove she's an employee?"

Simon raised his eyebrows. "You know our business is such that we don't keep a lot of records." He paused, thinking. "I know. Ruby, get your business cards."

Ruby panicked a little, trying not to show it. Did he know about the fake cards she'd run up to get into Yetitown? They wouldn't stand up to a side by side comparison to his own cards. She looked at Simon with growing desperation, then noticed Dr. Fortunato, sitting next to him, casually waggling her hand the way she had in the hallway. *Ah!*

Ruby reached into her pocket. "Sorry, I was just trying to remember where I put 'em." She flipped the little leather wallet open and glanced at the card behind the plastic window before passing it over to Dr. Sin. The agency logo, nicely embossed, with her name above the word *"Apprentice,"* and a phone number and email address. It was even a little worn-looking, as if she'd been carrying it for a while.

Dr. Sin dug into the pocket behind the display window and took out more cards to pass to the others. The Sasquatch pocketed his. Ruby wondered, with a strange hilarity, whether he planned to hire her for something.

"It seems to be in order," the yellow plastic woman murmured. "Does the agency answer for the charges, then?"

"I'm authorized to recruit mundanes, at need, on my discretion," Simon said. "As in this case."

Dr. Sin turned to Ruby. "What about Detective Garbers? You couldn't have had instructions for that."

Ruby had been wondering if anyone would even bother to ask her anything. "No, I had to decide on the spot."

"Which was justified," Kadopolous cut in, "to save his life. Does anyone dispute this?"

"Interfering in my investigation," Captain Urbana said, starting to sound a little desperate. "House arrest."

"Captain." Dr. Sin gave her a warning look.

Kadopolous flipped a page in his notes. "Leaving aside for a moment the question of whether she interfered or aided the investigation, let's discuss exactly when Miss Park was notified that an investigation was in progress...."

The proceedings went on for another hour and a half, Kadopolous doing most of the talking. Ruby started to relax a bit. It looked like success counted for much with these judges, and they didn't seem to doubt that things would've turned out badly if she hadn't acted. In the end, they put their heads together for a few minutes, then Dr. Sin announced the verdict.

"As breaking house arrest is admitted, we find against the defendant on that charge, with mitigating circumstances. The other charges were not proven. The sentence is three weeks home confinement, less time served."

Captain Urbana looked furious but left without speaking. Hezphaia's sheet of plastic went flat, and Dr. Sin folded it up, while the Sasquatch came up to her and looked down with mild brown eyes.

"I apologithe that our brother attacked you, He hath shamed uth all, and we thank you for expothing him." He handed her a small card, printed on fancy linen stock. "If I can help you, call on me."

Dr. Sin also paused on his way out. "Nice work. But next time, perhaps you could try a little harder to color within the lines."

Once everyone was gone but Ruby, Simon, and Wally—who'd fallen asleep in a chair—Simon came over and held out his arms. Ruby ran a couple of steps and threw her arms around him, her cheek against the cool silk of his tie. She didn't trust herself to speak.

Simon squeezed firmly, then used his hand on her shoulder to propel her toward the door.

"Where are we going?"

"Kitchen. I'm faint from hunger."

"What happened to the bad Sasquatch? I've been shut up here, and nobody tells me anything." Ruby walked ahead of him down the hallway, half turned around to keep talking. "I saw on the news about his confession letter and the supposed suicide off the bridge and the victim remains they found in the apartment house basement. I gave the Guardians those, by the way. The Skohlars had saved them."

"You've probably figured out as much as they've told me, then."

Simon opened the fridge and rummaged inside. "It's secret Guardian business. One thing I do know, the Sasquatch's body will never turn up, no matter how much they drag the river." Simon set things on the counter and reached up for a cutting board. "If you want some, cut extra." He turned to the stove. "Why are there no clean skillets?"

"Um, try the dishwasher."

"We unload the dishwasher when it's done. So anyway, you know my news. Things have been pretty quiet in prison. What've you been up to?"

"It's been quiet here, too. Me and Marissa...."

"Marissa and *I.*"

"Marissa and Kirk and Wally and *I* have started a band. We're writing songs to put online. I'm not very good yet, so they write easy guitar parts for me." Ruby scraped chopped onions into a bowl and reached for the mushrooms.

"Does your band have a name?"

"We're negotiating. Me and... Marissa and *I* like 'Surprise in the Dark,' but Kirk is holding out for 'Gizmo Government.' Wally doesn't care."

"They're both good. Sausage next. I'm surprised there's actually some decent food in the house."

"Should've seen it yesterday. Alice went shopping when she heard they were letting you go." Ruby set a sausage on the cutting board and stared at it.

Not hearing chopping, Simon turned to look at her, spatula in hand. "Something on your mind?"

Ruby resumed cutting. Over the last few days, she'd kept returning to the Sasquatch's claim that Simon had known what was going on, remembering Simon standing in the garden saying he couldn't stand rodents. The Sasquatch had obviously been lying, saying anything to convince her to erase her evidence. Right? But still, she wanted to hear it from Simon's own lips.

She looked at him. He, sensing her gaze, looked again at her. Ruby decided she was never going to ask. "Yeah, I've been thinking… once I'm a free woman again, I'd like to visit my folks."

"Oh? Good! You're not angry with them anymore?"

"No, I'm still angry. But they're my folks. Besides," she said brightly, "I have more in common with them now. We can compare prisons." She waved her hands at the surrounding house. "Discuss the merits of different techniques of building demolition."

"But you wouldn't really tell them about…." He waved the spatula vaguely.

"Oh, *hell*, no. They'd just worry. I'll tell them all I'm doing for you is making appointments and filing."

"I'd like to keep it to that, in fact, for now. Until you get a little more training."

"What, you weren't kidding with the business cards? I'm really an apprentice?"

"Gotta make good on my statements in court, don't I? It'd look funny if people didn't see you working for me now." He snapped his fingers. "Hey! Sausage! Up the pace."

Grinning, Ruby picked up the knife. "What's the starting salary for an apprentice?"

"Don't push it."

The End

Or is it…?

Are you on the Scene?

the Goodnight Agency

Find out more about Ruby, Simon, and their peculiar clients at https://tylertork.com/gn1

or scan the code with your phone!

Techie guy by day, crime fighter by night. But when crime is slow, as it often is in his quiet hometown of Plymouth, Minnesota, Tyler puts away the mask, cape, and ocelot, and finds a corner to scribble in. The victim of a dark destiny, he whirls through life with a set of shaky assumptions and a mug of rapidly-cooling java. Bewildered, scattered, querulous (some say curmudgeonly), he nonetheless attempts to entertain and inform. Someday, his alien masters will return for him. Until then, buy his books.